THE COLLECTIVE

FROM THE MINDS OF BLACK AUTHORS (VOLUME 1)

JAMES H ROBY   ALEX CAGE   JONATHAN STALEY

STEVEN VAN PATTEN   RYAN D. PATTERSON SR.

Copyright Page

This book is a work of fiction. The characters, places, and situations were all created from the author's imagination or used in a fictitious manner and are not to be interpreted as real. Any parallels to actual people, places, or situations, living or dead, is completely unintentional.

The Collective. From The Minds of Black Authors (Volume 1). Copyright © 2024. All rights reserved.

THE COLLECTIVE

CONTENT

PREFACE

Thriller: a work of fiction or drama designed to hold the interest by the use of a high degree of intrigue, adventure, or suspense.
- Merriam-Webster

Back in 1995, I saw *Devil in a Blue Dress*. I remember feeling so smart because this was the first time I had read the book before I saw the movie it was based on. I picked up the novel by Walter Mosley when I heard the movie was coming out. I wasn't a big reader at the time, but the idea that there was a BLACK hero written by a BLACK author... man, that was too good to let pass.

There I was, watching Denzel Washington and Don Cheadle, comparing what was in the movie and not in the book and vice versa. I had no idea what I was watching was nothing short of history. At that time, there weren't very many African American male heroes. To my knowledge, there weren't very many other authors like Mosley. That's not to say they don't exist. Black authors have been penning tales for Black readers throughout the history of the Union. But try to find them? Today? Good luck with that.

Most Black heroes were relegated to the role of sidekick or 'reformed' criminal. Their primary purpose was, quite frankly, to die.

His death would motivate the hero, usually a white man, to seek revenge or justice for his poor dead friend. Sometimes the Black hero was a mirror image of his white counterpart serving in the same military unit or coming up in the ranks of the police department...but for some reason, our Black hero just isn't as good as the white lead. This was especially true in the movies.

Since that time, Black readership has increased and in response, so has the number of black writers. Like so many endeavors, the road has been long and hard. Most books written by Black authors have been in the genre of romance, history and tales of the *struggle*. Most were written by Black women for Black women, and all of these are worthwhile achievements. Think of how poorer the world would be without the likes of Maya Angelou, Toni Morrison or Terry McMillan.

Such was the state of affairs for the Black action hero in the latter half of the 20th Century – guys who look like me.... especially in books. Sure, in the movies we got a Denzel or a Wesley or a Will – never at the same time, but that's another issue – but in the printed form our best bet was the sidekick.

Of course, there were exceptions: a pair of very famous heroes have cemented their impressions onto the American psyche; to be fair, it was mostly due to their movie presence. John Shaft and Alex Cross are definitely well known African American literature heroes. However, in both cases, they were created by white men, Ernest Tidyman and James Patterson, respectively.

But, as Willie Hutch and Public Enemy said, brothers gonna work it out.

A casual stroll through Amazon's 'thriller' or 'action' novels with the search option of 'Black author' added, you get a result consisting mostly of Black female authors and even an occasional white author either writing about Black characters or having the word 'Black' in the title.

Still, very few brothers.

When I started my writing journey, all I wanted was to tell my story. To share with the world my particular brand of thriller and adventure. I have been influenced by famous characters, like Mike Hammer, Sam Spade, James Bond and, of course, John Shaft (Mr.

Gordon Parks' version, of course) and my own life experiences growing up in Detroit and as an Air Force officer. I'll pause here to say I am very disappointed the late, great Mr. Carl Weathers' character, Action Jackson, never got a sequel (Dangerous Passion doesn't count). I won't bore you with the details of the horrors of trying to get my book noticed. I knew being a Black writer...a Black male writer...a Black male writer in a genre dominated by white male authors like Tom Clancy, Lee Childs and Clive Cussler would be a tough nut to crack. To say it was a lonely path is a mastery of understatement.

So, one day, minding my own business, scrolling through social media, I came across a Black author writing a thriller book in a similar vein as mine. After bumping into him a few times, I thought to reach out to him – find out if he was having as hard a time as I. We talked and concluded, in the spirit of many hands make light work, maybe we should join forces. Soon, we encountered other like-minded brothers in the same genre. These brothers ultimately became the Collective.

As I hope you'll discover as you read the stories in this anthology, the mission of the Collective is to present male African American heroes in a positive light. While forming this collaboration, there were few rules as to what the content of each story should be. Two of them were, the story had to be a thriller or adventure tale and, most importantly, the main character had to have agency and not be a victim of society. He had to stand for something.

So tasked, the brothers united have met and exceeded these requirements. In the upcoming pages, you will encounter no less than three hard-boiled detectives crafted by myself, fellow Detroiter, Johnathan Staley, and Alex Cage. Ryan D. Patterson Sr. has cranked out a psychological nail biter while Steven Van Patten has produced a tale of magic and mayhem.

Our efforts are to present to you, dear reader, an alternate view of characters, situations, and theme common in the thriller genre. We're not against anyone or are writing to get back at oppression, perceived or real. Our goal is to share our stories with you. We hope you enjoy this journey into our Collective.

James H. Roby

GHOST GUNS

The UrbanKnights

James H Roby

CHAPTER 1

A New Deal

Yo, Tyler!"

It always happened like this. Always right after midnight. They would come. This time, however, it would be different. Tyler Cooper was not interested in what would happen next but he might as well get it over with. He looked at his phone before answering. It was just after four AM, and as usual, his third shift crew was done with their assigned work.

He left his cubicle just off the factory floor and headed for the building's rear. One of the crew members was rolling up the garage door and as expected, a Cadillac Escalade came into view. A quick trio of bursts from sounded the horn. The other five guys on the shift smiled and clapped their hands. The Caddy's appearance always meant they were about to get paid.

"Hey, what's this?" Harold Garfield asked.

He looked at Cooper as an unexpected vehicle backed up to the entrance just behind the Caddy. He had been with Samson Industrial Works longer than anyone else. He probably should have been the shift supervisor, but Cooper had an associate degree. In any case, the others looked at him as the second in command.

Cooper stared for a moment as the trailer of a semi breached the rear of the building. Realizing Harold was expecting an answer, Cooper merely shrugged his shoulders. He walked over to the driver side of the Caddy just as Sabastian bounded out. The other three doors of the vehicle opened as the usual crew appeared. They were Sabastian's guys and like him, they were all muscle-bound. Two of them were white and the last guy was black.

"Hey, fellas," Sabastian said as his hand went up in a wave to the third shift crew of Samson Industrial. "Relax. Relax. They're with me."

As he made the announcement, two more giants came out of the semi like a pair of ghosts floating in from the dark. They came into the brightly lit floor of the factory but their twin dour expressions did nothing to relax the crew.

"Relax," Sabastian said again.

He walked over to a pair of shipping containers just as he had done every other time he visited Loveland, Ohio. Cooper fell in step beside him. As he had done during every visit, he lifted the lid of the chest high containers. Within and beneath thick styrofoam were five handguns; the second box had the exact same contents. Sabastian lifted one of the weapons and sighted into an empty corner.

"Beautiful," he said, nodding slowly in appreciation of the fine craftsmanship of the polymer weapon.

He looked over to the night crew. They had formed a line several feet away, awaiting their customer's judgment.

"Just beautiful." Sabastian extended his arm and gave the weapon a gentle shake. "This right here is a freaking work of art."

Harold and the others laughed and gave each other self-congratulatory hi-fives.

Sabastian turned to Cooper and asked, "So, what? Ten?" It wasn't really a question but a bit of theater.

"Yeah," Cooper said. "Just like always."

Sabastian tapped the barrel of the weapon on the side of his head, his eyes going up to the ceiling.

"Let's say, though...let's say I'd needed more. A lot more," Sabastian said.

Harold braved a step forward.

"What cha' talking about, Marty?"

Sabastian whirled to Harold then back to Cooper.

"Oh, I don't know. Hundred...hundred fifty..."

Harold looked back to the others, just as the crew was passing glances to each other. His broad face was still smiling but his eyes held nervousness. Their eyes all finally landed on Cooper.

Trails of sweat appeared at Cooper's temples, the first sign his mind was trying its best to warn his team of what was coming – but they just remained rooted in their spots.

Harold said, "We can't do that. We can crank out ten, no sweat. But any more than that the company will notice the missing material. Plus, the time..."

Sabastian folded his arms across his black leather jacket. He nodded, sympathetic to the plight laid out before him. Cooper felt a pit in his stomach grow to unimaginable dimensions. He walked slowly until he was behind Sabastian. He knew what was coming, but that didn't mean he wanted to see it.

"I see your point," Sabastian said.

He returned the gun back to its case. As he did so, Cooper turned slightly to get a look at Sabastian. The look in his eye would haunt Cooper for the remainder of his days. Cold. Indifferent. Pitiless.

Still looking at Cooper, Sabastian said, "Well, I guess we'll just have to take the printers."

Cooper turned to face a far blank wall as noises of confusion and doubt came from his guys. This was all cut short with the explosion of automatic fire echoing from all round. Flashes of lights played across the walls in time with the deadly discharges. It only lasted a few seconds, but the roar of weapons intermixed with the screams of his friends seemed to go on forever.

The horrible noises stopped and the echoes finally died. He knew what he'd see, all the same, something unnamed within him forced him to turn to verify. Without surprise, five dead bodies lie among streaks of crimson. A blueish haze lingered in the air like some sort of demented fog. Five men. Five men he knew, drank and laughed with. Just last week Harold had –

"Ty!" Sabastian said.

Cooper broke out of his trance. He turned and Sabastian was impossibly close, less than an inch from his face.

Sabastian said, "What's done is done. Now c'mon. We gotta get these printers loaded 'fore the next shift."

Sabastian walked away and joined the men, busy with returning their weapons to their hiding places. He turned back to Cooper.

"Unless, of course, you want the same thing to happen to them..." Sabastian said.

It wasn't a threat. It was a damn promise. Cooper headed to the two massive 3D printers and started the process of loading them onto the truck.

CHAPTER 2

A Client Like No Other

Jordan Noble looked at his latest potential client through the glass door of the main conference room. She sat in the middle of the table, three chairs to either side of her. He had many female clients, but it was absolutely no exaggeration he concluded this was the most unique. This wasn't going to be just another morning in Detroit.

The dress was brown and faded, loose strings appeared at its edge. Undoubtably a hand me down. Her hair sported six braids, each going a direction separate than the others. Her brow was furrowed and displayed an anger and what he was sure was sorrow. Jordan had never seen on the face of a girl who couldn't be more than ten years old.

Beneath the seat of her chair, her legs swung like children's legs tend to do. A constant pace like the movement of a juvenile clock. Given the grim look on her face, it wasn't due to anticipation, but a nervous energy held in check by a growing frustration. He looked before her and found a box, a cigar box by the look of it, resting on the table. Jordan started to contemplate the continued existence of this type of box when a pair of low heels click-clopped to a stop next to him. He took his first sip from his mug of Earl Grey as his executive secretary, Mrs. Steed briefed him on his tiny visitor.

"She arrived before eight," the Polish woman started. "I couldn't just have her standing in front of the building so of course I let her in, appointment or no."

Jordan drew a breath as if to speak, but thinking wiser of it, sipped again from his cup.

"Her name is Kiara Reynolds. She attends Munger Elementary Middle School of which she is in the fifth grade."

Jordan smiled. Mrs. Steed was his first and most valued employee. Unfortunately, or maybe fortunately, given her advanced age, she operated under the impression she was not only Jordan's mother but just about everyone's at the UrbanKnights Investigation and Security Services. And as such, he knew she believed she was aware of any and all questions Jordan could formulate before he could speak them to life. She was almost always right.

"Did you contact the school?" Jordan asked.

"Not yet, sir. I'm on my way to do just –"

Jordan reached for the doorknob.

"Not just yet, Mrs. Steed. Kids don't ditch to go to an office unless there's a good reason. See if you can find something for her to eat."

Mrs. Steed said 'yes sir' to Jordan's back just as he closed the conference room door. Kiara's legs stopped pulsating as Jordan entered. She didn't smile as she put eyes on him, instead regarded him with a kind of disdain usually reserved for mortal enemies. Despite this, she was a pretty little girl with big deep brown eyes that practically screamed intelligence and wonder. She tracked him as he sat directly across the high polished oak table. Her nostrils flared in time with her breathing and Jordan was afraid she was going to mention a woman's name he may have known ten years ago.

"Hey. I'm Jordan Noble."

"I know who you are. Why you think I'm here?"

Jordan's chest sank. It was going to be like that. Well, at least at the closer distance, he didn't see any resemblance.

"All right, Kiara. Well, what is it I can do for you?"

The little girl flinched at Jordan calling her by name. Turnabout and all that... It only took her a moment to recompose herself.

"I want to find out who killed my daddy."

All the oxygen left the room. He was *not* expecting that. The harsh visage across the table was now understood.

"I'm sorry. I-"

"Don't tell me you sorry! Everybody's sorry! I want you to do something. Here!"

She pushed the cigar box and it made just beyond the table's center. From the rattling it produced in motion, Jordan reasoned it was more coins than bills inside. Kiara's chest heaved under the faded dress. Tears filled her eyes and the gentlest of motion could cause them to fall. She didn't need coddling or soothing. She needed justice. But she was still a child and Jordan couldn't launch an investigation based on the explosive unpredictability of an emotional girl. And her apparent life's saving on the table or not, he wasn't having a child yelling at him.

Jordan held up a finger.

"Everyone gets one."

The sentence was delivered even and calm. There was no threat, only the statement of fact. For her part, Kiara's emotion went from a ten to one hundred and eight. For a second. Jordan was still and looked directly at her – his brown eyes on hers. Kiara's anger was like a raging inferno. But without any fuel to sustain it, it burned out instantly. She blew out a sigh and crossed her arms.

"Sorry."

She spoke the word as if it cost her a measure of life.

Inwardly, Jordan smiled but he kept his face at neutral, displaying no feeling. He reached into his suit's inside pocket and drew out a notepad and a silver Cross Century II pen.

"OK. Now, tell me about your father. What's his name?"

"Dedrick Foster. We ain't got the same name. He wasn't married to my momma."

Jordan smiled.

"That's all right. Now, tell me what happened."

Kiara came forward, her elbows on the table as her hands struggled to craft a reality that made sense.

"I don't know. He was coming home from work. He wasn't doing nothing. Just coming home. He was coming to get me. It was Wednesday. He comes and get me on Wednesdays."

The anger was making way for sorrow. The tiny face was contorting into a mask of itself, reflecting the struggle the mind was having coming to grips with the impossibility now her reality. Jordan spoke, hoping to stem the tide of the flood yet to come.

"What happens on Wednesday?"

Her arms came across her tiny chest. A lower lip jetted out.

"Piano. Before school."

"Before?"

Jordan stopped taking notes and looked up. He was rewarded with a sigh.

"Yes." Long and exasperated. "My school let's me 'cause I'm so good. Why? What do you care?"

Jordan bounced a shoulder before going back to his notes.

"Just getting an idea about you and your environment. Where'd he work?"

Kiara looked at him, surprised at the sudden change in subject. The distraction kept her from travelling further into the black hole of despair.

"Up on Warren and Livernois. They got trucks and stuff up there," Kiara said. The emotion overcame her. "He was a good daddy! He wasn't doing anything! He was working like he was supposed to! He wasn't a bad man!"

She drew the back of a hand across her face and the emotion died down. She took in a trio of breaths in rapid order. "What else you need to know?"

Everything, Jordan thought.

Just the same, he had already formed a sort of idea of what she was talking about. Wednesday, there was a shooting at the intersection she mentioned. Three men died in a drive-by shooting. No motive. Another random act of violence those outside of Detroit's 142 square miles believe occurred every day. To be honest, the past four weeks were doing a lot to contribute to that misconception. Six more seemingly random killings had happened at equally random locations throughout the city – all drivebys.

Jordan hunted down some more details – time, if it was a driveby – to ensure it was the same event. Kiara's answers verified it was.

"Can you do it?" Kiara asked. Another arm sliding across her face. "Can find who did this? Don't lie. If you can't, you can't. You ain't got to lie because I'm a kid."

Jordan's head was down, continuing to take notes.

"I don't lie to clients."

Kiara pointed at the cigar box, now closer to Jordan than her.

"You ain't even check my box. I got money…"

Jordan looked up. He smiled slightly. Ever since a mission with the Defense Intelligence Agency in Japan, Jordan had very little need of money from minors.

"I think this one will be pro bono."

Kiara's nose wrinkled.

"Pro what?"

"Pro bono. In short, it will be free."

In a move she must have seen her mother do, Kiara crossed her arms and rotated her neck and hips.

"Unh uh. You ain't doing nothing for me you don't do for anybody else. Don't be treating me different 'cause I'm a kid!"

Jordan sighed.

"Look, I told you it's free. Check with Mrs. Steed if you don't believe me."

Hands went to hips now.

"That old lady? Hmph. I don't trust her any more than I trust you."

Jordan stood up, no humor in his eyes. He understood the trauma the girl had just suffered, but he would not have this back and forth. She was going to have to be a grown-up for the duration of this case.

"Kiara. You came to me. You're asking me for help. You're a kid but if you don't want me to treat you like one, then you're going to have to be at least polite."

Kiara's features hardened as she prepared a retort. But a swift realization came over her again. One apology was no doubt her max for the day so instead she just softened her approach.

"OK, OK. You don't have to be so damn -"

"And watch your mouth," Jordan said pointing a finger at her. Unwillingly, he got an image of his father addressing him at a similar age. A chill followed. "I'm not one of your little friends!"

Kiara drew in a breath to counter when a sing-song voice came from the door.

"Who's ready to eat?" Mrs. Steed asked.

The battle forgotten, Kiara got to her feet and made for the door. Just behind Mrs. Steed came the gigantic form of Poppa Joe. The man with the coal black skin had a friendly smile rivaling his stomach in size. Joe owned the restaurant directly across the street from the UrbanKnights' back door so him visiting was far from rare.

"'Morning, there, Mr. Jordan," the booming voice of Poppa Joe said.

He wore a brown Carhartt jacket over his usual apron and beat up toque blanche. He balanced a stack of carry-out containers as he made his way to the conference room table.

"Now then," he went on. "Who up in here is hungry?"

Kiara was at his elbow.

"Me! Me! I am!"

Joe laughed as he began opening the containers.

"Well, now. I didn't rightly know what to bring so I gots me some eggs, bacon, grits, pancakes..."

Kiara grabbed the closest container and returned to her seat. The three adults stood watching the girl destroy the eggs and bacon.

Jordan turned to his secretary.

"Let her eat her full, then get her over to school."

"I'll take her there myself," Mrs. Steed said.

Jordan smiled.

"And Joe, thanks."

"No problem, Mr. Jordan," Poppa Joe said. "No charge."

He gave Jordan a wink, no doubt acknowledging Jordan couldn't be charged as he was an owner of the restaurant – a secret shared between only him and Joe. Jordan made for the door when Mrs. Steed caught him gently by the arm.

"So, Mr. Noble. Are you going to be able to help this young lady?"

"Yeah," Jordan said. "I got a quick stop to make first, but she's definitely hired the UrbanKnights."

CHAPTER 3

A Problem for the Police

1301 Third Street had more than the usual number of vehicles surrounding it. The headquarters of Detroit's Fire and Police Departments was under a literal siege. And little wonder.

Over the last four weeks, the spike in murders put the police under the intense spotlight of the media. It wasn't just the sheer number of murders but the similarities. All were drive-bys. All victims were men. All shootings were committed in daylight. Early morning to afternoon. Answers were needed. Answered the cops didn't have.

Stanley Clarke's 'East River Drive' played on the satellite radio as Jordan parked his Shelby GT 500 in the nearby casino's parking structure. He walked the two blocks against a wind of moderate force back to the Police Headquarters. The breeze wasn't too bad, but it was enough to drop the temperature to the 40s and have Jordan pull up the collar of his London carcoat. Spring was still getting its footing in the Motor City.

At the rod iron fence surrounding his destination, Jordan found the news vans from all of the local networks and a couple from the largest cable networks. He frowned. News was news, he got it. But that didn't mean he had to like these descending vultures picking at the hide of his hometown.

The news crews were inside their respective trucks. A haze of auto fumes mirroring the cloudy skies overhead surrounded the vehicles as they sat in watch for any news. Jordan was unmolested by the crew as he passed and went into the building. They were waiting for the big story.

Once he verified he had an appointment, the officer at the front desk directed him to the office of the Deputy Chief. Jordan opted for the stairs. Traversing the halls, Detroit's Finest were amped higher than their usual levels. The epicenter of this excitement centered on the floor of the executives. Jordan was ushered in by a secretary and a moment later, he knocked on the glass door of Deputy Chief William Ford.

Ford, on the phone, looked up from his call and waved in Jordan. It was like the office of any high-ranking official – a wall with plaques and awards...pictures of family on an impressively large wooden desk. Unique, however, was the number of weapons and devices crafted to look like weapons, on the desk and walls as recognition for past actions only found in the dangerous career of law enforcement.

A TV hanging in a corner showed the mayor of Detroit, Ronald Turner. The handsome, almost pretty, brown-skinned man was in the middle of a press conference – fingers pointing and grim visage staring into the cameras. A banner at the screen's bottom read something about the city being behind the mayor and his approval growing.

Jordan sat in a chair before the desk. Ford's call consisted mostly of 'yes, ma'am' 'no, ma'am.' He terminated the call and turned to his guest. William Ford was a thirty-year veteran of Detroit's peacekeepers. His skin of deep brown offset a nearly completely snow-white mane. Any and all wrinkles on his face were more concentrated in direct relation to the city's crisis.

"Hey, Jay," Ford said. He came up in the department with Jordan's father and knew Jordan as a child and as such, referred to the detective by his childhood name.

"Deputy Chief," Jordan said.

He didn't like elements of his personal life, especially a bygone personal life, intruding in his professional life. Ford, however, as a family friend and ranking police officer was given considerable slack.

"Look," the chief went on, "you can see we're pretty busy here, so unless this is important..."

Catching the chief's meaning, Jordan cut to the heart of it.

"I have a client who is the relative of one of the murder victims."

That got Ford's attention and he leaned back in his high-back chair.

"Well, that got you a few minutes. Care to tell me who?"

Jordan shook his head. Ford, in response, nodded his head. If Jordan was any other private detective, familiar connections to the police or no, he would have been politely asked to leave. But Jordan was a private detective with a direct line to the Department of Homeland Security and some undefined connection to military intelligence. Ford didn't know Jordan was a human intelligence operative of the Defense Intelligence Agency, but he did know Jordan could and often did find out things most couldn't.

This allowed Jordan's visit to continue.

"Fine," Ford said. "Client confidentiality or something like that? Whatever. You don't share – why should I?"

Ford's lips twisted under a snow-white mustache. Jordan answered it with a wry grin.

"Speed and efficiency. Your hands are kept clean by the...direct action this case will need to be completed quickly."

Ford leaned back.

"Who says I need it completed quickly?"

Jordan held back a laugh and pointed a thumb behind him and through the doors leading to the hall.

"All the news van outside waiting for something, anything they can put out to make you look bad." He pointed to the phone on the desk. "And that phone call you just got off of – didn't sound none too friendly. Who was it – mayor?"

The eyebrows on Ford's face threatened to come together. He calmed down enough to speak.

"The chief."

He sighed then checked the door to see if his assistant was in earshot. She, like everyone else in the building, was focused on the case. Ford moved forward and Jordan mirrored him.

"Quietly," Ford said.

Jordan bounced a shoulder.

"You know me."

Ford nodded.

"Yeah, I do. I also know you got some real cloak and dagger stuff surrounding you." He shook a finger in Jordan's face. "We gonna have to get to the bottom of that, one day."

Jordan blew a sigh of his own. He respected this man, but it would be a warm day in December at Minot Air Force Base before he told anything classified to the Deputy Chief.

"What you got, Chief?"

Ford looked around like he trying to come to a conclusion. Jordan, meanwhile, knew the urgency of the situation would loosen Ford's tongue.

"What do you know about ghost guns?"

That caught Jordan off guard. He stared off into a corner as he accessed his memories.

"You talking home-made guns?"

Ford nodded again.

"The ballistics we found at each crime scene didn't match any known weapons." He leaned back in his chair as his finger tapped out a nervous rhythm on his blotter.

Jordan said, "Is it possible they came from a weapon you're not familiar with?"

Ford slowly turned his eyes back to his guest. The words that followed seemed to almost be forced out.

"We're the Detroit Police Department. Guns is what we know."

"Gotcha," Jordan said. The two men both had knowing smiles now. "Any suspects?"

Ford shook his head again.

"Nothing connecting the victims. No demands. No crazies coming out of the woodwork. Your client...whoever it is may have something. Just to let you know – we've interviewed all the family and friends... good luck getting anything new."

Jordan stood and Ford followed suit. The Deputy Chief reached across the desk and shook Jordan's hand.

"You never know," Jordan told him. "But this...ghost gun angle. There may be something to that."

CHAPTER 4

All Hands On Deck

The Pharcyde lamented "She Keeps On Passing Me By" in Don Ross' ears. The thunderous rhythms of the Old School Classic almost caused him to miss his phone ringing, but he saw it on the corner of his desk, dancing as it vibrated.

"UrbanKnights."

"Young Don Ross." The voice was Jordan Noble, using the same greeting he'd used since high school.

"What up doe?" Don said in the most Detroit manner.

"Can't call it. Put Malcolm on the line."

Don put down the phone to switch to his desk phone, intending on paging Malcolm. The final member of the Special Investigation Unit just happened to be coming through the office door. Don switched his phone to speaker.

"We here," Don said.

"What's up?" Malcolm asked, taking a seat before Don's desk. "Who you talking to?"

"Malcolm, it's me," Jordan said over the line.

Malcolm leaned toward the phone.

"Yo, boss, what's up?"

"Plenty," Jordan said. He then went into a brief recap of the conversation with the Deputy Chief.

"I'm in the car," he said, finishing up, "Heading back to the office, but I wanted to know if you two had any leads on people in the ghost gun business.

Don and Malcolm looked up and locked eyes. Malcolm scoffed. He was the smallest of the three men and had been down with the group since college. Though he never graduated, he gained a kind of knowledge not found in any books. His cocky little smile at Jordan's questions set Don's eyes rolling.

"Now, Jordan, you know me," Malcolm said.

A laugh came out of the phone before Jordan went on. "Yes, Malcolm, I know you."

Malcolm leaned back into his chair, his hands behind his head and propped his feet on Don's desk.

"There's a few people in the game," Malcolm said. "but the dudes over in Livonia are probably the biggest. Real Second Amendment types."

"Sounds like a fun bunch," Jordan said.

Don stopped to consult his computer. He typed feverishly as his partners talked. Don was the biggest and tallest, the physical mirror image of Malcolm. Don knew Malcolm since grade school but a combination of fate and dumb luck brought the two back together just in time for Jordan to join the crew.

While Malcolm's thing was his network of people he knew, Don was the tech geek. Self-taught, if it had something to do with computers or the internet, Don knew enough about it to be dangerous.

"Mitchell's Industrial Creations," Don said in a voice a hair above a whisper. It was his way.

Malcolm whirled to the sound of Don.

"Yeah, how'd you know?" Incredulity was dripping with every word.

Without another word, Don gestured to his computer. Malcolm frowned and drew his fists into balls. It wasn't enough he thought he knew everyone, he also had to be the smartest one in the room. Before he could draw breath to speak, Jordan cut him off.

"Look, if you two are finished out doing each other, maybe you could go to this Mitchell and find out what's up."

Malcolm stared hard at Don behind his round glasses.

"Yeah, Jordan. We'll get on it," Don said with a victor's smile.

"And be careful. Don't just roll up in there accusing them of the biggest murder spree in Detroit history," Jordan said

Malcolm smiled at the phone.

"Aw, be cool, Jordan. Me 'n Mitchell go way back. He ain't involved in this."

"Mitchell and I," Jordan said.

"Whatever, Encyclopedia Brown. We got this."

Jordan chuckled.

"Right. OK, I'm going to have a chat with the family. Don't think I'll find anything, but you never know. See ya."

Malcolm picked up Don's phone and ended the call. Don took a calming breath. Between Malcolm's feet on the desk and turning off his phone, Don knew Malcolm was just being Malcolm. He was a jerk but it was a 'he's our jerk' kind of thing. By the time the breath escaped his nostrils, Don was ready to deal with Malcolm again.

"All right," Don said, "so who is this guy?"

"Told you," Malcolm said, "and you found him on the internet. He's a small manufacturing type who reinvented his business by getting into 3D printing."

Malcolm got up and headed for the door of the office. As he got to the hall, he gestured for Don to follow. Recognizing another bit of Malcolm's charm, Don shut down his computer and went to the corner to get his jacket in Piston blue from a coat tree. By the time he got to the hall, Malcolm was returning from his next-door office. now sporting his Letterman style brown coat. The two men fell into step and headed for the stairs.

Malcolm went on.

"Pete Mitchell's one of them diehard Republican. Every other sentence is either about guns or someone trying to take his guns. He found out he could use his printers to make ghost guns and thought he died and gone to heaven."

"Ghost guns?" Don said. "Jordan said something about that."

The two headed down the stairs to the main floor. In a bygone time, this level was the home of the majority of the detective agency. Some twenty agents entertained the clients which represented most of the agency's work. Now, all of them plus ten more occupied the building to the west and the Special Investigation Unit were the original building's sole occupants. All this came about when Jordan did some work for his old boss in the Defense Intelligence Agency and stopped an international arms dealer. A ton of government and classified work started heading the UrbanKnights' way after that.

But that's another story.

Malcolm sighed at the question and rolled his eyes.

"Ghost guns are privately made guns. 3D printers make it a lot easier. Uncle Sam thinks only licensed manufacturers should be allowed to make guns but private gun advocate citizens disagree."

The two men made their way through the empty floor with only the sound of Art Porter's "Inside Myself" to accompany them. They were exiting the building's kitchen via the employee entrance when they literally ran into Mrs. Steed. The executive assistant's eyes went big as she bounced off Don's chest.

"Sorry, Mrs. Steed," Don said.

"Well, that's quite all right," Mrs. Steed said, composing herself. "And where are you two off to?"

Malcolm pointed a thumb into the parking lot beyond the door.

"Heading out to get on this case with Jordan," he said.

"Ah. Well, make sure to get to the bottom of this with all due haste." Mrs. Steed's blue eyes held an intensity Don couldn't remember ever seeing before.

She went on. "I just dropped off our young client, Kiara Reynolds, back at her school. A brash type to be certain, but her walls crumbled at the insertion of a selection from Poppa Joe's."

Don and Malcolm turned to each other and then back to Mrs. Steed.

"His cooking will do that," Don said.

"Yeah," Malcolm said agreeing. "Though he makes too many pork products."

It was Don and Mrs. Steed's turn to exchange looks. Reluctant smiles came to their faces as Don was sure they were both recalling Malcolm's on-again, off-again relationship with the Nation of Islam, thus the origin of his pork products complaint. They let it go.

"Yes, well," Mrs. Steed said. She moved into the building as the detective exited. "She is quite devastated by the death of her father. Such an ordeal will have a ghastly effect on so young a girl. Do what you can to bring a measure of justice to her, won't you?"

The men got no chance to answer as the steel security door swung shut.

CHAPTER 5

Ladies of the House

"Yeah?"

He was about twenty; lanky and tall. He stood in the doorway, face glued to his phone's screen.

"I'm Jordan."

The young man stepped aside, neither setting eyes on Jordan nor asking any further questions. Past the house's sole guardian, Jordan could see the interior was just as crowded as the street before it. Mrs. Steed provided him with Kiara's address on Wetherby over by Livernois. It was standard procedure for a private detective to question the family, but Jordan was pretty sure he wouldn't get much here.

The house was a small colonial Detroit was known for. It seemed all the smaller, thanks to the thirty-odd people crammed in its living room and kitchen. Like the young man at the door, most of the occupants studied the contents of their phones. A TV was in the kitchen – another news story about Mayor Turner's handling of the current crisis.

As such, Jordan moved more or less unchallenged until he reached a couch. On it sat three women – the two on the flanks comforting the central figure. She was in her mid-twenties and in sweats. No doubt her attire since learning of Derrick's death. Jordan figured she was Cecilia, lady of the house and Kiara's mother.

Jordan stood before the trio for a handful of seconds before Cecilia raised her head to meet Jordan's eyes. She had the look of a woman who was beautiful but a combination of life and bad choices had beat her down. Her hair was hidden under a pink shower cap while her brown eyes were overshadowed by the bags beneath them.

"Cecilia?" Jordan asked.

Her eyes cast suspicion as they traversed Jordan's gray Tom Ford suit before returning to his eyes.

"Who you?"

"My name is Jordan Noble. I'm with the UrbanKnights Detective Agency."

The woman to Cecilia's left stiffened. She was an older version of Cecilia and clearly her mother.

"I know who you is," she said. The crack in her voice betrayed a lifetime of smoking. "I saw you on TikTok. Y'all had something to do with what was going down at the Motown Magic."

Jordan nodded. Sometimes the high-profile cases did help and you don't get more high profile than an attempted Chinese takeover of an American casino.

But that's a story for another time.

The woman on Ceilia's right leveled sad eyes at Jordan but didn't speak. For the second she looked at the detective, Jordan saw some of Kiara in her face and placed her as the other grandmother and Derrick's mother.

"My condolences for your loss," Jordan said.

Cecilia said, "What you want? You ain't no cop."

The voice was marred with grief and an incomplete education that stung like a slap to the face.

"Hush now," the woman on her right said. She turned to Jordan and extended a hand. "I'm Marge. This here is my daughter, Cecilia – but you probably figured that."

Jordan smiled but said nothing. This wasn't about him and how clever he was. He shook Marge's hand.

"That there is Velma," Marge said. "She's...well, Derrick was her boy."

Velma looked up again and opened her mouth. Any words she would have spoken were choked out of existence by sadness. Jordan squatted down to be eye level with the ladies. He turned to each before he spoke. He finally landed his eyes on Velma.

"I won't be long. I have a...client who is interested in finding Derrick -"

"Ricky." Velma's word was as soft as a whisper. "We...I called him Ricky."

Jordan and the woman locked eyes. He could see that they had been beautiful once, but that was a long time ago. He smiled before he spoke again.

"Ricky. Why would anyone want to hurt him?"

It was the job. He had to ask questions. Get information. But no one ever said it would be easy or pleasant. Velma's eyes watered over. Any voice she had was again stolen by emotion. Cecilia, however, had no such issue.

"Oh, so this was your big plan?" she said. "Come up in here and upset people?"

Her voice was loud enough to free the surrounding zombies from the spell cast by their phones...for a moment, anyway.

The moment of excitement vanished and the collective heads turned away. Jordan went on.

"I'll need information if I'm going to find out anything." He turned to each woman in turn again. "If I'm going to find out who did this to your loved one."

"What about what we need, huh?" Ceilia exploded and got to her feet. Jordan rose as well, taking a step back. The zombies were reengaged. Some of them focusing cameras on the confrontation.

"Aw, yeah," someone said, "This going up on Insta!"

Ceilia's finger stabbed in Jordan's face.

"What you thinking, coming up in here? That Ricky was some criminal? That he had it coming? All up in here with your fancy ass suit and shit – thinking you better than us!"

Jordan knew there was nothing to be gained here. Silently, he hoped his partners were doing better. His immediate concern turned to getting out of there without further incident. Velma arose. The sad face had an edge to it now. A kind of fatigue mixed with annoyance – and it was not for Jordan. As she got to her full height, she turned to Ceilia and gently placed a hand on each of her shoulders. Ceilia looked at her, just as the soft downward pressure returned her to her seat. As she sank, Marge took her hands – the gesture implying she didn't know what else to do. Mother and daughter both looked at Velma with confusion. Velma seemingly having enough with this pair turned back to Jordan.

"Can you find who did this to my boy?"

Jordan drew in a breath. The short scene was very telling. Ceilia and Marge were the emotional ones, saying and doing what they wanted. Velma had probably tolerated it to keep the peace in this family of sorts. But now, her son was dead and she didn't have the time or energy to deal with foolishness.

"I'll do everything I can," Jordan told her.

The words were true. He had said them before to women not too different from Velma. And while it took nothing to make a promise, when he got his sights on his prey, justice was always served. For Velma's part, she heard the words. Words, in a world where men of every stripe seem to have an endless supply of them. They were all Jordan had...today. They would have to do.

"My son was a good man," Velma said. "He made his share of mistakes," Velma's eyes glided down toward the women next to her, again speaking volumes without saying a word, "but all men have."

"Yes, ma'am," Jordan said, hoping his face lacked enough emotions to not reveal his own demons coming to the surface.

"He was just going to work. I don't know who did this to him."

Jordan sighed. This was a waste of time. It only confirmed what he already suspected. Derrick was just a man minding his own business, getting ready to take his daughter to her piano lesson when the world decided to reach out and grab him, taking a son and a father. Jordan started to say something...appropriate. Another meaningless apology when Velma grabbed his forearm.

"I don't know you," she said, "but you come in here promising something...well, I'm holding you to it."

"You have my word," Jordan told her.

She scoffed. Again, just more words. The breath had scarcely left her body when she froze. She caught that look in Jordan's eyes, a resolution for more powerful than any words. He had done what he came to do. His intentions plain, Jordan nodded his good-bye and left.

The young man at the door opened it for Jordan, face still locked on the Pied Piper of technology in his hand. Jordan was on the house's front porch for less than a second before the door slammed shut again. This was a waste of time, he knew, but leave no stone unturned. He just hoped Don and Malcolm were having better luck.

CHAPTER 6

Second Amendment Nuts

As Detroit went, so did the entire region of southwest Michigan. Suburbs that swelled with the success of the city's growth, felt the same bitterness, albeit somewhat delayed, of the Motor City's decline. However, Detroit's fortunes were changing again and the cities bound to its western boundaries, too, found reason to celebrate. Livonia was one such place. A string of small to mid-size industrial sites off of the Middlebelt corridor saw a sprinkle of business bloom like the first bounties of spring.

Don turned his red BMW 3 Series behind one of these businesses. The vehicle rumbled down the alley usually dominated by box trucks.

"Right here," Malcolm said from his usual spot as passenger. "Where it says 'Mitchell's Industrial Creations.'"

Don complied, but as his hand rotated the wheels into a parking space he said, "It says employee only."

Malcolm made a dismissive gesture as the car nosed its way to the white wall at the building's rear.

"Don't worry about it. We'll just be here a minute. Besides, me 'n Pete go back."

Don's eyes rolled as he switched off the car and exited. He didn't know who this 'Pete' was, but if he was anything like any of Malcolm's other contacts, they could be greeted with welcoming arms or gunfire. He met Malcolm at the front of the car and joined him through a door also marked for employees only.

Once inside, they were assaulted by manmade thunder of series industrial scaled machines. They groaned and clanked as raw material went in the front and screws, springs and bolts came out the other. They formed roughly a semi-circle on a dim and dingy factory floor – each one apparently tooling the part for the next machine's use. Two or three men were stationed at each machine, so focused at their task at hand, none took notice to the new arrivals.

Don saw on either side of the door they entered, a white and relatively clean machine humming quietly, as opposed to the racket their older, larger brethren were producing. From the machine on his right, came a short man.

"Oh, no," he said. "Not you, not now!"

He was all of five feet tall, brown hair competing with gray sprouting from under his yellow safety helmet. A fat digit pointed at Malcolm and Don had no doubt this was Pete.

"Aw, come on, Pete," Malcolm said, rearing back and arms extended. "Don't be like that."

Pete continued toward them. A few of the workers noticed this but stayed at their workstations. Pete got to Malcolm and his finger impacted Malcolm's chest with each word spoken.

"I don't need this shit right now. I want you outta my shop...now!"

Malcolm lowered his arms.

"Seriously, Pete? Why you coming at me like that? Besides, we know this ain't your shop."

The scene started to turn humorous. It was rare to see someone shorter than Malcolm. Add to that, the bright shade of red Pete was turning gave it a cartoony quality. That, plus the bushy mustache beneath his nose, had Don wondering if the man's next sentence would start off with '*Itsa* me...'

"Really? Really?" Pete trembled and Don wondered if he was going to have to break up a fight. "This is how you gonna talk to me? In *my* shop?"

Malcolm's hand came forward in surrender.

"OK, OK. My bad. Sorry. Cool?"

Pete seemed to relax slightly but was still in attack mode. Malcolm went on before he could say anything.

"So, what? The cops been here? Hitting you up about this shooting thing?"

"How do you know about that?" Pete's anger went down another notch.

"I know they think ghost guns are involved."

Pete inflated his chest.

"Privately manufactured firearms."

"Yeah, yeah. That's what I said. Anyway, I was just telling my partner here, I said, Don, man, Pete can't be wrapped up in all this. Ain't that what I said?"

Malcolm turned to Don for less than a second before he was back at it with Pete again.

"I mean, you been down with the ghos- er, privately manufactured firearms since 3D printing made it popular."

Pete's finger raised to Malcolm's face.

"So, here we go! A man executes his FIRST Amendment right to express his support for the SECOND Amendment, and suddenly, he's this," he made air quotes, "gun nut who wants to put guns in the hands of criminals and dismiss proper and responsible gun ownership!" His left hand karate chopped the palm of his right. "Well, let me tell you, my friend -"

Malcolm interrupted.

"Bruh..." Malcolm, rather dramatically, swept his hand up and above the door they had entered.

Don followed Malcolm's hand and saw, for the first time, a banner nearly thirty feet in length. He took a step back so he could read it. In red letters on a white background it read, 'SECOND AMENDMENT LEGIONNAIRES.' On the leftmost end was a logo of two crossed assault rifles over a target. Don went back to the conversation. Pete's cheeks flushed again and his mouth opened and closed silently.

"I mean," Malcolm said, "you literally got the 'we love guns' banner. If it ain't you –"

"I have a right to associate with whomever I please!" Pete said.

Don shook his head. Malcolm brought this out in people and they could be at this for a while. He wandered over to one of the 3D printers, wondering if, since these things were at the center of this issue, maybe something about the case could be revealed. At the machine, he found a chamber with a clear lid over it. Within, a laser, connected to a robotic arm, fired downward over a block of what looked like plastic. The beam traveled in an apparent set pattern as if carving out something. This fit with what he knew about this device from what he had seen and read on the internet. What this particular device was forming, he had no idea, but it wasn't a gun.

Don stroked his chin. 3D printer shops could be found all over the city. What made this one so special? Well, there was Malcolm. He thought there was some likelihood this particular shop had a connection. And there was the giant banner showing love to the Second Amendment. As much as Don hated to admit, Malcolm was right more often than he was wrong.

Don found a laptop affixed to the printer. Its screen displayed the company's logo. Don reached and drew his finger across the mouse pad. The screen went black, save for a box at its center requesting a username and password.

Don smiled. He had few vices and a computer asking for credentials was one of them. He wasn't a hacker, per se, but he had self-trained and dabbled enough in that realm to give himself some credibility. He stole a look at Malcolm and Pete. They were still verbally sparring. He lunged for the keyboard.

"Hey!"

Don's head popped up. Pete had disengaged from Malcolm and was stomping Don's way. Don's hands were hovering over the keyboard and lines of text filled the screen. He had forgotten how engrossed in the world of ones and zeros he could get. It seemed like a moment, but given the amount of data before him, he must have been typing away for several minutes.

Pete reached Don and gave him a hard shove, hard enough to make him back away from the laptop several steps. Malcolm got Pete by the arm.

"All right, all right," Malcolm said. "Ain't no call for all that."

As if time had no meaning, Pete's eyes went to Malcolm's, to where Malcolm held him by the arm, then back to Malcolm's eyes again.

"You gonna lay hands on me?" Pete said. "In *my* place, with *my* crew around?"

Don didn't get Pete's meaning until he looked behind him to the factory floor. The machines were still banging away, but the teams of men working on them had abandoned their posts. As one massive being, they descended on the two detectives. All Don could see was his face leading the evening news with another tales of 'senseless violence.'

"Uh, Malcolm," Don said, still tracking the crew of men, faces devoid of any discernable emotion moving their way. "I think it'll be a good idea if we..."

"I feel you, Don," Malcolm said. He slowly took his hands off of Pete.

"So, it's gonna be like that, huh?" Malcolm asked Pete. Don noticed a trace of sorrow in his eyes, but it could have been an act.

Pete raised his head.

"Get outta here, Malcolm. I ain't got nothing to say to you."

The twin slams of the BMW's doors were the sweetest sounds Don ever heard. The scrum of men spilled out of the employee entrance – the diminutive Pete leading the pack. Don started the engine and with much greater speed than they came, bounced down the alley onto the street.

Malcolm didn't say anything until they got to Seven Mile Road. Then it was a string of profanity.

"What?" Don asked.

Beneath his glasses, Malcolm's eyes got as big as his mouth opening in growing shock.

"What do you mean, '*what*?" Malcolm turned in his seat to face the driver. "What is it with you and computers? Do they call to you or something?"

The corners of Don's mouth went down.

"No."

"Then what is it?" Malcolm's hands flew up in exasperation. "I had him all calm down. He was starting to talk."

"What you find out?"

Malcolm rubbed his chin. "Not much. The police had questioned him. They wanted to examine his printers, but, without a warrant, he wasn't having any of that."

"So, he's hiding something?" Don glanced at Malcolm.

Malcolm's eyes went down as he considered.

"No...no, I don't think so. I would have gotten more if you had been all over his computer. I swear, you need to seek help. You and them damn computers!"

They stopped at a light just at Middle Belt and I-96. The radio was off so only the engine's rumble kept them company. The light switched to green and once traffic cleared, Don turned to get on the freeway and ultimately back to the city.

"I got something," Don said. His voice was soft like he spoke in whispers, which, quite frankly, was a good way to describe it.

"What!" Malcolm's voice, however, was not a whisper. "What do you mean, you got something?"

"I -"

Malcolm's hands went up, patting the air between him and Don.

"Yeah, yeah, yeah! I heard what you said. Just spill what you got!"

Don was all smiles now. He leaned back into his seat – the wrist of his right hand casually resting on the steering wheel.

"The computer at the printer was on a network with all the others in the building. It was an HP running Microsoft Windows. I had a backdoor password for -"

Malcolm broke in.

"Ain't nobody interested in all that! What do you know?"

Don slowly looked back at Malcolm, an arched eyebrow at the tone of his last words. Malcolm, whose body language had been suggesting movement and impatience, deflated a bit and took a more passive demeanor. Satisfied, Don went back to the freeway's less than hectic mid-morning traffic.

"You called out Pete about his 'Second Amendment Legionaries and acted like one of them was more likely to be involved in making these guns."

"Yeah?"

"Well, after I got into the system, I looked at Pete's emails – keyword searched, 'second amendment' 'privately manufactured' and, just for fun, 'witch hunt'. Turns out Pete and these Legionaries been chatting nonstop since these shooting started."

"Shit!" Malcolm clenched his fist. He could see Don heading to a conclusion close to his own.

Don maneuvered to the leftmost lanes, the express to the city. He went on.

"From what I can see, there's about twelve of them. They've been going back and forth for the last week or so."

"About what?"

Don bounced a shoulder. "Seemed like getting ready for more cops coming at them. Getting their stories straight...stuff like that."

Malcolm nodded. "You got all that in that little bit of time?"

Don looked at his passenger again.

"I just skimmed, you know. Didn't have a lot of time to go into details."

Several moments passed in silence. Don knew Malcolm was processing but more importantly, he knew Malcolm was impressed. Don had, in a matter of a few minutes gathered a lot of intel. In and of itself, not very useful, but there was more. He was going to make Malcolm ask for it. For Malcolm, admitting he didn't know something was a little less painful than pulling off his own arm.

"*Aaaaand?*" Malcolm finally asked.

His victory delivered, Don allowed a self-congratulating smile.

"There's twelve of them. But only eleven have been active in the email thread over the last four days. Lots of subject lines like: You still there? What's going on?"

"Really?" Malcolm said. "That's nothing really. Anything could have happened."

Don bounced his shoulder again.

"I know. Still. All I could find out."

More silence and only the rush of German engineering slicing toward the city could be heard.

Malcolm asked, "What's the name of the company?"

Don's eyes went up for a second, then he responded.

"Heavy Machinery and Pressing."

Malcolm nodded.

"Heard of them." He reached into his jacket's inside pocket and fished out his phone. "They're over on the Eastside...over by East-pointe, I think."

A few more seconds passed and Malcolm had the address.

"It might be nothing, but since Jordan's over on that side of town, I'll tell him and he can go and check it out."

"Cool," Don said, eyes focused on the road ahead.

"You hungry?" Malcolm asked.

Don and Malcolm turned to each other. Smirks formed as if Malcolm had voiced the dumbest question ever.

"My bad," Malcolm said. "Head for a Coney Island."

CHAPTER 7

Honor Among Thieves

Cooper admired the simplicity of the printer. The near stillness of the laser as it traveled on its predetermined path. It stitched out a path over and over again and in its wake, it left something behind. Something perfect. The printer and its laser didn't care what it was, it was just doing what it was told. But it did it perfectly. Repeatedly. There was a kind of beauty; a kind of...peace in that. The printer didn't care if it was crafting a machine part for an automobile, or the trigger assembly for an assault rifle. It wasn't hampered by guilt or conscience. It did its job. Perfectly. Every time.

Cooper wished he had such clarity.

He turned away from the huge white machine, its constant whir from its laser like a siren song. He looked to the right where the machine's twin set. Three men from Sabastian's crew surrounded it. They nodded silently coming to an agreement. Cooper knew what it was. They were all on one accord. The machines were running great. The location they hid in was great. Everything was going to plan.

———

Plan. What a joke. Cooper's life hadn't had anything like a plan for years. After high school, all Cooper wanted was to get a good job, marry his sweetheart, Marion, and live happily ever after. And it seemed to be going that way. He got a job at the factory, he got a little apartment and Marion had moved in. Then the bottom fell out. Marion wanted more. More attention, more jewelry, more square footage. And guys who could provide those things started hanging around.

Cooper, like any young man on a mission to keep his girl, worked harder. Got some more shifts at the factory – eventually, he started to bring home more money. But that wasn't enough. When the factory bought a pair of 3D printers, Cooper got an associate degree in the subject. He was hired as a technician. Then lead technician. Then finally, the shift supervisor.

But it was never enough. Marion always seemed to want more. The pressure got to Cooper and a beer with the boys wasn't cutting it. He needed something a little harder – just to, you know, take the edge off. The meth started as an every other day. Then every day. Then several times a day. When the landlord came pounding on the door complaining of late rent, Marion no longer wasn't getting enough – she *had* enough and disappeared with one of her suitors.

Cooper found himself in a deepening hole of debt. He was just scraping by. He was working nonstop around the clock, picking up every shift he could and still lived in constant fear of being evicted. Finally, when he was at his lowest point, Sabastian walked in.

Sabastian found Cooper at a local bar. It was a dive but it was where Cooper met his dealer and got his score. Sabastian breezed through the front door like he owned the place. He sat at a stool next to Cooper. A conversation started. Cooper didn't remember how they got on 3D printers and all they can do. He just remembered Sabastian asking if he was interested in making a little extra money. That very night, at the end of his shift, Cooper programmed one of the printers to create a few dozen bullets from a blueprint Sabastian provided. It was no big deal. The shift had made its quota for the day. The next day, Sabastian received his product and gave Cooper one hundred dollars.

"Wanna make some more money, kid?" Sabastian asked.

And away they went.

It was small jobs at first. Then bigger. Then illegal. Within two months, Cooper was forming small handguns in 9mm caliber out of polymer. One a night. When Sabastian asked if Cooper could do five every Thursday, Cooper admitted he couldn't...not without the rest of the shift finding out. Sabastian reached into his jacket pocket.

"Bring 'em on board," he said, a knot of five thousand dollars in his hand.

———

"Yo, Ty!"

Cooper snapped out of his thought and found Sabastian walking toward him. He had no reason to be, but Cooper was afraid. To be honest, he was always a little afraid around Sabastian. He had a way of making things happen; getting what he wanted...like this factory. Off on Detroit's far eastside. It just happened to be empty and available to Sabastian. Of course, Sabastian said he worked security here for a while. Maybe, Cooper leaving Ohio and coming up here with Sabastian and his crew was timed with when this building would be empty.

"So, what's up?" Sabastian asked.

He was a big guy. The type that looked like he lifted weights or something. All thick under his black jacket and T-shirt, through the shoulders and neck. He smiled a lot, still, there was something about those pale blue eyes of his. The way they seemed to pierce your soul under those fat blond eyebrows.

"It's all good, Marty."

Cooper forced a smile as Sabastian finally stopped. He was standing in Cooper's personal space despite the fact the factory floor was at least 30,000 square feet. There were still several presses and other heavy equipment left behind, but only he, Sabastian and the four guys in his crew were there.

"The programs are set. The power supply is steady." Cooper raised his shoulders. "Even your guys have picked up on how to work the printers." Cooper paused and bit his lips as he thought some more... mentally running down a list of things needed to continue working the machines. He couldn't think of anything else, so he pumped his shoulders again.

"I think we're good if we don't have to move anymore."

Sabastian gave that cold, dead eye smile of his.

"Good. Good! That's my boy!"

He slapped Cooper's shoulder and the smaller man stumbled forward a step. Sabastian turned to the other men over at the second printer.

"Yo! We're good, fellas. Go ahead a crank 'er up! Full speed." Sabastian turned back to Cooper with blond brows raised and wrinkled. "I mean, we are good, right, Ty?"

Honestly, Cooper didn't know. Technically, there shouldn't be any problems running the machine full out. It just hadn't been done before. Industrial standards and all that.

"I mean," Cooper started, "sure, I guess. No real reason not to."

Sabastian struck him again. This time, a playful punch to the shoulder.

"My man!"

Sabastian lifted his hand and made a circular motion over his head. One of the men nodded and twisted a knob on the printer. Its hum went up in pitch. Sabastian smiled again at Cooper and started to walk away.

"Hey, Sabastian."

Cooper reached out toward Sabastian, but made no real effort to touch him. Sabastian stopped short and turned back. The smile was gone and he looked a little surprised. Like he couldn't believe Cooper had called him.

"So,uh," Cooper summoned the courage to ask a question that had been nagging him. "You know, now that we're all set up, I been wondering...what's all the guns for? And, you know, why do we need them so quick?"

Sabastian pulled in his lips and breathed out a sigh. Just as quick, the smile returned and he took Cooper by the shoulders.

"Now, don't you worry 'bout that." He raised his hand over his head. "Way above your pay grade, see?" More smiling along with a pat to the shoulders.

Cooper's face twisted. He wanted to know. He needed to know. Since coming to Detroit, they had been cranking out guns, especially the assault rifles. While he was almost always high, even while setting up the printers, he still caught wind of some shooting going on around the city.

"Yeah but, you know, I mean, I'm in. You know I'm in. It's just that..."

Cooper trailed off. He was getting close to making a demand for information and wasn't quite over his fear of Sabastian to do that. Especially, now that Sabastian's smile, chilling as it was, vanished from his face.

"You're in, Cooper," Sabastian said. His voice was cruel and almost threatening, "'cause you ain't got no way to go." The man's large chest expanded with the drawing in of a deep breath. "Look, Ty." Another smile. "Here's the deal. There's a lot of moving pieces, see? Lots of people involved. People who would rather remain...anonymous. Now," He put his left arm around Cooper's shoulder and started walking toward the front of the building. "I understand you may feel a little... left out, especially given how important you've been to the operation so far. How about this?"

Sabastian's right hand went into his jacket's inside pocket. Cooper went stiff as a board, fearing one of the pistols he had created was going to appear. Instead, another knot of money formed in Sabastian's hand and this one was larger than any he had been given. Cooper's eyes widened and suddenly he didn't care who was involved with this caper or what they were going to do with the guns. He took the money and just studied it like it was some jewel unearthed from a pharaoh's tomb.

Cooper looked away from his latest treasure and turned to Sabastian. As he did, the purr of a phone came from another one of Sabastian's pockets. He held up a finger, withdrew the device and swiftly walked away. As Sabastian grew further away, Cooper's focus returned to his hands. The money was just what he needed. Sure, he was 'dead' as far as the world was concerned and he didn't need to bother with trivial details like rent and car note, but he could sure use a hit.

Cooper had already set up with a dealer not too far from the factory. He could probably grab a car, head to the city, get his score and he back before anyone even missed him. Driven by his addiction's call, Cooper headed for the front of the factory. Beyond the floor was a storage area and then a hall leading to the front door. Sabastian and the team always had a couple of cars out front. Cooper had just made it to the metal scaffolding several feet high and still holding whatever equipment this facility used in its legitimate days. He glanced back to Sabastian and the big guy just stared at him with those dead eyes. He raised his arm in acknowledgment. Cooper turned back around and walked with a bit more purpose if for no other reason than to get away from his creepy boss.

He was just about to round the first roll of storage when a loud sound echoed through the cavernous shop floor. That wouldn't have bothered Cooper so much if it hadn't been accompanied by a sudden sharp burning pain in his midsection. He looked down and in the center of his chest a growing blossom of blood appeared. His brain registered what happened when the sound came again, two in quick succession. His knees gave out and his arm stabbed forward to keep his head from crashing to the floor. It was a useless gesture, for a moment later, he was a crumbled heap on the concrete floor.

He trembled as if he was cold but he didn't really understand why. Of course, Cooper had never been shot before. He heard footsteps and figured, hoped really, someone was coming to help. At the appearance of Sabastian's face in his field of view, all hope was dashed. A smile, of all things, was on his face, and this time, it looked...genuine. Joy was in his eye. He almost looked human.

"I'll be taking that," Sabastian said, bending down and ripping the knot of money he had just given to Sabastian out of his hand.

Cooper wanted to swear at Sabastian but as he stepped out of view, Cooper saw the crew from his shift. He thought they'd be mad at him, but instead they all just grinned.

Harold Garfield made a beckoning gesture.

"Come on, man."

Cooper got to his feet and joined his crew.

CHAPTER 8

Bearded in Their Own Lair

The moment Jordan entered the building, he knew something was wrong. He parked his car in the circular drive just before the door. Once inside, it was quiet – deathly so. But that wasn't it. The lobby was cramped. A box of a room with a pair of chairs to the left, a sliding window to a secretary on the right and a door straight ahead. He peeped through the window. Beyond it was a desk with the expected phone and a mess of papers; forms and colored copies spread out in no pattern. There was a sense of sudden departure. Like a bell rang and the occupants just got up and left.

He reached for the door's handle before him and with a twist, it opened. A short hall followed with a line of plaques and awards along the right wall and a break room on the left. At the end was the main factory floor. The ceiling was high and metal racks held whatever it is industrial manufacturers keep around. A forklift set just before one of the racks doing nothing and, again, seemingly just abandoned. Jordan stood still listening to the silence. There was nothing. He moved through the storage area, heading for the workspace proper. He was still trying to figure out what made the building so unsettling when it hit him. The taste of it more than the smell. The coppery tang getting him at the back of the throat. His eyes panned left and right into those racks now towering overhead. He saw exactly what he expected. A stain of dark crimson on the floor ahead. His left hand found his faithful Heckler & Koch P7M semi-automatic pistol as he rounded the corridor. The floorspace opened up to a concrete floored room populated by conveyor belts and equipment. Overhead, halogen lights' buzz no longer competed with the ratchet of the apparatus they illuminated. By his feet lay a man's mortal remains.

Jordan knelt down; fingers reaching for the man's neck. His eyes still searched the room for whoever had visited this fate on the stranger below him. With no surprise, Jordan did not find the rhythm of life under his fingers.

"Who are you?" Jordan asked the still form.

He turned over the facedown man by the shoulder to get a look at his face. A young blond with a few days' growth on his chin was revealed. He lowered the corpse to its resting place and started for the factory's equipment. He stepped lightly but quickly. In the still his footfalls sounded like thunder to him. He got to an enclosed workstation. It was a cement box with a wood paneled interior with walls littered with safety notices and bulletins. It was just big enough for a manager to have a desk. Something close and accessible to the employees of the factory. It too was unkempt and abandoned. He was checking the room's contents when the first sound reached out to him.

It was a cough or maybe a loud exhale. Whatever it was, it could only be made by a human. Someone who would know about the dead man. Silently as possible, Jordan came around the huge presses, stamps and whatever the hell the other devices scattered around were. He moved on, encountering no one but hearing more sounds. Breathing. Moving. And finally, a voice. He was near the rear of the building and again, it opened up into an empty space. At the far wall, a garage door for delivery vehicles. And at the center most door, a knot of men before the open maw of a truck's trailer.

Five men, four facing Jordan's direction, were all focused on a fifth. A snatch of a word reached him, but Jordan couldn't tell what they were saying. Another workstation was at Jordan's left, so he made for it. He hoped once at the far side, the angle would prevent him from being seen.

"Hey!" One of the men shouted.

Shit.

No such luck.

They all turned to Jordan. The man the other four formed on turned first. As he did so, an assault rifle appeared. A thunderous discharge followed just as Jordan got behind the workstation. It was made of sterner stuff as the bullets impacting did not exit on Jordan's side. He readied his weapon, but as he listened there was something...odd.

Jordan had heard his share of gunplay in his day and while no expert, he knew something was wrong. The assault rifle the apparent leader was firing sounded like an AK-47 but not quite. The other weapons made up a chorus of background noise like a lethal version of Boyz II Men.

Within the noise there was a break. Jordan dared a peek. The guy with the assault rifle (definitely not an AK-47) backpedaled to the relative safety of a support pillar. Jordan switched his view to the others. Each one had some sort of machine pistol, the likes Jordan had never seen. They too were on the backfoot but stood in the middle of the empty space. Jordan took aim at one. His head was down, reloading. The P7M roared twice and leaden death sprang forth. It was followed by a scream of pain, the slap of a body hitting the cement floor.

On to the next one. Jordan fired twin missiles at another man, who, at his comrade's fall, ducked down creating a smaller target. The bullet flew wide, striking whatever large, white piece of equipment filled the rear of the truck. Jordan snarled and went on to the next man – but he and the last of the crew jumped behind another pillar.

Jordan felt he had stuck his head out long enough and ducked back behind the wall shielding him. Just in time too as the assault rifle reentered the fray. The resulting gunfire sounded like a buzzsaw on steroids.

What the hell is that *thing?* Jordan thought.

More shouting. This time from the leader.

"Pick that son of bitch up! Get him in the truck!"

Then, more buzzsaws. Only this time in shorter bursts. Jordan ran back and around the workstation. Appearing on the other side, he saw exactly what he expected. One man half dragging the victim of Jordan's first shots. The only two were backing up, their weapons on where Jordan had been. Assault Rifle swept his weapon in an arch toward Jordan. The detective met his opponent's eyes for just a moment. Blond hair. Small pale eyes above a narrow nose and mouth. There was something about the bearing in the body beneath the leather jacket and jeans then Jordan could not quite place. And nor would he as he again dipped back just as what sounded like all the bees in the world descending on him.

The bursts went on with an occasional report from the machine pistols. Next was the sound of a transmission engaging and the roll of the rear door of a truck slamming into place. Finally, the peel of tires.

Jordan jogged to the spot where his foes were just a moment ago. He approached cautiously and arrived just in time to see a box truck leave a trash strewn alley and hit the nearest street on two wheels. A breath mixed with the frustration of allowing his queries to escape and the rapture of still being alive fled from his lungs. He stopped to examine the battlescape. His right brow arched up. A splash of crimson stretched across the otherwise clean polished concrete floor where two of his shots had met their mark. But nothing else. Given the rate the assault rifle was pushing out rounds, the ground should have been littered with shell casing like popcorn in a movie theater after the opening of a Marvel movie – before *Endgame,* that is. Instead...nothing. Not even from the machine pistols discharges.

Jordan got over his shock long enough to sweep the room again. Just to make sure he was truly alone. That confirmed, he holstered his weapon and said the only thing he could in this situation.

"What the fuck, over?"

CHAPTER 9

Closing In

Standing at Heavy Machinery and Pressing's loading dock, Jordan waved at Don's BMW. The car cruised to a parking space and Jordan's two partners bounded out. Malcolm was readying one of his usual tirades, but Jordan jumped in before he could get started.

"We got to hurry up," he said, his thumb pointing behind him deeper into the factory. "I got to call the cops soon."

"Well, that can't be good," Malcolm said.

Don and Malcolm both leaped onto the dock. They marched into the factory, heads swiveling in every direction.

"I remember this place," Malcolm said, "used to be with the Big Three. Made doorknobs or something."

Don looked over to Malcolm and nodded. They were all old enough to remember at least the end of the era where Detroit was full of factories feeding the three major car manufacturers. Jordan hadn't thought about it, mostly because he was fighting for his life, but this building was something from that era. It didn't matter. They were on a case and needed to get to business.

Jordan led them through the docking area to the storage rack area. His partners didn't have to go far when they saw the body. Malcolm reacted by taking a step back. Don instead, cocked his head to one side, regarding the body.

"Who this?" Don asked.

"That's why you're here," Jordan said with a half-smile. "Do that computer thing you do."

Don knelt down. He looked for a few seconds at the fair-skinned corpse getting fairer. Jordan reached and as before, gently lifted the young man's face off of the floor. Don nodded a thanks as he produced his computer tablet. He snapped a quick series of photos of the man and without a word, stepped away. Jordan returned the dead man to his original position. He didn't want to disrupt the scene too much for the police. He was aware he needed to report shooting someone, even in self-defense, to the cops but he wanted his guys to get a crack at it first. Malcolm was typing on his phone. Jordan glanced at Don, his face also glued to his electronic device of choice. Jordan decided to go with the lesser of two evils and try to engage with Malcolm.

"What you got?"

Malcolm turned to Jordan. He gestured around the room.

"So, this joint here? It was one of them car parts places. Of course, like everyone else, they went belly up. So, they switched to making other shit — parts for washing machines, screws...any contract they could get their hands on."

Jordan regarded the equipment on the floor. They did look decades old and the building had a sense of disrepair and just age weighing on it. He cocked an eye back at Malcolm, who was, as usual, caught up in the rapture of being in the know. To be honest, Jordan didn't know exactly how Malcolm knew what he knew, or even if he was right, but so far, everything seemed to match his story.

"Eventually," Malcolm went on, "they got into this 'private weapons manufacturing' thing." His head dipped down to his phone as if verifying with some internet source. Then with a nod of his head, he looked up again, a cocky little smile at being right.

"They didn't have the 3D printers some of the other gun nuts like my boy Pete did, so they cut corners, took some under the table deals, anything to make some scratch, you know what I'm saying?" He flashed a look at Jordan the last part.

"Go on," Jordan said.

"Well, looks like they were playing all loose with the law and shit, cutting Uncle Sam out of his ill-gotten treasure." Another glance at Jordan with a toothy, knowing smile. "Taxes. State ain't having none of that, so *BAM*. The great state of Michigan shut them down."

Jordan put his hands on his hips and narrowed his eyes.

"Never mind the question of how you know all this, but what does that do for us?"

Malcolm made a high-pitch noise that was his laugh.

"Dog, you know I know people. Besides, I don't know, maybe someone who was up in here is involved in this ghost gun shit. Using this empty building as their secret evil lair or something."

It was a wild idea, but it was better than what they had. Jordan didn't respond when Don called him. He walked up to the other two, still tapping on his tablet's screen.

"Yo," Jordan said, spurring Don on.

"That guy is Tyler Cooper. He's been missing for the last three weeks outta Ohio. His picture was a partial match on the FBI Missing Person page."

"Ohio?" Malcolm said. His voice was high with tension and surprise. "How the hell he get here?"

Don shrugged.

"He and his whole shift disappeared while working at Samson Industrial Works."

Jordan said, "Let me guess: they do 3D printing."

"Yup," Don said with a nod. "Two of their machines are missing. Couple of SmartMake 1200s." He twisted his lips. "Mid-range in terms of industry standards."

"Could they make rifles and handguns that fire caseless shells?" Jordan asked.

Don cocked his head to one side. The term 'caseless shells' threw him. It wasn't in his wheelhouse to know about a configuration of weapon cartridges eliminating the part that typically holds the primer, propellant and projectile together.

"Caseless...what?" Malcolm asked.

Jordan looked over his shoulder to Malcolm.

"Had a gunfight right here and one of the guys tried to shoot every bullet in the world at me." He waved his hand over the concrete floor of the loading area behind them. The *empty* floor behind them.

"No casings. So probably our ghost guns."

"Could be," Don finally answered Jordan's question. "I mean, with the right program and materials, you could make anything."

"Yeah," Malcolm said, "and there's nothing illegal about the stuff you'd need to make the guns – plastic, polymer, I don't know, some other shit, I guess."

Jordan nodded to all this. Still, they were going to need something to point to where this Smart-thingamajig was...*now*. And all they had was a dead guy the cops needed to know about.

Malcolm said, "Maybe if we knew who was here...Jordan, did you get a look at any of them?"

The leader of the UrbanKnights sighed.

"I don't know. We weren't having tea."

Malcolm stood next to him. He held up his phone.

"Here. I got a list of everyone who used to work here. One might be your guy with all them bullets."

Jordan took the phone from his partner. The screen displayed a website for Heavy Machinery and Press. The words, 'Working Hard, Building Better' were at the top of the page above the heading STAFF. Jordan scrolled through a few rows of smiling employees when he stopped.

"Well, shit."

Malcolm leaned in.

"What?"

Jordan put his finger under the picture of a blond man with short military style haircut. He had deep set dark eyes and his smile looked like it was hurting him. Jordan read the name.

"Martin Sabastian."

Malcolm coughed out a laugh as he took back his phone. He looked at his partners with arms outstretched and mouth agape. The look lasted a few more seconds and when no recognition came, Jordan and Don looked at each other. Still no answers appeared so they looked back to Malcolm.

"Marty Sabastian was Detroit PD. Before that he was in the Army or something. Anyway, he was a cop for about six years before he got bounced."

"For what?" Jordan asked.

A laugh accompanied Malcolm's words as he said, "Name something! This dude was into everything. Planting evidence, assault...it wasn't until he got caught with his pants around his ankles with a hooker over on Belle Isle that his services were no longer required."

"Sounds like a nice guy," Don said.

Jordan drew out his cell phone. He turned to each of his friends. His brow was tight and his voice came out in a firm clipped tone. That military way of talking Jordan had when he was on point and in a hurry.

"This is good intel, but we're running out of time. Sabastian's in the wind and I gotta tell the cops about this dead guy here." Jordan jerked his head in the general direction of the dead guy in question. "So, we got until about five minutes after I call 'em to figure out where he is."

CHAPTER 10

The Final Rampart

Joe wasn't going to make it.

This was supposed to be a simple job. Sabastian had been 'contracted' to find a way to get some guns into the hands of criminals. The old-fashioned way of stealing or buying them wasn't going to work. They had to be completely untraceable. It seemed Sabastian was the perfect guy to make that happen. He got them to their secondary location – that was always the plan. The circumstances they got here certainly were not.

Sabastian had done a stretch in the Army and then was a cop for a while. Sure, he took some...*liberties* with the rules, but, overall, he was a good cop. Not necessarily legal... In any event, after he and Detroit PD parted ways, he took a few security gigs before ending up at Samson Industrial. While there, he discovered they were doing some inroads into the whole 'privately manufactured gun' bit. The guys here all ran around yelling about the Second Amendment but in reality, guns just got their nut off. When he was contacted by his silent and mysterious employer, Samson had gone the way of the dodo. The governor had found out about all of Samson's side gigs of making guns and shut them down. Still, Sabastian figured he could track down someone who could get the job done. The Second Amendment Legionnaires were the first choice but surprisingly they spurned the idea. Sabastian dug around and while he found no company willing to make some untraceable guns, no questions asked, there was Tyler Cooper.

Joe thrashed around on the table the other guys had laid him on. Sabastian was about twenty feet away, watching Trent and Keith try to keep Joe still. Brian stood a little further away, holding one of those machine pistols Cooper had made for them, all the while looking out the door into the hallway beyond. The room had been an office or something. Pretty good size too. Used to the foreman's office. Blood was everywhere. And blood was evidence. Joe had bled all over the inside of the truck they used to get the printer out of Heavy Machinery. Sabastian punched the wall next to him as he realized a perfectly good plan was collapsing all around him.

Cooper worked in a 3D printing company, and a pretty good one. They weren't in the gun game, but they had some SmartMake 12Ks – old Heavy Machinery would have killed to get them. Cooper was the weak link. He had some possession charges and a quick check later, Sabastian found that old Ty was getting tweaked. A lot. And one thing meth heads need is a lot of money. Sabastian offered him a lifeline to get his hands on some quick cash and the rest, as they say, was history.

Now this.

Joe cried out in pain and arched his back again in some vain attempt to free himself from his comrades' grasps. If there was a less appropriate location for a dying man Sabastian couldn't think of it. Joe was atop an old desk. The lighting was spotty to say the least. There were three lamps overhead but only one worked. Dust floated in the air like clouds. Sabastian could only imagine the amount of dust, dirt and germs falling into Joe's open wounds.

They were always going to lose Heavy Machinery and Press – it was part of the plan. The plan, however, was for the cops to find Cooper's dead body and go around thinking it was him and his missing crew behind the random killings throughout Detroit. The motive would be a thing of debate for months if not years and in the meantime, Sabastian and his bunch could slip away. But all that had gone to shit now, thanks to the fucking cowboy who had shown up. Who the hell was he anyway?

Trent turned pleading eyes to Sabastian.

"Do something, man!"

It was Keith's turn to get into the act. He screamed something as well, but it wasn't really clear as it was competing with Joe's anguished cries. Brian nervously looked at his dying partner, to Sabastian, then back to the hallway again. The three of them, white, mid-twenties, seemed like good guys, but no soldiers or cops. From what he could gather about what the contractor told him, these three and Joe were in this caper just for a chance to shoot Black guys. Not that he had a problem with that, but it usually doesn't make for the most tactical thinkers.

Trent was right, though. Sabastian had to do something. He couldn't take Joe to a hospital. He'd talk. Sooner or later. Definitely couldn't leave him here. He'd die eventually but, in the meantime, he would scream bloody murder. Then the other three would get in their feelings. One thing would lead to another and, well, it wouldn't be good. Sabastian decided to just cut to the chase.

On a workbench next to him, Joe had laid his assault rifle. It was like an AK 47 but different in so many ways. First it had a larger magazine capacity. More importantly, it fired larger unique caseless rounds. The thing was a beast. He gazed down at it. Whatever else Cooper was, he was a goddamn genius when it came to that 3D printer. This gun was a freaking work of art.

"Sabastian! Seriously!" Trent said.

Sabastian looked over to his team. Joe's thrashing slowed. It would be over soon. This only made the three others all the more desperate. Sabastian sighed and lifted the gun off the table. They were again focused on Joe, screaming his name as blood turned their hands and forearms red. He leveled the weapon at the back of Keith's head.

"For the love of God, Do – Hey!"

Trent had pulled his face away from the ruined body of his comrade just in time to see Sabastian squeeze off the first round. Thunder filled the air, accompanied by the flashes from the weapon's muzzle illuminating the space like some demonic rave. Keith died instantly as the first burst entered his head and exited like some kind of stampede.

Trent fell as a barrage of bullets slammed into his head and chest. The body of Joe caught more than a few rounds, speeding him to the inevitable end. Sabastian switched targets as death and fire raced toward Brian. He tried to return fire, but his aim or lack thereof showed he wasn't the best of marksmen. More noise and flashing discharges filled the room.

Sabastian stepped closer to Joe's desk, using it for cover. Brian ducked in and out of the room, desperately trying to get a bead on his target. But he was no former cop or soldier. And Sabastian was. There was a buzz saw of bullets, a scream truncated by the finality of death and it was over.

A haze of smoke swelled in the room, but no sound emerged after the orgy of noise. None, except Sabastian's ragged breathing. He stumbled out of the room like the taking of the lives of his former comrades had drained him. Beyond the office, Sabastian was again in the cavernous openness of another factory building, long since fallen into disuse. More loading bay doors were off to his right. The truck he and his newly murdered team had escaped in was at the center bay.

Sabastian took a moment to steady himself. The assault rifle slipped from his fingers and clanged to the floor. He took a couple more steps. It had been a while since he killed someone. Well, besides Cooper, but that didn't really count. There was no way Cooper could have harmed him. He got the killing out of the forefront of his mind and considered his situation. Cooper was always going to die at Heavy Machinery but no one was supposed to know it was an inside job. Now, like a row of dominoes slightly askew, the rest of the plan was not moving as expected.

Now what? The only thing that mattered was him getting away. Fuck the plan. It was nuts anyway. How could driving around, killing guys with untraceable guns help?

There was a sound. Like a creak or a...Sabastian didn't know. It wasn't something natural. Like something made by a person. His first thought was it was either from Joe or the others, but he had put nearly the whole mag in them. If they were moving around, he had bigger problems.

Another noise rose from the building and this was definitely a footfall. Sabastian froze but only for a moment. Confusion and shock rooted him in his spot as he could not believe anyone could be there. A figure appeared from a hall on his left. Sabastian was suddenly not surprised.

"How did you get here?" Sabastian asked the guy just an hour before he had been in a gunfight.

A grin formed on the man's face as he continued closer. He was armed with a pistol and Sabastian had to admit, the suit he wore was pretty nice. The hall led from the front of the building and like the rest of the building, it was in a woeful state of disrepair. No one would look at this place and think it was occupied. This gun wielding, fancy suit, *pain in the ass* came here directly from Heavy Machinery and finding that was a fucking miracle. A new question formed in Sabastian's mind.

"Who are you?"

The guy was closer now – maybe thirty feet away. He was a black guy, probably mid-30s but the shorter distance did not make his identity more apparent.

"Doesn't matter who I am, Martin."

Hearing his name from this stranger killed any hope of getting away free and clear. His heart pounded with a manic new energy.

"As to how I found you." He paused for a scoff of a laugh. "It was a matter of connecting the dots. From the crime scenes of your murders, the bullets were clearly custom jobs. So, I tracked down sites that could do that."

Sabastian stabbed a finger at his opponent.

"Heavy Machinery ain't have none of that!"

The man rotated. In a couple of steps, he was across the hallway from Sabastian. He was too far away to reach, but just off to Sabastian's left was the assault rifle. If he could distract the guy for just a second...

"All you nut jobs were in the Second Amendment Legion. It was a matter of eliminating the one who couldn't or wouldn't be involved in this." The guy smiled broader now, like he knew something no one else did. "I have a source who narrowed that down a bit for me. You jokers were left."

Sabastian didn't even know this guy but that cocky little grin of his was starting to piss him off. He glanced at the rifle again. He tried to calculate how long it would take him to dive for it, get the barrel fixed on his target and fire. Second and a half...two seconds...

Sabastian said, "Even so, how'd you find this place? It ain't connected to none of that stuff."

Sabastian was nearly ready to make a dive for the gun. A quick distraction for this cocky mother...

"Once I got your identity, it was a matter of figuring out where you had to go. You had some holdings online to hide your purchases during this whole mess. I got a guy to figure that out, too. One of them had purchased a building in Detroit.... with factory production space and the electricity requirements to run a couple of industrial 3D printers. *This* building in Detroit. It was simple really. Don't do that."

The last line surprised Sabastian. He was on a razor's edge between determination and outright panic.

"Don't do what?"

The gunman quickly nodded his head at the assault rifle on the floor.

"Go for the gun. You won't make it."

The wild heartrate skyrocketed. Sabastian knew one certainty. He could not go to jail. A cop? Even a former cop? He wouldn't last a week in general population. Whatever happened, he had to get that gun. And he could *not* go to jail. He tried one last gambit – one last attempt at distraction.

"I don't know what you're talking about. I don't even know who you are. Why are you so interested in this?"

The man adjusted his aim, bringing his right hand beneath his left. He had done this sort of thing before.

"I'm a private investigator. This is my case. You killed my client's father."

"Hold on!" Sabastian's hands came out, palms forward. "I didn't kill anyone. But, I know everything. Who's involved...who's running this thing. You want to know that, right?"

There it was. This private investigator lost focus for a moment. He did want to know and pulled his head back in mild shock. Sabastian moved. He jumped for the discarded gun. Got his right hand on the weapon's pistol grip. Whirled the business end of the thing on target.

There was a pair of flashes. Two cracks of thunder. And then there was nothing.

CHAPTER 11

A Father's Last Wish

Jordan had long gotten over the feeling of being overdressed. When he entered the hall among a sea of T-shirts contrasted to his Brioni Midnight blue windowpane, wool-silk suit, he had not a moment of discomfort. The T-shirts all displayed the face of Dedrick bracketed by his sunrise date at the top and sunset date on the bottom. There were ten tables with seating for ten each. A banquet table was positioned along a far wall. A line of people waited for meals prepared by family and friends. Someone at one of the tables was watching the news on his phone. Something about the mayor's approval rating going up. In short, exactly what was expected from a repast.

Sabastian really shouldn't have made a move for the gun. It was like he was in slow motion bending down and diving for the weapon. If it had been a pistol, maybe. But a big ass assault rifle? Jordan had more than enough time to aim and squeeze off a pair of shots before the gun got anywhere close to being a danger.

For the second time in an hour, Jordan called Deputy Chief Ford. The first call was to inform the police about Heavy Machinery and Press and the accompanying dead body. The UrbanKnights all had left that scene before Detroit's Finest's arrival. After Jordan had dispatched Sabastian, a second call was in order.

"Martin Sabastian?" Ford asked.

He, along with a flotilla of police, stormed the halls of Metro Dynamics, a small, long shuttered production facility on Concord, just south of East Grand Boulevard. A perfect location for a disgraced former cop to operate out of. The cops did what cops do while Jordan and Ford had a discussion.

"Do I want to know how you and your guys found all this out?" Ford asked.

"Probably not."

There were a few more questions but only two really mattered.

"Why?" Ford said as he ran a hand through his salt and pepper hair. "And who was calling the shots? Couldn't be Sabastian...never was that bright."

"Don't know."

It was an honest answer but Jordan had a theory.

Jordan moved through the crowd as unseen speakers played an assortment of songs from Dedrick's life. Usher's "Yeah" came on. Two women reared back their heads in thunderous cackling.

"Jumped up every time he heard it."

"Couldn't dance a step!"

Laughter disguised pain.

From the crowd, Velma appeared. Unlike the others, she wore no T-shirt. Instead, she sported a black knee-length dress, accented only by a single string of pearls. She walked among the tables, bending over to the diners, thanking them for coming and receiving condolences. She lifted her head with a sigh on her lips and locked in on Jordan. She smiled with those once beautiful, could be beautiful again, eyes of hers. Arms outstretched, she came to Jordan. She took him by the face, drew him close and kissed his cheek.

They parted and Jordan took in those eyes. He wondered what kind of woman she was ten, twenty years ago – and what in the intervening years tried so hard yet failed to dim the light of her beauty.

"Mr. Noble...Jordan," Velma said, tears pooling beneath her brown spheres. "Thank you. I know you can't bring him back..."

Jordan reached and took her hands in each of his. He gave them a tight squeeze, conveying more than mere words could. She returned the gesture with the same meaning.

"I haven't done much," Jordan said.

She slid her hands from his.

"You caught the man who killed my son. More than the police did." She narrowed her brows as if a thought came to her. "But, this seemed, I don't know, complicated. Like..."

She drifted off in thought. Words weren't coming to her immediately. Jordan caught her meaning. Men driving around the city, randomly shooting people. As much as those far from Detroit's borders would like to believe such a thing, it was way too much trouble for no visible gains.

She looked back to Jordan like some clarity had fallen upon her. Her lips parted to speak, but a soulful rendition of "Take My Hand, Precious Lord" filled the air. Velma cocked an ear in the direction of the nearest speaker. She laughed softly.

"He wasn't much for church, but he did love this song."

"Then it's better than anything I could say," Jordan said. She looked back at him. "Goodbye, Velma. And God bless."

He found what he was looking for in a corner of the room. She was as he had met her. Legs swinging at a piston's pace in a chair, this time a folding one, feet hovering above the floor. Kiara wore the same T-shirt, emblazed with the image of her father. Almost on instinct, Jordan looked for her mother. Ceilia was a dozen feet away, engrossed in a conversation with a young man, arms displaying an array of inkwork. A scoff left Jordan. He wanted to believe Ceilia was just mingling with well-wishers, but something in the closeness of the two...that, and the looks from a gaggle of ladies at a nearby table screaming contempt.

It wasn't his problem. He was here to see his client. He was right in front of her before the legs stopped their enteral motion and her eyes lifted to his. A smile came to her lips for the briefest of moments. But girls from Detroit aren't supposed to smile so the expected scowl returned. She folded her arms.

"I guess you here about yo' money, huh?"

Jordan put his hands in his pockets. He waited a beat before answering. She didn't know any better and her bravado was all she had to shield herself and her pre-teen emotions. She turned away when he didn't reply to attitude with attitude. A moment passed as she looked at him again.

"Yeah, about that," Jordan said. "I thought I told you this was a pro bono job."

Her eyes sought out the floor.

"I looked that up," she said. "It's like a good deed or something."

"Something like that."

Awkward seconds crept by as "Un-thinkable" by Alicia Keys floated in the air. Someone screamed out, 'That's my jam!'

Kiara found courage and spoke.

"I don't want you to have something over me. Like you done did me a favor or something."

Jordan stroked his chin as if in thought but really hiding a smile. It was like she was reading from a script she was so predictable.

"I gotta say." Jordan looked at the child like she was an adult and he, having provided a service, was concerned with being made whole. "I mean, I did do a lot of work here. Gun battles and all that. Not exactly pro bono stuff."

Kiara reacted with a sudden surprise. She, as a precocious child, had every right to speak to an adult any way she pleased. How dare he speak to her in kind?

"I don't think you have anywhere near the funds to meet my requirements."

Jordan folded his arms and shook his head a little. Her face clouded as the sting of his words stuck and she drew breath for a retort but Jordan was faster.

"Yet."

The one word froze whatever comeback she had. Jordan reached into his jacket pocket and handed her an envelope. Kiara's eyes went to it, to Jordan and back again. The envelope was before her just at eye level. Finally, she took it, opened it and unfolded its contents. He watched her face and knowing what the letter within proclaimed, was not surprised by the slowly growing grin.

"Are you for real?" Kiara asked.

"Of course I'm for real," Jordan said. The two-page letter in her hands was from Detroit's Edward "Duke" Ellington Conservatory of Music and Art. The school had applications from all over the city. Selections were limited and conducted by a lottery. Everyone who graduated was more or less guaranteed admission into the college of their choice. Kiara had a flash of emotion again but remembering her role as a hardened girl of the city, she again put on her blank expression.

"So what? I'm supposed to go to this fancy school, get a job and be rich or something?" She leaned back in her chair. "And then give it all to you?" Her lips twisted and she again folded her arms. Even still, her resolve was weakening.

"We'll worry about that when it comes," Jordan said.

She didn't respond, arms still folded. Jordan turned. It was a lifetime of training he was trying to overcome. He couldn't expect her to be a bundle of joy no matter how grand the gesture.

"Think of it as your father's last wish," Jordan said over his shoulder.

He was sure that last line would break her emotional walls. Instead, her eyes stayed focused on something unseen in the corner. He shrugged and turned to leave. Maybe he could pry Ceilia away from her male admirer long enough to tell about her daughter's good fortune.

"Mr. Jordan!"

He turned at the sound of his name just in time to be captured by a waist high bear hug. Kiara embraced him for several seconds before it ended just as quickly as it had begun. The emotional display over, she sat back down and reviewed the contents of her letter. Needing no further clue, Jordan left the hall.

He emerged onto Seven Mile near Middlebelt. The hall hosting the repaste was a low squat building proceeded by a parking lot. Malcolm and Don awaited Jordan's return beside a Lincoln Navigator the UrbanKnights owned for just an occasion.

"You all set?" Malcolm asked from the far side of the SUV.

"Yeah," Jordan said.

He stopped for a moment to look back at the hall. The faintest sounds of the gathering's music could just be heard. A wind whispered, drowned out by Seven Mile's traffic.

"You all right?" This time from Don.

Jordan turned back to his friends – men he had known for years through good times and bad – literally life and death. He cracked a smile as it had again dawned on him his success and quite possibly his life, depended heavily on these two men. He moved to the driver's door. At his approach, the doors unlocked.

"I'm good. Just...thinking."

"The waste of it all?" Malcolm was never one to let a poignant moment go by. Jordan's head slowly nodded.

"There's that," he said, "But..." he paused again before looking at his friends on the other side of the SUV. "There's the most important question."

Don and Malcolm exchanged looks before going back to Jordan.

"Why," Jordan said. "Senseless murders. All behind the theft of valuable machinery...employing several men, traveling back and forth to Bum Fuck, Ohio."

Don said, "Yeah. That's...that's got to be pretty expensive."

It was Malcolm's turn. "Yeah, man. Like you said, why?"

The whistle of traffic filled the void between them.

"Cui bono?" Jordan said lowering into the car.

From the Navigator's rear passenger side, Don asked Malcolm, "Cui who?"

"Cui Bono," Malcolm repeated. "Who benefits. Who profits."

EPILOGUE

Mayor Ronald Turner stood at the exit of the Coleman A. Young Building facing Larned Street. Ms. Kennedy, his executive assistant, handed him a stack of paper he was sure she thought was important. And they very well may have been but the mayor's mind was somewhere else.

It was a good plan and by all accounts, it should have worked. The timing was perfect... everything was just as it should have been. But what happened?

One of the police sergeants, doubling as the mayor's security detail, opened the rear door of the black Cadillac Escalade, which served as the mayor's personal vehicle. As always, his eyes scanned the street looking for dangers that certainly weren't there. Still, it was the job.

Turner's time as mayor was coming to a close. He knew this. Too many schemes...the wrong allies. They had cost him the windfall he needed to go into the next election cycle well ahead of any possible opponents. The failure of his *Phoenix Project* topped off with the disaster at the Motor City Magic Casino and he would need something. Something big to get the voters' attention.

The sergeant beckoned the mayor forward. Kennedy reached and opened the building's glass door for him. Turner nodded a good-bye and went into the street. A gust of wind created by the city's manmade caverns struck him and he hurried through the open door and into the dark cocoon of the vehicle.

Crime hung over Detroit's head like a cloud that wouldn't move, no matter the season. The downtown area and a few other selected areas had escaped this shadow but the majority of the city fell under its cold embrace. Turner had no delusion of 'fixing' the city. That was impossible. It was what it was.

The sergeant jumped into the front passenger seat. His considerable size made the SUV dip under his weight. The driver, with rehearsed precision, rotated the wheel, executing a U turn and took them eastward.

Turner tapped out a nervous rhythm of his door's armrest. It was simple. An *if you can't beat them, join them* kind of thing. He would cause crime in Detroit to skyrocket. Drive-bys...guns on the streets. No one would suspect it was artificially being raised. That idiot Martin Sabastian was perfect. He had so many convictions for gun related crimes. And the unlicensed guns the company he worked at made? Perfect. The introduction of Tyler Cooper was just icing on the cake. Sabastian and his crew of lunatics would go through the city shooting on sight. They were even instructed to only kill adult Black males. No women. No kids. There would outrage, but not *too* much outrage. The national press would get in on the act. What will the city do? Who can turn the tide?

Why Mayor Turner, of course. At the right time, he would direct the police to the crime scene. The lair of the villains and the foul machines they used to bring this plague on this already beleaguered city. And what would they find there? Cooper – dead by his own hand. A fate fitting for the lowest of the low. Que the applause of a grateful city. It. Was. *Perfect*.

The SUV got up to speed and Turner began to thumb through Ms. Kennedy's stack. The first item was a letter from a parents' group. He tossed the whole stack onto the seat next to him. He knew what went wrong. *How* was the bigger question. This guy was starting to become a problem. A problem he was going to have to deal with – and soon. Between the murder of former Deputy Police Chief Banner and the affair at the Motown Magic Casino, Jordan Noble was getting too close to some dangerous truths. Turner sighed. He was overreacting. Jordan Noble was just a lucky gumshoe with a mysterious past. If Noble bothered him again, Turner would just go about shedding some light into that past.

Turner leaned back into the leather seat. He had a more pressing issue to occupy his mind. He was just starting to focus on the 24-year-old lovely issue he was speeding his way to, when he just happened to glance out the window. He popped forward, almost putting his nose to the glass. The windows were smoked, no one outside could possibly see him. Yet there he was – at the corner of Randolph and Larned. Like a conjured ghost in a jet-black suit staring at the mayor's car as if he could look into the eyes of the rider in the back. Turner jerked back from the window.

"How..?"

The question bounced around in his skull as his car turned left on Randolph and deeper into the city.

———

On the corner, Jordan Noble stared at the armored city vehicle until it disappeared into traffic.

"This isn't over, Turner," he said.

JAMES H ROBY

About the Author

James H. Roby is a Detroit son, born and raised. He served in the US Air Force as a commissioned officer – tours included Mobile, AL Peterson AFB, CO, Clear AK and four years, three months, twenty-three days, seventeen hours as a Missile Launch Officer in the 91st Missile Wing, Minot AFB, ND.

James has a bachelor's degree from Michigan State University and a master's from Central Michigan University. He's been to World Cities like London and Toronto, seen three icebergs come together 500 miles above the Arctic Circle, and watched dolphins play in the Caribbean. Still, no matter what, even when he's not in Detroit, Detroit is in him.

jameshroby.com
jameshroby@gmail.com

A DEADLY CHANCE

A Chance Freeman Thriller

Alex Cage

CHAPTER ONE

The first time I saw her, I was sitting at a bar top, ordering hot wings, crinkle cut fries, and a club soda with grapefruit juice. The jazz club's door opened, and she floated across the floor toward me. Sounds from the saxophone, guitar, and piano all dampened as she approached. It was hard to take my eyes away from her. She wore a v-neck, navy-colored wrap midi dress with a slit. Sparkles emitted from her wrist as light struck her diamond-speckled gold bracelet. I glanced away briefly, but my eyes quickly returned to her alluring strides. We fixed on each other when she reached the empty bar. Her baby brown eyes complemented her mocha skin. She sucked in her lips and smoothed her dress before sitting one stool away from me.

"What can I get you, ma'am?" Robby, the bartender, asked.

"For now, I'll just have a Coke," the woman said in a gentle tone which kept the words lingering for seconds after she spoke them.

"You got it," Robby said before turning away.

He glanced at me while shrugging his lips and nodding. It was a gesture he and I used for years to suggest the appreciation we had for a female's appearance. The woman's shoulder-length, curly, natural hair bounced as she adjusted herself on the stool. She brushed a bundle of curls behind her ear, exposing her sharp cheekbone and narrow jawline.

She smiled at me.

I smiled back. "How you doin'?" I asked.

Her eyes widened, and her smile grew. She threw a hand over her mouth as she laughed. A soft, enchanting giggle.

I continued smiling. "Happy my question makes you smile and laugh," I said.

She raised her palm and patted the air between us while continuing to laugh. "No, no, no," she struggled to say. "It's just—you have a unique, deep voice. Has anyone ever told you that you sound like Barry White?"

"I may have heard it a few times," I said.

Robby settled a napkin and a dew-dripping glass of Coke in front of her. "Sounds like Barry White and would look like him if he wasn't bald and had more weight on him."

I pointed my thumb at Robby. "See this?" I said. "I've been dealing with it since grade school."

"So, you two went to school together?" she asked.

"Yep. Right here in Tampa," Robby answered.

"Oh, okay."

"My name's Robby, by the way. Let me know if you need anything else," Robby said before looking at me. "Your food will be out shortly, Mr. Barry White. The taller, leaner, bald version."

She giggled. "You have the voice; you have the full beard. If you had more weight, some hair, and was a little shorter, you could go for Barry White's son."

I chuckled, then smiled.

"But," she continued while fixing on my face, "a bald man with a deep voice is a weakness of mine."

"You don't say," I said, leaning toward her. "Because a mocha woman with natural hair and full lips, filling a dress like the one you're wearing, is a weakness of mine."

She glanced away and gently traced her hand down the side of her neck. "You use that line before?" she asked.

"I was just gonna ask you the same thing."

We laughed. I was just about to hit her with one of my best lines, but my phone rang.

"One sec," I told her before removing my phone.

The screen showed a missed call from Keith, my cousin. Not a very close cousin, but close enough to where he felt comfortable calling me when he needed something. Yeah, I was sure he needed something and it could wait, so I figured I'd just call him back later.

"Sorry about that," I said to the woman, placing the phone back inside my pocket. "Now, where were we?"

"You were telling me how you used that same full lips, filling a dress line on other women."

My eyebrows furrowed. "I think we moved past that," I said, half-smiling.

She cocked her head to the side playfully. "Did we?" she asked.

My phone rang again, Keith's number on the screen.

I sighed. "I'm gonna take this," I said before slowly looking her up and down. "Don't wanna but have to."

"Okay."

She smiled and kept her eyes on me as I stood and made my way toward the same door she used to enter. I stepped outside onto the sidewalk and under the cloud-blotted night sky. Pedestrians hoofed the sidewalk and cars whizzed past on the street. I found a spot near the jazz club's entrance and leaned against the wall.

"Yeah, Keith?" I said with the phone to my ear.

"Hi, cuz, I need a favor."

I rolled my eyes. "Naw, really? Here I am thinking you were just calling to check on me."

"You got jokes, but I'm serious, man."

"I was in the middle of sumpin'."

"Look, it's a job."

"You know I don't like doing jobs for family."

"Yeah, yeah, I know. But you're the best at what you do, and this one could be a nice payday."

I sighed but said nothing.

"You'ca put it toward that downtown condo you been saving for."

I inhaled, then slowly exhaled, hoping I wouldn't regret what I was about to do. "What is it? And it betta not be nothing shady," I said.

"No—well, it's a watch."

"A wristwatch?"

"A Rolex. Uncle Eugene gave it to me."

I felt my eyebrows furrow. "Rich Uncle Eugene? I haven't seen him in years. Not since he left Florida. Why would he give you that?"

"He gave it to me when I went to visit him a little while back."

"You hustled it from him?"

"No, no, promise. He told me I can have it and sell it, or do whatever I wanted with it, I promise."

"Uh-huh. How much is the watch worth?" I asked.

"Well, you know it kinda fluctuates depending—"

"Keith, how much?"

"Ahh. Probably forty stacks."

"Whoa! And you lost it?"

"More like someone took it."

I chuckled. "I don't know what Uncle Eugene was thinking, giving you sumpin' like that."

"He didn't care. He has way more where that came from."

"Where's the watch, Keith?"

Keith sighed. "Terrell has it," he answered.

"Wait. The only Terrell I know is the one who wanna be a thug."

I heard Keith shrug through the phone. "Him and a couple of his boys jacked me."

I laughed. I remembered when Terrell was a little snotty nose punk who wanted to be like me. Not exactly sure why he fell off and became a menace to society.

"Yo, not funny," Keith continued.

"Who could've imagined?" I said, tempering myself. "Little Terrell robbing you. You know where he stay?"

"He bounces around, but I know where he's at now."

"Where?"

"Bernini's Pizza."

"Here in Ybor City?"

"Yep."

"Man, that's just up the street from where—wait a minute—you knew I was at my spot."

"I mean, you go there a lot."

I scoffed. "You a trip," I said, shaking my head.

"Will you go get it? I know a man in Sarasota who wanna buy it."

"I got you, but I want half."

"Half?"

"Did I stutter? If you're my client, you're paying like one."

"Whateva, man. I just want it back."

"Guns?" I asked.

"What?"

"Did they have any guns?"

"Yeah, Terrell's boy had one. A skinny guy with a nappy fro and a nappy goatee. He needs to comb that mess."

"But yet they got your watch," I said. "I'm heading there now, half."

I ended the call, then walked back inside.

Robby had his elbows on the bar top, leaning toward the woman, talking.

"So, he came back home after that," is all I heard him say as I approached and took my seat.

"That was quick," Robby said.

"Apparently not quick enough," I said.

"What's that supposed to mean?"

"I didn't know you were a detective in Los Angeles," the woman said.

"That's what I mean," I told Robby.

Robby threw me a dismissal wave. "Your food's about ready," he said before walking toward the kitchen door.

"Hey, just keep it warm for me."

"Alright," Robby said with a shrug.

"I wasn't a detective," I informed the woman.

She winced.

"I passed the detective's exam, but never worked as a detective. Was on LAPD SWAT though."

"Well, aren't you just full of surprises, Mr. Chance Freeman?"

"Oh, he told you my name, too."

She nodded. "Um-hum."

"How long are you going to be here?"

She bit her lower lip and hunched her shoulders. "Not sure."

"Look, I hafta make a quick run, but I'll be back soon, Ms?"

"My name," she said playfully. "I guess you'll find that out when you get back."

"You think that's fair? You knowing my name and me not knowing yours."

She sucked in her lips and shrugged.

"I'll be back soon," I said standing and adjusting my jacket. "And don't believe everything Robby tells you while I'm gone," I continued as I made my way toward the door.

CHAPTER TWO

My mind was on the mystery woman the entire seven-minute hike to Bernini's Pizza. I stood outside the sparsely crowded hole in the wall, wondering what stories Robby was telling her. Thinking about her plump lips and... I jolted my head. Had to get focused, being I was on a job. A simple job, more like a favor for a family member, but a job nonetheless.

As I entered the restaurant, the aroma from buttery bread and sweet tomato sauce struck my nose. Booths lined the walls and square tables filled the checker-tiled floor.

"How many, sir?" a petite, blonde waitress asked as I scanned the restaurant.

I saw Terrell sitting in a booth near the back wall. He had his hair cut in a low box fade. A small scar underlined the right eye of his scowling face. Next to him sat a skinny man whose reputation did truly proceeded him.

"Yeah, he needs to comb his nappy head and face," I said to myself.

"What was that, sir?" the waitress asked.

"I'm here with my friends," I said, pointing and walking in Terrell's direction.

I caught pieces of conversation and chitchat from patrons as I threaded through tables and approached Terrell's booth. A bald man sat across from Terrell and the guy with the nappy hair.

"Terrell, what's up?" I said.

He winced, then squinted as he fixed on my face. "Chance?" he said, a slight chuckle in his voice.

I shrugged. "Yep. It's me."

Terrell leaned back in his seat. "Haven't seen you in a minute," he said.

I snatched a chair from a nearby table and slid it to the booth. "Saw you sitting and thought we should catch up," I said as I sat in the chair.

On the table sat a basket of garlic knots. I grabbed one and threw it in my mouth.

"Mmmmm."

The nappy-haired man looked me up and down. "Yo, who's this, T?" he asked.

"I grew up with him," Terrell said. "He wrestled in school. People liked him. I even looked up to him back in the day."

"This guy?" the bald man said.

"Yeah. Believe it or not, he was the man."

I nodded, swallowing a morsel of toasty, buttery goodness.

"That's until he became a cop," Terrell continued.

I looked at him.

"Dude's a cop?" Nappy said.

"Used to be," I corrected.

Terrell leaned toward me. "Now he's a lowly private eye."

I ran my tongue across my gums to remove any remaining debris from the garlic knots, kissing my teeth as I did. "I have my PI license, but I'm not a private investigator."

"Then what are you?" the bald man asked.

"I'm what you'd call a... retrieval consultant."

"Retrieval what?" Nappy said. "That sounds made up."

I noticed the Rolex on Terrell's wrist. "That's a nice watch," I said. "Reminds me of a family heirloom."

Terrell winced. "What?"

"Oh, I forgot. You dropped outta high school and started selling drugs, so you probably don't know what heirloom means." I shared my gaze between Nappy and the bald guy. "And that was way before I became a cop, you know, a bad role model," I said, making air quotes with the last sentence.

Terrell glared at me with bulging eyes and tense jaws. I looked at him with a nonchalant gaze, then kissed my teeth again.

"What you wanna do, Terrell?" Nappy asked.

I eyed him.

"Do you know who you talking to?" Terrell asked me.

I sighed. "Look, I don't have all night," I said, shaking my head. "I know you took that watch from my cousin, so give it to me and we can all go about the rest of our nights."

"Your cousin talks too much, so now it's my watch."

Terrell nodded at Nappy. The skinny man glowered at me, then reached toward his waist and went to stand. Before his butt could leave the seat, I shoved the table into his stomach, then jabbed him in the nose. The bald guy rose from his seat. I rammed the table into his lower abdomen. He arched toward the table as I delivered a devastating right cross to his jaw. The bald man toppled to his side before falling to the floor. Nappy held his nose with his head bowed toward the table. I removed the gun from his hip and yanked him from the booth. As he squirmed on the floor, clenching his bloody nose, I stepped over him and took his seat in the booth right next to Terrell. He stared at me, mouth and eyes wide open.

"The watch," I said with the gun aimed at him under the table.

Terrell removed the watch and handed it to me. I inspected it before placing it into my pocket.

Terrell shrugged. "Now what?"

"Stay away from me, my family, or anyone close to us," I said. "Or it won't end well for you."

Terrell poked his lips and stared at me. I pushed the gun into his side. He grunted.

"Got it?" I said.

"Yeah, yeah I got it."

I ejected the magazine, then pulled the slide, allowing the bullet in the chamber to clink to the floor. Giving Terrell the magazine, I slid from the booth and stepped around his boys on the floor. Terrell told them about my wrestling days but failed to mention I was a golden glove champ back in the day.

"I'll hold on to the gun," I told him.

As I walked to the front of the restaurant, I noticed eyes on me.

I stopped. "Imma cop," I informed everyone before leaving. Which wasn't a hundred percent true, but it wasn't a hundred percent false either.

Once outside, I tossed the gun into a garbage bin and removed my phone. *Got it*, I texted Keith.

The phone rang with a number I didn't recognize.

"Freeman," I answered.

"Ah, Mr. Freeman," a man's voice came through. "I hope it's not too late."

"Who's this?"

"A... a prospect."

"Well, office hours are closed."

The man chuckled. "I understand, but I'll make it worth your while."

"I tell you what, call tomorrow during business hours and we'll talk."

"I'll do that, Mr. Freeman. Talk with you tomorrow."

"Didn't catch your name."

"We'll talk tomorrow."

The call ended. I didn't care for after-hour calls from people I'd never met. Gotta get Darla to have the calls forwarded directly to voicemail, I thought on my way back to the jazz club.

CHAPTER THREE

I made it back just in time to catch the woman standing from the bar.

"Leaving already?" I asked as I approached.

She winced as if my presence surprised her. "Oh, you," she said, adjusting her dress. "Yeah, I have to go."

I shrugged. "Okay. Let me walk you out."

She looked at me, at the door, then at me again. "Ahh—sure…"

Robby placed a steaming plastic bag on the bar top. "Here's your food," he said to me. "Figured you'd want it to go."

I grabbed the bag. "Thanks, Robby," I said, guiding the woman toward the door.

"Nice to meet you, ma'am," Robby said.

She responded with a quick wave. "Same here."

When we stepped outside, her head was on a swivel.

"You alright?" I asked.

She smiled. "Yeah. Just keeping an eye out for my Uber," she said before looking at her phone. "Should be here any minute now."

"Perfect," I said, extending my hand to her. "Let me hold your phone."

"Why?"

"Trust me."

"That deep voice."

She handed me her phone. I dialed my number and hung up when I felt my phone vibrate inside my pocket.

"Now you have my number," I said, giving her back the phone. "And since you know my name, you can add me to your contacts."

"I'll be sure to do that."

"Speaking of names, you never gave me yours."

She stared at me with a half smile. "Eve," she said. "Eve St—Price, Eve Price."

"Well, nice to meet you, Eve Price," I said while extending my hand.

Her hand seemed to disappear in the expanse of mine as we shook. It was soft and smooth.

"Same here, Chance Freeman."

The heart-shaped diamonds in her bracelet discharged a glint as we released each other's hand. A car pulled to the curb. Eve glanced at the vehicle, then her phone. "Well, that's my ride."

I brushed past her and opened the car's back door.

"Such a gentleman," she said as she slid into the back seat. "Thank you."

"Anytime, babe."

We exchanged smiles. I shut the door, then watched as the car veered into traffic. The glowing taillights shrunk with each passing moment.

Now that's a woman, I thought before walking to my black Cadillac XTS and driving home.

Home was an Aquanaut Drifter 1250 docked at a marina on Harbour Island. Older model boat, but she held her luxurious appeal. Got it from a rich client at a steal. Equipped with a small kitchen, bathroom, and bedroom, it was all I required for a short-term living arrangement. A specific condo downtown had my name on it, that is, once I saved enough to pay cash for it.

Inside the boat, I placed my bag of food on the counter near the kitchen area. Removing the Rolex from my pocket, I sat on my bed and studied the expensive piece of jewelry.

I felt a grin cross my face. "One step closer to the condo," I uttered to myself.

The next morning, I woke to the sun warming my face. Yawning, I leaned forward and rubbed my eyes. I went to the bathroom, relieved myself, washed up, then lotioned up before heading back into the living area and shrugging into some fresh threads: a khaki button up, short sleeve lapel shirt with navy slacks. While tossing the debris from my dinner into the trash, I grabbed my phone. Two missed messages waited for me on the screen.

Good looking out.

Let's meet up.

Both from Keith. *At one, the park by the aquarium*, I replied.

I slid the Rolex into my pocket and gave my living quarters one last glance before climbing from the boat and clunking across the dock toward my car as the sounds from spilling waves and squawking birds accompanied me.

———

My first stop was at a drive-through window where I ordered two sausage egg biscuits with hash browns and two coffees. Both with sugar and creamer. The next stop brought me to a small business plaza in Brandon. I parked and exited the car with food and cup carrier in hand. Nestled between a flower shop and a travel agency was my unit. There was no business name on the unit. And that was on purpose. Ninety-five percent of my clients came by referral, and I liked to stay as anonymous as possible. The office space serves as a place to handle back-office stuff and occasionally meet clients. Balancing the food and cup carrier in one hand, I removed my key and unlocked the door.

"You're late," a firm female voice said as I entered.

A small woman with glasses sat at a desk, behind a computer screen, typing.

"Good morning, Darla," I said, shutting and locking the door behind me.

I walked to her desk and placed the food and coffee on top.

"Careful. I'm trying to work here," she said before reaching for the bag. "What'd you get me?"

"A sausage egg biscuit."

She looked at me with her lips poked. "I told you I'm cutting back on that stuff."

"What was I supposed to get you, avocado toast?"

"Yeah," she said, rolling her eyes.

I hired Darla a couple of years back to help with things around the office. And she was very good at it. She had worked as an executive assistant for a big-time law firm downtown but didn't like how the men treated the women. She was efficient, smart, and easy on the eyes. I was lucky to have her. But I never allowed her name, glasses, pretty face, shoulder-length hair, or the way she spoke to fool me. Darla was from around the way, and I knew she was packing.

My phone buzzed. Keith liked the text I sent him earlier.

"Who's that?" Darla asked. "One of your floozies?"

"Keith. Floozies? Somebody's jealous."

Darla scoffed. "Yeah, right."

I grabbed my coffee and biscuit sandwich. "I'll be in my office," I said.

"Oh—someone's here for you."

"Where? In my office?"

"Yeah."

I contorted my lips and cocked my head to the side. "And you just now telling me?"

"He just got here a few minutes before you."

"Well, who is—you know what—I'll find out myself. Oh, can you forward the after-hour calls to voicemail?" I said on the way to my office.

The door was already open. Inside, a fit man wearing a dark gray suit sat in a chair opposite my desk with his legs crossed and his hands clenched in his lap. The man stood as I placed my coffee and sandwich on my desk. His height put him eye level with my shoulders, so I could see the top of his head, which was filled with short, curly hair. Above his lips and around his chin, tiny hairs protruded from his light-brown skin.

"Mr. Freeman," he said, extending his hand while smiling with some of the straightest pearly whites I'd ever seen.

"Yes, and you are?" I asked as we shook hands.

"Patrick Stevenson. I called you last night."

"Right," I said, circling behind my desk. "Sorry if I was abrupt, but it was after hours, and I was working a case."

Stevenson shrugged. "If you're as good as I hear, then I guess you can afford to be abrupt."

"So, who referred me?"

"Charles West."

"Chuck? Really?"

Stevenson nodded.

Charles West was the rich client in Miami who sold me my houseboat. Nice man. He and I were on good terms.

I gestured for Stevenson to sit as I did the same. I placed my elbows on the desk and clenched my hands together. "So how do you know Chuck?" I asked.

"Years ago, we worked a deal together."

I nodded.

Stevenson adjusted in his chair and leaned forward while tugging his blazer's lapels. "Look, Mr. Freeman," he said, "time is of the essence. I have a job for you and I'm willing to pay a lot for its completion."

"Okay," I said, reclining in my chair. "What do you need me to retrieve?"

"A person."

I chuckled. "Mr. Stevenson, I'm in the business of collecting things, not people. I'm sure Chuck mentioned that."

"Yes, he made it clear you specialize in the procurement of personal articles, but I don't want you to collect the individual. Just locate them."

"Why me? Sounds like a missing person's case." I hunched my shoulders. "Why not just go to the police?"

"The situation is... well, the situation is delicate."

I scoffed and shook my head. "Delicate?"

"I'll pay fifty thousand up front and another fifty once the job is complete."

I leaned forward. Now he really had my attention.

"One hundred thousand?" I asked to confirm.

Stevenson nodded. "I'll even throw in an extra ten percent for any supplies you may need."

I drummed my fingers on the desk and felt my eyes squint. My experience taught me when something sounded too good to be true, it probably was. But then I felt a nudge from the condo owner inside of me, urging me to take a chance. You only live once. Plus, I'd seen rich people spend a lot more money on things less suspicious.

"When was the last time you saw this person?" I asked.

"Does that mean you're taken the job?" Stevenson asked.

"Probably."

"Well, then, three weeks ago. New York."

"You live in New York?"

"I do a lot of business in New York, so I have a home there, yes."

"New York? What makes you think this person is in Tampa?"

"The previous contractor I hired tracked them here."

"So, you already hired someone?"

Stevenson shook his head. "They're no longer working for me. We had a disagreement."

I stared at him in a moment of awkward silence. "Your case seems complicated, Mr. Stevenson," I said.

"I guess you can say that."

Looking at him, I reclined in my chair and rubbed my chin. I wanted to give the impression that I was possibly considering passing on the job.

"One hundred thousand," I said. "Just to locate this person?"

Stevenson nodded. "That's it," he said, a slight chuckle in his voice.

"Alright. Half up front, and I'm going to need details about this missing individual," I said while reaching for a pen and pad on my desk.

"Certainly," Stevenson said, as he reached into his blazer's inside pocket and removed a check. He slid it across the desk. "That's half," he continued before reaching into his opposite pocket and producing a photo. "And this is her," he said, sliding it toward me.

The picture was upside down. As I grabbed the photo, I spun it right side up, and my eyes widened when I recognized the person in the picture.

"That's my wife," Stevenson said. "Eve."

CHAPTER FOUR

Eve looked the same in the photo as she did the night before at the jazz club. Except in the picture, she was wearing what appeared to be a white wedding dress.

"Your wife?" I asked, wanting to make sure I heard him correctly.

"Yes," Stevenson said. "That picture was taken at our wedding two years ago."

"Eve? Eve Stevenson?"

Stevenson chuckled. "Yes. And I would like you to find her."

"I don't get it. You know she's here in Tampa. Why not just call her? She is your wife."

"It's not that easy. She's already changed her number twice."

I shook my head. "Don't know, Mr. Stevenson. Sounds like she doesn't want to be found."

"You work for her or me?"

"Neither at this point. Not until I have more details at least," I said while sliding the check back toward Stevenson.

He sighed. "What else do you need to know?"

"Any idea why she would come to Tampa?"

Stevenson hunched his shoulder. "My only guess is she's familiar with the area. Her family used to vacation here a lot when she was younger."

"Speaking of family, does she have any here?"

"Not that I know of," Stevenson said while folding his arms. "Which is why I'm hiring you. To figure all this out."

"What happened in New York three weeks ago?"

"What do you mean?"

"You said the last time you saw your wife was in New York three weeks ago. What happened before she headed south?"

"That's personal. Suffice it to say, we had a minor disagreement."

"You certainly have a lot of disagreements, Mr. Stevenson."

"Do you want the job or not?"

Part of me wanted to say no. This whole situation stunk of complications. Not to mention it bordered on a conflict of interest, considering I had already met Eve and all. But the condo owner inside of me didn't want to pass on the chance to make a hundred grand.

I nodded. "I'll take the job," I said.

"Great," Stevenson said, clapping his palms together, then sliding the check back toward me.

"Is there anything else I should know, Mr. Stevenson?"

Stevenson shrugged his lips and stood. "Nope," he said, adjusting his blazer. "You have my number, so let me know as soon as you find anything."

"Of course," I said while standing.

As I circled around my desk, Stevenson exited my office. I stood just outside the office door and watched as he exited the unit. When the door shut behind him, Darla stared at me. She adjusted her glasses as if she was expecting an explanation. I shrugged, then returned to my desk. I usually told Darla everything, and this situation would be no different. Just wasn't ready to tell her right then.

I ate my sandwich and finished half of my coffee while considering how to approach the case. Giving Mrs. Eve Price, or rather Eve Stevenson, a call would probably be a good place to start. It could be a breach of her trust, though. Not to mention a breach of my client Mr. Stevenson's trust. I thought maybe I'd just have a conversation with her and see what's going on. If the water was too murky, I'd back out of the job without receiving the final payment. I felt good about that plan.

"Darla," I called as I exited my office.

She looked at me.

"I'm stepping out. Can you do me a favor, sweetheart?"

She cocked her head to the side and poked her lips. "What is it, Chance?"

"Can you find out as much as you can about Patrick Stevenson? And his wife, Eve Stevenson. Try Eve Price, too. I believe that's her maiden name."

"Where're you goin'?" Darla asked.

"The bank. Call me when you have something," I said before locking and shutting the door on my way out.

I eased behind the wheel of my Caddy, then pushed the ignition button, and she purred to life. The drive to the bank took less than ten minutes, and it took about the same to get inside and deposit the check. A smile arched on my face when I looked at the deposit receipt and saw my account fifty thousand dollars fatter. Once back inside my car, I figured it was time to start the job, so I removed my phone and dialed Eve's number.

"Hello," a male's voice answered.

"Sorry," I said. "Think I dialed the wrong number."

"Are you looking for Eve Stevenson?"

"Maybe. Why you ask?"

"Who are you?"

"Just some good-looking guy she picked up last night. Who are you? Where's Eve?"

"Detective Greg Hiller with the Tampa PD."

I winced at the phone. Many questions flooded my mind, but I kept cool and listened.

"Not sure where Eve is," Hiller continued. "But since you're one of our only leads, maybe you can answer some questions for us."

"I'll think about it," I said before ending the call.

My eyebrows furrowed as I held and stared at the phone. "What's goin' on?" I said aloud.

CHAPTER FIVE

Greg Hiller. I worked with the Tampa PD almost every day and the name didn't ring a bell. So, I figured I'd pay a cop buddy of mine a visit down at the station. When I arrived at the station, the officer at the front desk immediately greeted me.

"What's goin' on, Chance?" he said as he buzzed me in.

"What's up, Jeff?" I said, opening the door. "Just another day in paradise for me. How's the wife and boys?"

"Good, man. Everybody's good."

I nodded. "Good. Hey, is Ed around?"

"Yeah, I think I saw him earlier."

"Thanks," I said before passing through the door.

I entered a large room filled with desks, many occupied by officers typing away at their computers. A few of the officers engaged in conversations with civilians sitting opposite their desks. On my way to a glass-walled office near the back, I passed some desks and dodged a handcuffed man arguing with his police escort. The office blinds were closed, so I knocked on the door with the plaque, *Sgt. Edward McCoach*. After five knocks and no response, I opened the door and peeked inside to find the office empty.

"Hi, Chance," a soft voice said to my back.

I turned and behind me stood a tall, slender woman in a police uniform. No name tag. She wore her hair pixied with curls, and her dimples cut into her almond-toned cheeks as she smiled at me.

"Hi," I said, trying to remember her name and confused at how I could forget such a woman's name.

"Looking for Sergeant McCoach?" she asked.

"Yes, I am, pretty thang."

She giggled. "Pretty thang. I have a name, you know."

"Of course you do."

"What is it?"

I chuckled. "C'mon now."

"You don't remember. You're something else, Chance Freeman."

"Remind me."

She winced at my request. "It won't be that easy," she said. "Follow me."

We threaded across the floor and into a hallway. In a huddle room at the end of the hall, we found McCoach, in uniform, alone. His buzzed-cut head bobbed as he wrote on a whiteboard.

"Sergeant McCoach," the female officer said.

McCoach turned to us. His bushy eyebrows furrowed, and his thick mustache arched above his pouty lips. As long as I'd known him, he'd always had a gruff demeanor but was a good cop and friend.

"Chance is here to see you," the lady officer continued.

"Thanks," McCoach said in his husky voice.

She smiled at me. "And don't tell him my name," she said before leaving the room.

"That lady's something else," I said, walking between a line of chairs on my way to McCoach. "Don't know why a woman like that would want to hang around a police station with a bunch of middle-aged white men like yourself."

McCoach shook his head and chuckled. "You said that the last two times you saw her," he said before turning back to the whiteboard. "What's going on, Freeman? I have a briefing to prepare for."

"Was wondering if you could help me sort out some details on my case."

"What case?"

"I'm looking for someone."

"You find things, not people," McCoach said as he wrote on the board.

"This case is a little different."

McCoach faced me. "Different how?"

"Well... It's..."

As I struggled to explain myself, the door opened, and a group of officers entered the room.

"Let's talk later," McCoach said.

"Morning, Detective Sergeant," one officer said as he sat in a chair upfront.

McCoach nodded.

I found a chair near the back of the room as more people entered. McCoach went through roll call. There were only about nine officers in the room, so it wasn't long before he called, "Detective Hiller."

"Present," an athletically built man said.

Unlike most of the other officers in the room, I'd never seen him before. He had tanned skin and slicked-back, dirty-blond hair. Looked like he spent more time on the beach than in the police station.

After roll call, McCoach had every officer give an update on their case. I leaned back in my chair and paid little attention until he called on Hiller.

"Sir," Hiller said to McCoach. "I've closed the Langford case. Turns out their missing daughter was just a rebellious runaway. She returned home when she ran short on cash. The Dunn case appears to be a situation where the husband doesn't want to be found. Think we have the identity and location of his mistress. I imagine we'll have that one wrapped up by the end of the week."

"Hey, new guy," a woman officer said to Hiller. "What about the case that came in a few days ago?"

"Yeah, I was getting to that one. Looks like a case of the wife just not wanting to be found but may be more complicated," Hiller said.

McCoach's forehead wrinkled. "What makes you so sure?" he asked.

Hiller hunched his shoulders. "Well, according to the private investigator," he said, looking at the ceiling, then tapping his index finger against his chin. "What's his name? Ahh, Jacob Finley. When he filed the missing person's report, he stated the husband was looking for her, but she didn't act like she wanted to be found—by her husband, at least."

"Wow. No one wants to be married these days," the female officer said.

"Don't worry, someone will marry you," one male officer told her.

"Just like I'm sure there's some woman desperate enough to marry you."

The group laughed.

"Okay, everyone, calm down," McCoach said. "What makes you say there're more complications?" he asked, directing his question at Hiller.

"Not entirely sure, just seems—strange," Hiller said. "We knew the motel where she was staying, thanks to Finley. So, we thought it would be a good idea to check on her ourselves to confirm if a crime was actually committed. But when we arrived there this morning, we found her door open and the room disheveled, like she left in a hurry."

I sat up in my chair.

"She left behind some clothes and a few personal items, including her phone," Hiller continued. "The motel clerk said she never checked out."

McCoach cuffed his chin. "Interesting. Any more leads?"

Hiller shrugged. "I've reached out to Finley but haven't been able to get him," he said before sighing. "I was planning on running by his office today." Hiller wagged his index finger in the air. "There is another possible lead. As we were storing her phone into evidence, it rang. I answered the call and a man with a deep voice said he was looking for Eve."

"Eve's the missing person?" the female officer asked.

"Yeah. Eve Stevenson. But anyway, I guess the man met her the night before."

"A booty call!" one officer blurted. "You answered her booty call."

The group laughed, and I took it as my cue to leave, so I stood from my chair and headed for the door.

"Everybody, quiet," McCoach said. "Have we identified this man?"

"Not yet," Hiller said. "But I have the guys looking into the number."

When I made it to the door, McCoach noticed. I gave him a hand gesture that suggested I'd talk with him later, then exited the room.

CHAPTER SIX

While sitting at a red light, I removed my phone and called Darla.

"Don't have any information on the Stevensons yet," she answered. "Was just about to look into it."

"Before you do that, I have a different person," I said.

"Okay. Who?"

"See if you can find a phone number and address for Jacob Finley."

"Finley?"

"Yeah. He's a PI."

"Alright. I'll see what I can find."

"Thanks, baby doll."

"Chance, we've had this talk already. Darla is my name."

"Fine. Thanks, Darla."

"Much better. I'll let you know what I find."

The call ended, and I continued my drive to the jazz club. When I arrived, a few cars pulled in around the back of the building. I parked the Caddy at the curb, then walked along the building's side. Cigarette smoke struck my nose when I made it halfway to the back. A group of men hummed while unloading footlockers from a van and carrying them into the building's back doors.

"You're a little early, aren't you, Chance?" one of them said.

"What, no shows before lunchtime?" I asked.

The man chuckled. "Naw, man, I'm afraid not," he said between cigarette puffs.

"Is Robby in yet?"

"Yeah, he's in the kitchen."

"I thought you were quitting," I said, pointing at the cigarette in his hand.

He shrugged. "I did—but you know—old habits. Like you and women."

I shook my head. "Watch it now," I said on my way through the back doors.

A dark hallway welcomed me. At the end of the hall, there was a stage and a dance floor. I continued across the dark, quiet space to the bar top. Clanking and ruffling flowed from the kitchen. I knocked on the bar top.

"Robby!"

The noise stopped. Seconds later, the kitchen door swung open, and Robby walked through.

"Chance. What're you doing here?" he said.

"Need to ask you something."

"Okay, go ahead."

"You remember that woman last night?"

Robby smiled. "Oh, yeah. How'd things go with you two?" he asked.

"Nothing went with us. We exchanged numbers. She got in her ride, then we went our separate ways."

Robby kissed his teeth. "Really?"

"Yep. Really."

"Imma check the front camera's video to make sure," Robby joked.

I pointed at him. "Do that. And send a copy to me."

Robby paused and stared at me. "You're serious. What's going on?"

I glanced around the jazz club, then waved Robby toward the kitchen door. "C'mon, let's go to the back and talk," I said, circling the bar top.

I spent five minutes catching Robby up with the situation.

"Boy, you sure know how to pick em," he said.

"Don't start," I told him. "I didn't pick her; she just happened to be here the same time as me."

"Why didn't you tell McCoach about her? He'll have your back."

"I'll let him know. Didn't want to complicate the situation."

"How complicated you think it's gonna be when he finds out on his own? They already have your phone number."

"It's a burner number."

"Either way, just a matter of time before he finds out. Might as well be from you."

I nodded. "I know. Hey, did she mention anything to you when I stepped away?"

Robby shrugged his lips. "No," he said, shaking his head. "I did most of the talking."

My phone vibrated. I removed it and saw a missed call from Darla.

"I hafta get outta here," I said on my way to the kitchen's door. "Don't forget to send me that video footage."

"I gotcha," Robby said as I exited the kitchen.

On the way to my car, I returned Darla's call. She gave me the address to Jacob Finley's private investigation practice in St. Petersburg, even texted me a picture of him. I drove on I-275 for twenty-seven minutes, then on I-175 for an additional two minutes before arriving in downtown St. Petersburg. Traffic was smooth, with only a few vehicles on the road. As I cruised along 4th Street, palm trees, shopping and restaurant outlets, and the occasional ten to twenty-story building surrounded me on either side. I parked at the curb across the street from Finley's office. It was a small, one-story industrial building sitting somewhat off to itself.

I made my way across the street, and as I approached the front door, I noticed it was ajar.

I knocked on the door. "Finley, Jacob Finley."

A loud thump followed by footsteps shuffling wafted to the door. I peeked through the opening and a rotten odor swept across my face. I knew the smell. It was the scent of death. I quickly entered a small receptionist foyer, where a desk greeted me. Behind the desk, a contemporary sitting area sat surrounded by offices and a conference room. A man lay on the floor near the sitting area. I raced to him and quickly recognized Jacob Finley.

"Finley," I said, but he didn't answer.

I'd seen many dead bodies and was positive I was looking at one. He had two bullet holes in his chest and one in his head. The blood had dried to his skin. As I kneeled to further inspect the body, a figure zipped from an office and down a hall near the back of the building.

"Hey!" I shouted as I gave chase.

Dashing into the hall, the figure shoved open the door at the opposite end. I increased my pace and shouldered through the door before it closed. Stumbling into an alley, I looked up as a garbage bin eclipsed the sun and descended toward me. The trash container struck my side and knocked me off balance. I smacked into a wall and trash from the bin littered the alley. As I pushed from the wall, I got a good look at the figure.

A man in a hoodie with a face band covering his mouth and nose stood in front of me, four inches shorter than my height. He flicked open a knife and rushed me. I raised my fist and my survival and boxing instincts kicked in. As the man thrust the blade at my chest, I parried his hand before throwing two jabs in quick succession. Both attacks struck his jaw, then out of pure muscle memory, I threw a left cross and connected with his right eye. My attacker stumbled backward, and his back slapped into a wall. With my fist raised, I shuffled toward him. He feinted a knife jab. I flinched, briefly leaving my left side open. The man slashed the blade and grazed my left shoulder. I hit him with another cross, then shoved him. My opponent raced through the alley with me behind him. As we approached the main road, the man knocked over a garbage bin. I dodged it but slipped and fell to one knee. In the couple of seconds it took me to recover, the man turned a corner at the intersecting street.

When I exited the alley, he was nowhere to be found.

"Great!" I grumbled, grabbing my left shoulder and inspecting it. My fingers brushed over a minor cut with a thin coat of blood. "That punk cut my shirt. What's goin' on here?"

I pondered the question during my short walk back to the car. Once inside, I immediately removed my phone and dialed.

"We need to talk!" I said before the person could greet me.

CHAPTER SEVEN

"What is it? You have something for me?" Stevenson asked.

"Yeah, I have something," I said. "Questions."

Stevenson released a nervous chuckle through the phone. "I've told you everything you need—"

"No, you didn't. Was Jacob Finley the PI you hired?"

"Well, Chance, I don't believe—"

"Stop playing with me, Stevenson. Yes or no."

"Yes, but I've already told you I hired someone."

"Finley was based in Florida. That means you already knew Eve was in Florida when you hired him."

"Was?"

"Yeah, was. Finley's dead."

Stevenson gasped. "What? Oh, my. How?"

"Looked like a professional hit."

Stevenson said nothing.

"You knew Eve was in Florida before hiring Finley? How?" I asked.

Stevenson sighed. "I had someone following her in New York. That investigator learned she was seeing a guy in Tampa."

"Wow."

"I know. Can you believe her?"

"Her? What about you? If you put as much time, money, and energy into understanding your wife as you do spying on her, you wouldn't have this problem."

Stevenson chuckled. "If you say so," he said. "Anyhow, the man she cheated with would come to New York and visit her a couple of times a month. I wanted to know more about the guy, but the investigator I hired in New York didn't work out of state. That's when I employed Finley. He dug up some information on the guy and provided surveillance when I needed it. So, when Eve left New York, Finley confirmed she met up with her little boy toy."

"Hmm. What was the disagreement between you and Finley?"

Stevenson drew in a long breath before slowly exhaling. "I may have made an unsavory suggestion, but I didn't mean it."

I shook my head at the phone. "Wishing death on you wife and her lover," I said. "Have to admit, Mr. Stevenson, this isn't looking good for you."

The line fell silent.

"Why did Eve leave New York? What did you two disagree on?" I said, putting specific emphasis on disagree.

"Like I told you before, it's personal."

"This whole situation smells. I'm seriously considering backing out of the job and handing everything over to my cop buddies."

"Wait, look, all I need from you is to locate her and you'll have an additional fifty grand. Plus another ten for any incidentals."

The condo owner inside of me once again reared his acquisitive head.

"I'll find her, but I need to know why she left New York to begin with."

Stevenson sighed into the phone. "All right, I'll tell you," he said. "Just not over the phone. Let's meet somewhere."

"Your day's pretty open?"

"Yeah."

"Okay. I'll call you back a little later with a place."

"Sounds good. Hey, did the cops find Finley's body?"

"They will," I said before ending the call. Figured the less

Stevenson knew, the better, since he was my client, and I didn't trust him.

The drive back to Tampa took me a little longer on account of traffic. During the entire ride, I wrestled with the thought of calling McCoach and telling him about Finley's dead body and all the events leading up to it, but ultimately, I decided it wasn't the right time. The situation had gotten messy, and I was slap in the middle of it. I stopped at a popular burger joint's drive thru near downtown and ordered a double cheeseburger and Coke. The food remained untouched until I made it to my destination—a sparsely crowded park just twenty yards from The Florida Aquarium. Finding parking was easy. I grabbed my burger and Coke before exiting the car, then strolled across the parking lot until I passed two immense palm trees and ended up in an open grassy field. I surveyed the area but didn't see Keith. Taking a bite from my burger, I circled a small playground, then found a seat at an empty bench.

Children's laughter mixed with parents' admonishments for safety chattered the air. I finished my burger and made it halfway through my Coke before I saw Keith. He grinned on his way to me. I ejected from the bench as he approached. Keith stood a few inches shorter than me. We had similar body builds and features except he was thinner and sported a faux hawk and fade.

"Hey, what's up, cuz?" he said, smiling.

"Don't what's up cuz me," I said. "You betta had not hustled Uncle Eugene outta his watch."

"I told you I didn't. He gave it to me. You know how rich people can get—sometimes they just give stuff away."

"Uh-huh, I bet," I said, clasping my cousin's hand, then pulling him in for a hug. "Come here, man. Haven't seen you in a while."

"Yeah, it's been a minute," Keith said as we released our embrace. His eyes squinted as he pointed to my left shoulder. "What happened?"

"Nothing, just a scratch," I said.

Keith shrugged.

"So, when do you plan on meeting your buyer?" I asked.

"Today. I can have your cut to you tomorrow."

With my head on a swivel, I reached into my pocket and removed the Rolex. "Half," I said while handing the watch to Keith.

Keith smiled as he placed the watch in his own pocket.

"Half," I repeated.

"Yeah, yeah, I got it," Keith said. "I hafta go if I wanna catch the buyer today. Whatchu doin the rest of the day?"

"My afternoon's full. Gotta client to meet."

We fist bumped.

"I'll let you know when I have it, cuz," Keith said before making his way across the park.

"You betta," I said.

When Keith disappeared from my view, I removed my phone and dialed Stevenson on the way to my car. He answered on the second ring, then I gave him the address to a diner in Valrico and told him to meet me there in an hour.

CHAPTER EIGHT

Thirty minutes later, I pulled into the diner's parking lot. Since I didn't trust Stevenson, I wanted to be early to case the place. I removed my Smith & Wesson M&P and its magazine from my glove compartment. After confirming the chamber was clear and inserting the magazine, I emerged from the car and stuffed the handgun in the back of my pants and made sure my shirt hid it. Once inside the diner, I sat at a table near the back. A petite waitress with short, curly hair checked on me periodically. Each time, I told her I didn't want anything and was waiting for a friend. But after twenty-five minutes of us doing that dance, I finally asked her to bring me a Coke. With small sips, I finished the soda twenty minutes later and there was no sign of Stevenson.

The waitress approached my table. "When is your friend coming?" she asked.

I hunched my shoulders. "They were supposed to be here like fifteen minutes ago." I smiled at her. "But I do appreciate you keeping me company, sweetheart."

She smiled. "Want a refill?"

I shook my head. "I'm good."

"Can I get you anything else?"

"Not right now. How much do I owe you?"

She threw me a dismissal wave. "It's on me."

"Why, thank you," I said, standing from the table.

"I hope you find your friend," the waitress said.

I shrugged before stepping to her and leaning toward her ear. "I think I like my new friend better," I whispered.

She giggled. I smiled at her, then eased toward the door. I glanced back and gave her one more smile as I exited the diner. On the way to my car, I dialed Stevenson. The phone rang until I got his voicemail. I ended the call before Stevenson's voice asked me to leave a message. I waited in my car for another ten minutes. Stevenson didn't show, so I left for my office. On the way, I called him a second time and once again got his voicemail.

"I don't know what he's tryna pull," I uttered to myself as I ended the call.

A ginger, garlicky aroma with a hint of soy sauce struck my nose as I entered the office. A steaming container sat on Darla's desk. The bathroom door thumped closed, and she emerged from the hall.

"You're back," she said on the way to her desk. "I was just about to have a late lunch. Would've ordered you something but figured you'd already ate."

"I did," I said with a sigh.

Darla stopped walking and pivoted away from her desk. "Everything alright?" she asked while walking toward me.

I pursed my lips and cocked my head to the side.

"Do you need to tell me something?" she asked.

I shrugged. "You know, baby doll. Just the normal hiccups cases like this bring."

Darla rolled her eyes and sighed before glancing at the floor, then my left shoulder. "Is that what that is?" she asked, pointing at the minor injury. "A hiccup? And no, I don't know. You left without telling me about this case."

"Well, we're about to change that now," I said, placing my hand on her back and guiding her toward her desk.

I spent eleven minutes telling Darla everything while sitting near her desk as she inspected and cleaned my cut.

"Well, you had a busy day," she said before shaking her head. "You and these women."

I said nothing, just flinched as she pressed a bandage on my cut.

"The good thing is," she continued, "you had a big payday today."

I felt a smile arch on my face. "Yeah, it's nice," I said while nodding.

"Good for you," Darla said before slapping my injury.

"Ouch! What was that for?"

"Not telling me sooner. I thought we were a team."

"We are a team, baby doll. I just wasn't sure what was goin' on. Still not. And this is good for us. You know I got you."

"Good," Darla said, standing from her desk with the first aid box in hand. "That means I may not have to work for you much longer." She walked toward the bathroom.

"You don't mean that, baby doll."

"Why do you insist on calling me that?"

I chuckled to myself as Darla disappeared into the bathroom. She came back a minute later, drying her hands with a paper towel as she sat back at her desk.

"Did you find anything on Eve or Stevenson today?" I asked her.

She shook her head while opening her container of food. "Nothing more than you already know, but I'll dig deeper now, obviously."

I nodded. "Also, Imma need you to work from home. Just until we get a handle on this situation."

Darla shrugged. "I get it," she said while sticking a fork into her stir fry chicken. She glanced at me. "You're gonna let McCoach know?" she asked before taking a bite.

"I will."

Darla stared at me.

"I will," I repeated.

"Okay."

"I know I asked to have the after-hour calls forwarded to voicemail—"

"They're still going to you," Darla said between chews.

"Good. And since you'll be keeping a low profile, have all the calls forwarded to me."

"You're sure?"

"Yep."

While Darla ate her late lunch, I went to my office and locked my desk and file cabinet drawers. When she finished, we locked up the rest of the office and I tailed her home. She lived in a luxury apartment building downtown with a concierge, plenty of restaurants and shops nearby, and security.

Parked at the curb across the street, I watched as she entered her parking garage. She called me to confirm she had made it to her unit. After leaving Darla's place, I drove five blocks to my future condo. It was a luxury building much like Darla's, expect it sat near the water. I eased the Caddy next to the curb, then watched the building. It helped me to think. My phone vibrated with a text from Robby.

I only sent the part where you helped her in the car.

I played the video below his text message. It showed me opening the car for Eve, us staring at each other, then me shutting the door and the car pulling off. I dropped my phone in the passenger seat and continued in my thoughts.

After five minutes, I pulled off. On the way home, I stopped for a pizza. I liked pizza because it meant I didn't have to do any dishes.

With the case being so shaky, I decided to drive the boat to another dock I rented about a nautical mile away from my primary marina. It was for emergencies and only a few people knew about it. I arrived there in under twenty minutes and secured my boat for the night.

After finishing my pizza, I called Stevenson, but again only got his voicemail. I tossed the phone on my bed, and everything else, I placed on the stand next to the bed, then went to the bathroom to wash up. When I made it back to the bedroom, my phone vibrated. A text message displayed on the screen.

I got all the cash, Keith's message read. *Same time, same place tomorrow?*

That should work, I replied before connecting the phone to its charger.

I lay on the bed, and three minutes later, my eyelids shut.

CHAPTER NINE

I woke to my phone ringing, my office forwarding number displayed on the screen.

"Hello," I answered.

"Freeman," McCoach's husky voice came on the line. "You still in bed?"

I groaned as I adjusted my position. "Well, it is just a quarter after eight."

McCoach scoffed. "I keep forgetting you work for yourself," he said. "A guy like me has to be up early, even after a late night."

"Caught another case last night?"

"I'm always catching cases, but yes."

I leaned forward and twisted to where my legs hung over the bedside and my feet rested on the chilled floor. "Oh, really?"

"Yeah. We had a body, but it was out of our jurisdiction, so had to play ping-pong with Saint Pete PD all evening."

I said nothing.

"Then this morning I thought of you."

I stayed quiet

"You came to me for help with your case, but we never talked about it. Figured I'd reach out to you before I got too busy today."

I sighed. "Yeah, we need to talk."

"I bet we do."

"You had breakfast yet?" I asked.

"Not yet."

"Let's meet for breakfast. In an hour."

"Sure. Jay's Cafe?"

"That's our place."

Fifty minutes later, I pulled into Jay's Cafe's parking lot. The cafe was a dark yellow, one-story stucco house converted into a restaurant. I placed my gun in the glove compartment and exited the car. Once inside the cafe, I spotted McCoach sitting in a booth with a steaming cup of coffee to his mouth. I threaded through the sparsely occupied dining room and slid into the booth across from him.

"You ordered yet?" I asked.

McCoach shook his head. "Just the coffee," he said. "Was waiting for you." He pointed at the table. "The waitress left a menu."

"I don't need it," I said. "I'm g'ttin' my usual."

McCoach shrugged. "I told her," he said before chuckling. "But didn't protest when she insisted on leaving it in case you wanted it."

"You always allowed women to push you around."

"And you always allowed women to get you in trouble."

I smirked. "Well, that's not always a bad thing," I said.

We both laughed.

McCoach took another sip of coffee. "So, tell me about this case you're working."

"It's a mess and doesn't look good."

"I bet."

I adjusted in my seat. "Where to start?" I sighed. "Yesterday I took a job from a wealthy, annoying, and kinda shady guy."

"Who?"

"Stevenson. Patrick Stevenson."

McCoach's eyebrows rose. "Have you seen him today?" he asked.

My eyebrows furrowed. "No, but interesting you asked because I was supposed to meet him yesterday and he ghosted me. Why? Do you know him?"

"I don't know him, but I know where he is."

I winced. "What? Where?"

"The hospital."

"The hospital? As in Tampa General Hospital?"

McCoach nodded. "Exactly," he said. "He was involved in a hit-and-run last night. An officer on the scene briefed me. Stevenson's pretty banged up."

My gaze fell to the table before flicking back to McCoach's face. "How did it happen?" I asked.

"A silver SUV ran a red light. Totaled his car. He's lucky to be alive."

"What about the driver in the SUV?"

McCoach shrugged. "Don't know. They fled the scene."

Once again, my gaze fell to the table.

"What's going on, Chance?" McCoach asked.

I looked at him and sighed. "I'll tell you what I know. But like I said, it's a mess, and doesn't look good."

It took me sixteen minutes to tell McCoach what I knew, and to show him the video Robby sent me. It would've taken less if not for the waitress' interruptions, but at that point, I had a cup of coffee in front of me and both McCoach and I had ordered our food.

McCoach placed his cup on the table after taking a sip. "The video shows you weren't the last person with Mrs. Stevenson when she left the jazz club," he said.

I nodded. "That's right."

McCoach cuffed his chin, then patted his cheek with that hand's index finger. "So, when you arrived at Finley's office, he was already dead and someone else was at the scene?"

I glanced around the cafe, then leaned toward McCoach. "Yes," I said, almost in a whisper. "He was dead."

"So, the other person there killed him?"

I shook my head. "I wouldn't say so. Finley was shot—looked like a professional hit. The guy I tussled with had a knife. He had some moves and all, but he didn't strike me as a stone-cold killer. Also, Finley had been dead for a while before I got there."

"What makes you say that?"

"His blood had already dried. Did your guys find any gun shells?"

McCoach shook his head.

"Yeah. I think whoever killed Finley is careful and wouldn't've made the mistake of returning to the scene."

"But we know for sure you and this other guy were there," McCoach said.

"What does that mean?"

"You said it yourself, Freeman. It doesn't look good."

"But you believe me, right?"

"Of course, but—"

The waitress approached and placed our plates on the table. "Anything else I can get for either of you?" she asked.

McCoach shook his head.

"No thanks," I told her.

She walked away, and I turned back to McCoach.

"But what?" I asked.

"There's procedures around these things. You know that," McCoach said.

"I'm gonna figure out what's going on."

McCoach took another sip of coffee. "I hope so. Hiller comes across a bit flaky, but it won't take him long to figure out you're involved. Your number is on both Stevenson's and Eve's phones. How long do you think it'll take him to find out it's your number?"

"Probably a while," I said.

McCoach's eyebrows furrowed.

"It's a burner," I continued.

McCoach sighed. "I didn't hear that," he said. "My point is, it won't take him long to realize Stevenson hired you." He sucked in his lips and looked up as if a thought came to him. "How much is he paying you, anyway?"

I shrugged. "That's client privilege."

McCoach chuckled. "Yeah, I bet it is. Well, I'm the Detective Sergeant on this case. That means you don't have much time to sort this out. I'd say you have twelve hours."

"Starting when?" I asked.

"Twenty minutes ago."

"Well, I guess I better eat fast."

We finished our food and left the cafe. McCoach reiterated he could only keep the heat off me until ten o'clock that night. And since he didn't owe me that, I thanked him and told him I'd be in touch soon.

The first stop I wanted to make was the hospital. I dialed Darla on my way there.

"I was wondering when you were going to call me," she said when she answered the phone.

"Why you wondering about me?" I asked in a teasing manner. "Thought you'd take advantage of this remote work situation—you know, lie around in your pajamas and eat cereal."

"You're half right. I'm in my pajamas, but not doing the cereal thing today."

"Well, I just wanted to call and check on you."

"Ahh, how sweet of you."

"I told McCoach."

"Really? How'd that go?"

"To put it short, I have less than twelve hours to get a grip on this thing."

"Hm. That was very lenient of him."

"Trust me, I'm not complaining," I said.

"Where are you heading now?"

"To the hospital. Stevenson is in the hospital."

Darla scoffed into the phone. "What's going on?"

"He was involved in a hit-and-run."

"It's getting stranger by the minute. But speaking of Stevenson, I did a little more research this morning, and did you know he owns a lot of properties in New York and New Jersey?"

I shrugged at the wheel. "He mentioned he does a lot of business in New York, so?"

"So why does he use various LLCs? I checked out five of his properties and two are in a corporation, two more in another, and the last property is in one by itself."

"A bit strange, but many business owners operate various LLCs."

Darla sighed. "Right, but two properties are literally up the street from one another and they're under different company names."

"That's a bit more unusual. You thinking shell companies?"

"Probably."

"Well, I'll be sure to ask Stevenson about that."

"Alright. I'll keep poking around," Darla said before ending the call.

CHAPTER TEN

After finding a spot in the hospital's parking garage, I took my gun from the glove compartment and stuffed it in the back of my pants as I emerged from the car. With the way the case was going, I wanted to be prepared for anything.

Inside the hospital, a full-figured woman sat behind the front receptionist counter. She smiled as I approached.

"You're here to see someone?" she asked.

"I am. But seeing your pretty face just made my day."

The receptionist's smile grew. "Who are you here to see?" she asked before glancing at the computer screen in front of her.

"Stevenson. Patrick Stevenson."

She stared at the screen while dragging and clicking her computer mouse. After a moment, she looked at me and said, "He's on the fourth floor. Room four twelve."

I smiled. "Thanks, beautiful."

She gave me a visitor's sticker, then I rode the elevator to the fourth floor and strolled the empty hall, following the signs to room four twelve. Stevenson had a room to himself. He lay on the bed with bandages wrapped around his head and bruises on his face. As I walked closer, I noticed his eyes were closed. Thinking he was unconscious, I pivoted away, and when I took my first step toward the door, Stevenson groaned. I turned to him. His eyes flickered open as whispers flowed from his moving lips. I stepped to his bedside and arched toward him.

He inhaled a labored breath before exhaling and mumbling, "Fi—find her. Mancini."

"Mancini?" I repeated.

Stevenson sighed, then closed his eyes, his breathing slowly regulating. I figured he was still on pain meds and wasn't all coherent, so I left the room. *Who's Mancini?* I thought on the elevator ride down. As I passed through the lobby, I saw Hiller talking to the nurse at the receptionist's counter. He didn't notice me, so I continued to the parking garage where I passed two more uniform officers on the way to my car.

I had a little under eleven hours left and no leads. While inside my car, I dialed Keith, figuring it would be a good idea to get my payment sooner rather than later and deposit it, just in case I ended up in jail before the end of the day.

"What's up, cuz?" Keith answered.

"Are you able to meet me sooner?" I asked.

"Yeah—yeah, when?"

"Twenty minutes."

"Cool. Same place?"

"Yep."

Seventeen minutes later, I pulled into the parking lot near The Florida Aquarium like I did the day before. To my surprise, Keith parked a few spaces from me a moment later. I left my gun in the glove compartment and exited the car.

I walked to Keith's car. "You're actually on time," I said to him as he stepped out from behind the wheel.

Keith shrugged. "I was in the neighborhood," he said before closing the car door. "It's back here."

I followed him to the trunk. While he opened it and leaned inside, I surveyed the area. A moment later, he emerged with a brown paper bag in hand.

"A paper bag?" I said as he handed it to me.

"Man, that's all I had at the time," Keith said before smiling and shutting the trunk. "But it's twenty stacks."

Inside the bag were two stacks of one hundred-dollar bills. Both stacks were separately banded with a paper bill strap indicating ten thousand was in each. I examined a few bills and immediately knew they were real. A skill I picked up during my time on the force and honed in my current line of work.

I placed the bag under my armpit. "Looks good," I said while pivoting toward my car.

Keith clapped his hands together. "Alright," he said, following me to the Caddy.

I popped my trunk and settled the bag in a hidden compartment off to the side.

"You gonna be able to get that condo in no time," Keith said.

I shut the trunk. "And whatchu gonna do with your portion?" I asked him.

"There's some other—investments I'm looking to make."

I shook my head. "Betta be legal and stable investments."

As I uttered those words, a familiar, 2012 Chevy Caprice cruised along the road on the opposite side of the parking lot. The vehicle was a pearl black with silver trimming and tinted windows.

"Were you followed?" I asked Keith.

Keith winced and said, "Nah, man," before following my gaze to the Caprice. "Wait. That's Terrell's car."

"I thought so."

"Chance, we gotta bounce."

"He's not stupid enough to try sumpin' in a public area."

The Caprice whipped into the parking lot and sped toward us.

"Maybe I'm wrong," I said. "Split up!"

Keith ran in the aquarium's direction while I darted toward the park. The car screeched to a stop. Terrell, the skinny guy with the nappy hair, and the bald man all emerged from the car. Terrell pointed toward me and yelled, "Get 'em," before rushing after Keith.

Nappy and the Baldy hustled in my direction. I bolted into the park and ran the paved pathway for fifty meters before veering across an open field and through a small, wooded area. I glanced over my shoulder and saw Nappy and Baldy hurrying across the field. Once out of the woods, I ran toward the public restrooms and hid behind the small building. I reached behind my back and felt disappointed when I realized I had left my gun in the car. *Guess Imma have to do this the old fashion way,* I thought.

As I peeked around the corner, I saw the men exit the woods. They stopped running and scanned the area with their heads on a swivel. The restroom building was the only standing structure close by, so they immediately turned their attention to it. I weaved my head behind the corner, then rested my back against the wall and listened. Footsteps and heavy panting breaths approached. I peeked around the corner and saw the two men near the front of the restrooms. Nappy held a pistol. Baldy's hands were empty.

"You think he went inside?" Baldy asked.

"I don't know," Nappy said. "Go see while I check the back."

He circled the building on my side. I eased behind the corner and waited. Nappy's footsteps crunched over leaves and twigs as he made his way closer to me. As his gun's barrel inched around the corner, I clenched it, then twisted my wrist as if I was turning a doorknob. The skinny man yelped as I yanked him toward me and delivered a devastating cross to his jaw.

Nappy went to sleep as he leaned to the side and fell to the ground. With the gun aimed, I eased along the wall toward the front of the building. As I turned the corner, the Baldy exited the women's restroom. He winced, then charged at me, ramming into me as I struggled to bring the gun to bear. The firearm flung from my hands and scraped across the pavement. I shoved him, then shuffled backward off the pavement onto the ground. He launched toward me with a wild punch. Bobbing under his attack, I struck his exposed ribcage with a right hook, then a left. Baldy immediately hugged his midsection and sunk toward the ground. With his face wide open, I connected a crushing cross to his jaw. His eyes closed, and he fell to the leaves and dirt.

"Weak chins," I uttered to myself, picking up the gun and jogging back into the woods.

I hustled through the park, back toward the aquarium, and in the direction I last saw Terrell chase after Keith. The track led me along the side of the aquarium and to the back, where a small plot of grass and a view of the Ybor Channel's still waters greeted me. With my head on a swivel, I surveyed the area and noticed a shabby deck leading to an old boat shed. As I made my way toward the shed, I heard voices flow from inside. I raced across the creaky dock and yanked the shed's door open in time to hear Terrell yell, "Ya'll think ya'll can punk me—" He had his gun trained on Keith, but as the door slammed behind me, he swung the pistol in my direction. While he pivoted toward me, I grabbed his firearm with my free hand, then pistol-slapped him with the gun in my other hand. Terrell stumbled toward the back of the shed. Keith dodged around the staggering man and circled to the door.

I pointed both guns at Terrell. "I thought I told you not to mess with me or my family," I said.

He stepped back with his chin raised and nose crinkled. "You tough with those guns, huh?" he said before shaking his head. "I ain't scared of you."

I cocked my head to the side, squinted at him, then looked at the guns. "You think I need these?" I said, a slight chuckle in my voice.

Terrell shrugged. I shook my head and walked toward a window at the shed's sidewall. Once there, I tossed the guns through the broken glass. The pistols splashed as they hit the water.

"You hafta be running low on guns," I said, walking back to Terrell. "That's three I've taken from you in less than forty-eight hours."

Terrell grimaced.

I shrugged. "No guns. Now what?"

Terrell nodded and raised his fists. "Okay."

He threw a jab. I weaved from the attack's path. Terrell followed up with a cross. I bobbed under the punch and struck him in the gut. He shuffled backward and doubled over.

"Done already?" I taunted him.

Terrell looked at me with gritted teeth. From his pocket, he removed a knife and flicked it open. Growling, he charged toward me with the blade drawn back above his shoulder. I stepped forward, hit his nose with a quick jab, then grabbed his knife-wielding arm and used his momentum to toss him over my hip and to the floor. Air huffed from his mouth as his back hit and splintered the wood beneath him.

"Whoa," Keith enthused.

With Terrell's arm still in my grip, I locked his elbow and took possession of the blade. As the thug lay sprawled on the floor, I closed the knife and placed it inside my pocket, then patted him down for any other weapons. I felt something jingle in his left pants pocket. I removed the item, and my mouth fell open when I recognized it.

CHAPTER ELEVEN

In my hand rested the same gold bracelet I saw Eve wearing the other night. It had the same heart-shaped diamonds. I was sure of it.

"Where did you get this?" I asked Terrell.

He leaned forward and coughed. "Nonna yo business," he said.

I kneeled and grabbed his collar. "You betta start talking," I said.

Terrell smirked.

I yanked his collar until he was a few inches off the floor, then slammed him back to the floor. Terrell gasped.

"Where'd you get it?" I said, wagging the bracelet in front of him.

He coughed. "From some chick. What's it to you?"

"What she look like?"

"I don't know. Curly hair. Plump lips. Plump butt. She was bad. Didn't wanna give me her number, so I made her give me the bracelet."

"Where was this?"

"You asking a lot of questions."

I yanked Terrell by his collar again.

"Wait, wait," he protested. "Near Riverview. Across the street from the mall—by the water where those new townhomes are."

"I know the place. Was she staying there?"

"I don't know. It was getting dark. Didn't see where she came from, but looked like she was heading toward the townhomes."

"You betta not be lying."

"I'm not."

I released Terrell's collar. "And when I say stay away from me and my family, I mean it," I told him before jabbing his face.

Terrell's head hit the floor, and he immediately took a nap. I stood and settled the bracelet in my pocket, then headed straight for the door.

"What's goin' on?" Keith asked, trailing behind me as we crossed the deck.

"I'll explain later. Let's get outta here."

When we made it back to the parking lot, I removed Terrell's knife and poked a hole in both back tires of his Caprice.

"That's gonna make him mad," Keith said.

"So?" I said.

Keith shook his head.

"Why don't you hang low for a couple of days?" I continued. "You know—stay outta sight."

Keith shrugged. "Okay."

I slid behind the wheel of the Caddy and started the engine. Keith entered his car and followed me onto the main street. I turned right, and he turned left. After driving a quarter of a mile, I dialed my cop buddy.

"McCoach," he answered.

"Hey, it's me," I said.

"Tell me you have something. You have nine and a half hours."

"Plenty of time. I may have something, but not sure."

"Tell me what it is."

I shook my head at the phone. "I will once I follow up on it. Want to confirm before I have you chasing down a dead lead."

"Okay then."

"But there is a suspicious group at the aquarium. They're driving a black Caprice. You may wanna check it out."

"Should I even ask?"

"Probably not."

McCoach chuckled. "I'll have a unit sent."

"Thanks. Hey, does the name Mancini mean anything to you?"

"Mancini, Mancini. The only Mancini I know are mobsters."

"The mob?"

"Yeah. They're big in New York City. An old friend of mine at the New York District Attorney's office has been working for years to shut them down. Why?"

"Stevenson mentioned the name. May be a good idea to put a security detail on him."

"I already did. Sent a unit this morning."

"Hiller?" I asked.

"No, a couple of uniforms. What are you thinking?"

"Not sure. But I'll let you know as soon as I figure it out."

"I'll be waiting."

I ended the call and headed for the Riverview Mall. On the way, I dialed Darla to have her look into any connections between the Stevensons and Mancinis. The mall's parking lot was sparse, so it was easy to find a spot facing the townhomes across the street. I had an unobstructed view of the community's entrance. The small neighborhood comprised of fifteen or twenty new waterfront units, with a few more under construction. Most looked empty, and the community was quiet with little activity. Not much vehicle traffic moved on the main road near the entrance, and very little foot traffic used the sidewalks. I looked down the street and saw a few old, dilapidated buildings maybe two blocks away.

Gentrification. I cracked the car windows, adjusted in my seat, and waited.

An hour passed when I looked in my rearview mirror and noticed a familiar figure leaving the mall. As the silhouette came closer, I knew without a doubt it was Eve. She wore a fitted white blouse and dark jeans. With a bag in her hand, she crossed the street and walked toward the townhome community. I grabbed my pistol and exited the car. Quickly stuffing the gun in my back waistband, I darted across the street and followed Eve onto the sidewalk at a distance. I increased my pace until we were only twenty feet away from each other.

She stopped walking. I ducked behind a unit and peeked around the corner. Eve surveyed her surroundings before continuing up the sidewalk. I followed. She walked to a home near the end of the community and removed a key. I made note of the house number, and when she unlocked the door, I rushed to her.

"Get in," I said, forcing her inside and shutting the door.

"Hey, wait," she protested.

"Hi, Eve," I said as we stood in a partially furnished living room.

A couch, a television, and a shelf with a few trophies occupied the space. One thing that really caught my attention was a poster with a stick and knife crossing. Eskrima was written at the top of the poster.

Eve's mouth fell open. "Chance? What—what are you doing here?" She spoke as if she was out of breath.

I circled her. "I could ask you the same thing. There's a lot of people looking for you, Eve."

Her eyes widened as footsteps approached behind me. "No, wait!" she said.

Before I could turn, something hard struck the back of my head, then blackness veiled my eyes.

CHAPTER TWELVE

As I opened my eyes, I realized I was on a carpeted floor in a room with one door and one window. I had a pounding headache. My hands were bound together. So were my legs. Both with cotton rope. Small slits of light squeezed through the closed window blinds and provided faint illumination to the empty room. I adjusted myself so my back sat against the wall. Voices flowed from the opposite side of the door. One voice I recognized as Eve's. She was arguing with a man.

A moment later, the room's door opened, and she stepped inside. As we stared at each other, I noticed the energy drain from her face. Like she was concerned or worried.

"Don't look at me like that," I said.

She took two steps toward me. "Are you okay?" she asked.

"You and your boyfriend knocked me out, then tied me up. Whatchu think?"

"I'm sorry." She walked to me and kneeled. "I tried to stop it."

I rolled my eyes and looked away. "Yeah."

"What are you doing here, Chance?"

"Looking for you."

Eve winced. "Why?"

"Your husband hired me to find you."

"What? No, he hired some investigator in St. Pete to find me."

Before I could respond, the room's door swung open. A familiar-looking man with an athletic built stood at the door. His bruised left jaw and black right eye sat prominently on his light-brown face.

The man placed a hand on top of his curly hair and slid his hand to his forehead. "That's what I've been tryna tell you," he said to Eve. "He's the guy from that PI's office."

"You mean the man you killed?" I taunted him.

He pointed at me. "Watch ya mouth. I didn't kill him. He was dead when I got there."

"Calm down, Will," Eve told the man.

"Will," I said before looking at Eve. "Is he your boyfriend? He looks like Patrick." I glanced at Will. "Yeah, you definitely have a type."

Will stepped into the room. "Keep talking and I'll cut ya tongue out."

"Sure, whateva."

"You think I'm playin' with you?"

Eve stood and walked to Will with her palms aimed at him. "Look. I need a word with him," she said.

"You betta tell him to watch his mouth."

"William!"

Will looked at Eve.

"Please give me a moment."

Will glanced at me, then Eve, before nodding and leaving the room.

"That boy's a piece of work," I said to Eve's back. "Just like your husband. You sure know how to pick'em. Was your father around when you were a little girl?"

She turned to me. "Chance. I need to know everything Patrick told you."

I shrugged. "He didn't tell me much. Said to just locate you."

"That's it? Anything else?"

"Oh. He also said you were cheating on him."

"This isn't funny, Chance. Someone came after me."

"At your motel?" I asked.

Eve's eyebrows furrowed.

"Why were you at a motel anyway when your boyfriend has a townhome?"

She glanced at the floor.

"Oh, I see. You were hiding something from Will. Or maybe you were planning on breaking up with him. Was that why you were at the bar? Looking for the next sucka?"

Eve jolted her head. "Y—you don't understand."

"I understand there's a dead private investigator and your husband is laid up in the hospital."

"What?" Eve said. Legitimate concern filled her eyes.

"You didn't hear? Some accident. Hit-and-run."

Eve paced the floor. "Okay, okay, okay," she mumbled before facing me. "You need to tell me everything you know."

"I did."

She shook her head. "No, you know more," she said while pointing at me.

"Sorry, babe. You know more than I do now. Tell me, why does he want to find you so bad?"

Eve pivoted toward the door. "I'll give you some time to think about it," she said with her back to me. "Then I'll send Will in. He knows martial arts. Good with knives. If you talk, he may untie you."

"Is that some kinda threat?"

Still with her back to me, she sighed. "It's not meant to be. I'll be back."

I shook my head as she left the room, and the door shut. Will may be good with a knife, but he lacked experience in this game. My keys, wallet, Eve's bracelet, and Terrell's knife were still in my pockets. Only my pistol was missing. Removing the knife from my pocket posed a bit of a challenge, mainly because my hands were big. Flipping it open was even more challenging, but positioning the blade at a part of the rope that wouldn't cut my hand was the most tricky part.

As I sawed the rope, I heard faint chatter from the room opposite the door. The voices fell silent and two brisk knocks flowed from the townhome's front door. Someone said something, but I found it difficult to make out what was being said. Footsteps rapidly approached the room. I dropped the knife to the floor and concealed it with my thigh. The door swung open, and Eve entered. Her eyes were wide, and concern stretched across her face.

She put a finger to her lips. "You need to be quiet," she said.

"First you want me to talk, now I hafta be quiet?" I said.

She exhaled and shook her head before grabbing a long, drape-looking cloth from the floor and tying it around my mouth, gagging me.

"Stay quiet," she said before leaving and closing the door.

I picked up the knife and continued cutting.

I was halfway through the rope when I heard more talking from the other room. Suddenly, a boisterous crash flowed from the door. Eve screamed. Shouting and stomps followed. I finished cutting through the rope, then quickly removed the gag and untied my legs. As I unwound the loose strands from my ankles, the roar of two gunshots smacked against the room's door. Eve's screams grew louder, then abruptly stopped. I zipped to the door and nudged it open. Peeking through the slit, I saw Will sprawled on the floor. A male figure dressed in dark clothing threw Eve over his shoulder and walked toward the front door. When the door closed behind them, I rushed to Will. Two bullet holes in his chest oozed blood.

"Ahh," he gurgled as a red bubble formed in his mouth and then popped.

I kneeled over him.

"A cop," he said before taking a final breath and closing his eyes.

My gun lay on the floor next to him. I inspected it. He hadn't fired it. Outside, a vehicle door thumped closed. I hurried to the door, and as my eyes adjusted to the light, a silver SUV with a dented front bumper, shattered headlight, and busted grill jetted past, stringing a trail of smoke behind it. I hustled through the community toward the main street. The SUV exited the community, bolting by as I crossed the street. When I reached my car, I brought the Caddy's engine to life and sped from the parking lot after the SUV. The vehicle was maybe thirty yards from me. It made a left at an intersection. I was sure I wouldn't catch it when the traffic ahead of me halted for a red light. I slammed the brakes and the car jerked to a stop. Gripping the steering wheel, I exhaled. After a minute, traffic eased forward, and I removed my phone. Ignoring the missed calls, I dialed McCoach.

"A little over eight hours left," he answered.

"Yeah, I'm not worried about that. I found her."

"Okay. Where is she?"

"With her kidnapper."

"What?"

"Someone took her. Killed her lover in the process."

"Where?" McCoach asked.

I gave him the location and number for the townhome.

"I tracked her there, and they got the drop on me. Shortly after I woke, someone entered the house, killed the boyfriend and took her."

"I'll send a couple of red and blues there. Where are you now?"

"Was in pursuit of the vehicle but lost them."

"Did you get the tag?"

"I didn't. They were moving too fast and trailing smoke."

"What kinda car was it?"

"Silver SUV. May have been an Explorer."

"Sounds like the vehicle that fled Stevenson's accident."

"Now that's interesting," I said.

"Thanks to CCTV footage, we got a number from the plate. The SUV belongs to a Benjamin Greer."

"So, he's your guy?"

"Well, he's the primary suspect for the hit-and-run, and now looks like we can add kidnapping."

"And murder."

"Yeah. And murder. Hiller went to Greer's home address. Should hear from him shortly—actually, I'll probably call him after I get off with you."

"What's the address?"

"If I tell you, am I gonna regret it?" McCoach said.

"My man, there's a lot about this you already regret. Just add it to my tab."

CHAPTER THIRTEEN

Fifteen minutes later, I turned onto a street heading toward Benjamin Greer's home. It was in a quiet neighborhood on the east side of Brandon. Large oak trees and stucco ranch-style homes with manicured yards rolled by as I cruised the freshly paved road. After driving a couple hundred yards, the road became bumpy and the yards unkempt. I eased down the street for another minute before seeing the number I was looking for. It was on a mailbox near the end of the street. The front yard was spacious, but untidy, littered with car parts, boxes, and a variety of other mechanical scraps. An older bungalow style home sat in the yard. The house had a screened porch and dirty tan vinyl siding with faded black trimming.

I parked by an empty field a little ways from the house. McCoach had told me not to do anything. Said to sit tight and wait for the cops. But since I didn't work for him, I took it as a suggestion. I grabbed my gun, then emerged from the Caddy and into the cool shade. Holding the gun to my side, I crept toward the house while surveying the area. I entered the yard and threaded around a rusted nineteen eight-six Pontiac Firebird frame on blocks.

Footsteps crunching over twigs and leaves flowed from the back. With my gun trained, I crept along the side of the house. On my way to the back, I noticed a defined vehicular path on the ground and a shabby car shed in the backyard. More footsteps from the back crushed the sticks and foliage beneath it. When I turned the corner, an athletic man in dark slacks and a polo shirt stood in front of me with his arms raised.

"Don't move," I said.

We stared at one another for a few seconds until we registered each other's face.

"Hiller," I said.

"Yeah. You're McCoach's friend, right?"

"Right," I said, slowly lowering my gun.

Hiller touched his chest. "You scared me," he said while using his free hand to rake his messy, dirty blond hair backward.

"We tracked a suspect to this address," Hiller said, nearly out of breath. "Doesn't appear anyone's here, though."

I nodded. "Okay," I said, walking closer to the house to inspect the back door.

It looked closed.

Panting, Hiller hunched over and touched his knees.

"You okay?" I asked.

"Yeah. I ran around the house earlier. Thought I heard footsteps, but it was a stray cat. Then you scared me and took what breath I had left."

My phone rang. I took a few steps away from the house and Hiller before removing it from my pocket.

"Yep," I answered.

"Did you not get my missed calls?" Darla said.

"Sorry, but a woman had me tied up."

"Hilarious. Listen, I looked into Stevenson and the Mancinis. And my hunch was right."

"Okay," I said into the phone while glancing at Hiller as he waved for my attention.

"Imma call this in," he mouthed before turning and heading to the side of the house.

"Seems many of those LLCs Stevenson owns are shell companies,"

Darla continued. "Victor Mancini is a member with him on several companies, so he has to be laundering Mancini's money."

"Okay, so Stevenson's dirty. That's no surprise. What does this have to do with Eve?"

"Hello, she's married to Stevenson. Maybe a deal with Mancini went sideways."

"Then why not just go directly after Stevenson?"

"The Mancinis are mobsters. Maybe they want to make an example."

"I get that, but there's more. Why go through all this trouble for an example?"

"It's no trouble for them," Darla said. "These people have connections all throughout the judicial system."

"I'm sure they're pretty connected."

"They are. It's nothing for them to have cops or maybe even judges in their pocket. Some months back, Stevenson and Victor Mancini were persons of interest in an NYPD Internal Affairs investigation involving a cop. Apparently, the detective was caught with a large bag of cash. The bag had one of Stevenson's and Mancini's companies' logo on it."

"Really?"

"Yep. It's amazing what you find when you dig deep enough."

"What happened to the cop?"

"You know how it goes. Suspended for a little while, then back to work."

"Who was the cop?" I asked, turning toward the car shed. *I didn't see his car!*

Out of pure instinct, I ducked.

"Greg Hiller," Darla's faint voice said as the phone dropped from my hand and a loud blast erupted behind me.

CHAPTER FOURTEEN

I dove to the ground while a cocktail of sounds flooded my ears. Darla calling to me through the phone, a bullet whizzing past my shoulder, and the thunderous echo from a gunshot. While falling toward the dirt and leaves, I spun and saw Hiller in a weaver stance with his pistol pointed in my direction—the white of his eyes exposed and his teeth gritted. His aim followed my descent, but I already had my gun trained on him. I fired a round before landing on the ground. A deafening roar swept across the yard as a bullet penetrated Hiller's shoulder, causing him to drop his gun.

I thrust myself from the ground and into a kneeling position to prepare for another shot. Hiller rushed me before I could bring my gun to bear. He grabbed me in a tackle and my gun flew from my hand as we both toppled to the ground. We rolled in the grass, grabbing and clawing. It ended with Hiller straddling me. He threw a punch. I parried his attack, then jabbed him in the nose before hooking the back of his head and slinging him to the ground. I rolled onto my belly and pushed myself up. Hiller did the same. As we stood, he wiped his nose with his sleeve.

"So, you're the Mancini's lapdog?" I said.

Hiller just gritted his teeth.

"You killed Finley and put Stevenson in the hospital."

Hiller smirked. "Yeah, I did. And after I kill you—I'm gonna take care of that woman, then finish what I started with Stevenson."

"So, she's still alive?"

"Don't worry about it," Hiller said, raising his fists. "You won't be alive long enough for it to matter."

I raised my fists, and we squared off. Hiller jabbed with a right. I weaved out of the attack's path. He followed up with a left jab, and I weaved to the opposite side before landing a jab on his forehead and following up with a cross to his jaw. He staggered backward.

I shook my head. "You won't beat me in a fistfight, my man. Especially with that injured shoulder. Stop this and turn yourself in."

Hiller growled and blitzed toward me. He grabbed me in a tackle and rammed my back against an oak tree.

He struck my right ribcage with a hook, then my left. I mushed his face. His head snapped back, and his body followed as he stumbled backward. I rubbed my elbows against my sides to soothe the stinging.

"How that feel?" Hiller taunted.

I set my chin and raised my fist. Hiller launched at me and threw a nearly perfect cross. He had his feet planted, his form was good, but he misjudged the distance between us and overextended his attack. I leaned back. The punch breezed past an inch away from my face. I slipped to Hiller's outside and delivered a devastating hook to his ribcage. As he shrunk under the pain, I followed up with another hook to his stomach.

Hiller hugged his lower body, leaving his upper body completely exposed. I hit his chin with a left cross, then his jaw with a right. Hiller flopped to the ground. He moaned as he rolled to his hands and knees. He whipped his head to the right. I followed his gaze and saw his gun. Hiller crawled toward the pistol. I scanned the ground and spotted my gun slightly burrowed under sticks and leaves. I ran and slid to the ground after my weapon. Grabbing the gun, I turned to Hiller. He spun toward me with his gun in hand. I aimed at him and pulled the trigger twice. The first round hit his chest and the second near his neck. Hiller dropped his gun, gasped, then fell backward and sprawled on the grass.

Wincing at the various aches shooting throughout my body, I stood and walked to Hiller. I kicked his gun away from him and kneeled to frisk him. I didn't find any other weapons or his pulse. Standing, I stuffed my gun in my back waistband, then scanned the ground for my phone. When I picked it up, Darla screamed my name.

"Okay, I'm here," I said into the phone

"Are you okay? What was that noise?" she asked.

"Death knocking on the door, but it wasn't for me."

"I'm calling the cops."

"No need. They're on the way."

"You sure?"

"Positive. I have to go. And thanks, baby doll. You saved my life."

"Oh my goodness, be careful."

"Aren't I always?"

I ended the call and surveyed the yard. My attention quickly went to the car shed. As I approached the shed, the faint sound of engines turning over and car doors shutting flowed from behind the structure. Looking behind the shed, I saw the parking lot of a popular department store past a wooded area in the distance. I returned to the front of the car shed and lifted the door. It rolled open and the scent of death struck my nose. Inside, the busted silver SUV stood parked front and center. In the back corner, a man sat on the floor, leaning against the wall. Swatting flies away, I hurried to him. While inspecting him for a pulse, I found a thin laceration circling his neck but no pulse.

Benjamin Greer, I figured.

Standing from the body, I noticed the SUV's trunk ajar. I raised the door a few inches before the hydraulics took over and opened the door completely. A black jacket and duffel bag sat on the floor. I unzipped the bag and stacks of one hundred-dollar bills fell from the bag. Before I could fully process what happened, the vehicle shook, and a muffled moan flowed from the back seat.

I circled to the passenger's side back door. When I opened the door, Eve lay in the seat with her hands duct-taped behind her. Her ankles were also tied together, and a strip of tape stretched across her mouth. I pulled the tape from her mouth.

"Chance!" she said. "You have to help me. He's—"

I stuck the tape back around her mouth. She didn't groan or fight, but her furrowed eyebrows said everything. With the knife from my pocket, I cut the tape from around her ankles and helped her out of the vehicle. I guided her outside the shed and sat her on the grass. I removed the tape from her mouth once more.

"You gonna untie my hands from behind me?"

I pressed the tape back on. She protested briefly before staring at me. Her eyes asked questions I didn't care to answer. I walked back inside the shed and grabbed the duffel bag from the SUV, then stepped outside and tossed the bag at her feet.

I removed the tape once again. "Now you may talk," I said before pointing at the bag. "Start with telling me about this."

Eve looked at the ground and sighed.

"Today, hon!" I said.

She looked at me. "I took it."

I nodded as if to say, no kidding.

"As you already know," she continued, "Patrick and I have had issues for a while."

"Issues? Meaning you cheated?"

"He cheated long before I stepped out on him. He's not the clean businessman he presents himself to be. Been stealing from the Mancinis long before I took this money."

I squinted.

"Oh, you didn't know? Patrick's been siphoning the Mancinis' money to offshore accounts for years. He did it in small amounts, so it didn't immediately raise any flags. He must've thought I was too stupid to understand the paperwork, because he knew I had access to the safe where he kept the documents." Eve chuckled. "I guess he forgot I majored in finance."

"You knew the money belonged to the Mancinis and took it anyway?"

Eve shrugged. "I needed to get away from Patrick for a fresh start. So, when I saw the bag in his office, I took it."

"This was three weeks ago?"

"Yeah, I guess so."

"How did Hiller end up with the money?"

"Hiller?"

"The guy that kidnapped you."

"He had to be the one who took it from my motel room. Took my cellphone too. At first, I thought the private investigator Patrick hired a while back had something to do with it."

"That's why you sent your boyfriend to his office. You thought he had the money."

Eve glanced at the ground, then back at me before nodding. "Yeah. But when Will got there, he found the man dead. Said he was shot. But I promise you, Chance, I didn't hurt anyone or mean for anyone to get hurt."

"That may be true, doll, but your boyfriend's dead and your husband's in the hospital."

Eve sighed. "Patrick," she said, shaking her head. "How'd we get here?"

"Easy. The Mancinis found about his scheme and wanted him dead." I shrugged. "I'm guessing they've known for a while. And with you being his wife, they may have thought you were involved, so when you took the money, they probably saw it as a play and decided to kill you two. I'm sure they've been keeping tabs on you for some time. You were never gonna get away and start fresh."

Sirens wailed in the distance.

Eve looked in that direction. "You used to be a cop. How bad does it look, Chance?" she asked.

I removed her bracelet from my pocket and walked to her. Kneeling, I placed it in her pocket, then stood. She stared at me like she wanted to ask a question but said nothing.

"Four people are dead, sweetheart. Doesn't look good," I told her.

She hung her head.

"Why did you come to the jazz club?"

She hunched her shoulders before looking at me, her eyes misty. "I just wanted to get away from it for a while."

"Running away from your double life. That's something."

"I didn't mean for you to get involved."

I believed her. "I'm sure you didn't, hon," I said. "But you were scheming, just like Patrick."

Eve nodded. "I was."

"But I think you're gonna be alright." I grinned. "Just remember to practice what you preach, though," I said, eliciting a forced smile from her.

My phone rang. I stepped away and answered it.

"Chance!" McCoach answered.

"What's up?"

"I had suspicions about Hiller's investigation, so I looked into him and found—"

"I know," I interrupted. "I'll see you when you get here," I told him before ending the call.

CHAPTER FIFTEEN

An hour later, the sun began its descent. I sat on the rear bumper of an ambulance parked in the middle of Greer's front yard with my eyes fixed on the gorgeous, slender, female paramedic disinfecting my cuts and bruises. She noticed me looking. I smiled. She smiled back.

"What?" she asked in a playful tone, her short, dark feathered hair bouncing as her chin dropped and her penetrating hazel eyes locked with mine.

I shrugged my mouth. "I was just wondering."

"Wondering what?" she asked, gently pressing a small bandage over a cut on my cheek.

"What time you get off?"

She cocked her head to the side and looked at me while removing her latex gloves and smiling. "We're finished," she said.

"No, not already."

"Yes, I'm sorry."

McCoach approached the ambulance. The paramedic turned to him.

"He checks out," she told McCoach before glancing back at me. "But I'll have to keep an eye on him," she continued before disappearing toward the front of the ambulance.

"You still haven't learned your lesson," McCoach said.

I shrugged.

"You were right," McCoach continued. "The body in the shed is Greer. We found Hiller's car parked at the department store on the other side of the woods. The working theory is he parked there and came over here to steal Greer's SUV."

"Greer has a record?"

"Yep. Robbery and attempted murder."

I nodded. "Makes sense. Hiller probably thought he'd make a good scapegoat."

"Right. But Hiller didn't get a chance to stage it." McCoach sighed. "With him dead, that makes four bodies."

"Could've been more."

"What makes you say that?"

"Myself and Eve. And then Stevenson, if you didn't send that security detail to the hospital."

"Maybe Stevenson and Eve. But I don't see you going down easily."

"Ain't that the truth," I said before staring at McCoach. "You know, I feel bad for Jacob Finley's family. He was just doing his job. And when he realized how deep it went, he handed the matter over to the authorities but still ended up dead."

"Is that your way of explaining why you didn't let the authorities know sooner? Your justification?"

I stood. "Like I mentioned, there was a crook in the department. If I had gone to Tampa PD too soon with this, I could've been the fifth dead body."

"I had my suspicions about Hiller but never investigated his past. You were a cop, so you know how it is. We want to assume the best of our fellow brothers." McCoach shook his head. "An oversight on my part."

"I wouldn't sweat that too much. The Mancinis probably have people around the country."

"Well, I plan to contact my district attorney friend in New York. With the Stevensons' testimony, I believe the DA's office can build a strong case against the Mancinis."

"What makes you think they'll testify?" I asked.

"When they see the charges we stack against them, they'll be ready to cut a deal."

I hunched my shoulders and nodded. "Smart play. Just know I won't be testifying."

McCoach sighed. "I can't make any promises," he said.

"I can."

McCoach shook his head. "Either way. I need you to come down to the station tomorrow. Still a lot more to sort out."

"I know the drill," I said, pivoting away from him and heading in my car's direction. "I'll be there right after I go to the hospital."

"You betta not be going to intimidate Stevenson into testifying. I want the pleasure of doing that."

I stopped walking and turned to McCoach. "The only thing I want from Stevenson and this entire situation is the rest of my money."

McCoach chuckled, then disappeared into the busyness of the crime scene, and I threaded around a few squad cars on the way to the Caddy. As I settled behind the wheel, an officer escorting Eve to a cruiser caught my eye. I watched as Eve paced to the vehicle in what seemed like slow-motion strides—her eyes bulging and watery, her mouth gaped. I couldn't believe she was the same woman I saw two nights prior.

I called Darla to let her know I was okay and to work the rest of the week from home. She offered to patch my wounds, but I informed her that a sweet young paramedic beat her to it.

"You haven't learned, have you?" she asked before abruptly ending the call.

I started the car and headed for the jazz club.

The band started their first set as I entered and ambled to my usual seat at the bar. Robby emerged from the kitchen. He stopped in front of the doors and winced.

"What happened to you?" he asked.

I cocked my head. "Just one of those days," I said.

"Right." Robby chuckled and leaned over the bar top toward me. "It has nothing to do with that woman?"

I shrugged. "How 'bout you cut me a break tonight?"

Robby chuckled. "Alright, alright," he said with his hands raised in a surrendered posture.

"Thank you."

Robby again leaned over the bar top. "So, did you at least get to the bottom of it?"

"Don't I always?"

Robby stood. "I guess. You wantcha usual?"

"Yeah, that sounds good."

"Coming right up, my brutha."

Robby poured me a club soda with grapefruit juice, then waved to someone across the room before disappearing into the kitchen. I sat with my drink and enjoyed the music while the band finished their set. The audience immediately clapped and cheered. Slowly, the hoots and applauses died down, and the club's front door opened. A tall, fit woman wearing a black bodycon dress entered. She had hazelnut skin and a short bob cut. A shorter woman with longer hair walked in behind her. The tall woman exchanged some words with her friend before glancing at me. I looked away, keeping my eyes on my drink as the two women made their way to the bar. They sat one stool away with the tall woman closest to me.

As they chit chatted, I kept my sights ahead and sipped my drink. Maybe McCoach and Darla were wrong. Maybe I had learned my lesson. After a few moments, the short woman stood and walked toward the bathrooms. In my peripheral, I saw the tall woman flick her hair, then glance at me. I fought to not look at her but couldn't resist. Felt like a motor was torquing my head in her direction. We locked eyes and she smiled. I smiled back.

Maybe I haven't learned my lesson.

ALEX CAGE

About the Author

Alex Cage is a thriller author and passionate wordsmith who loves to blend his fascination with martial arts and travel with high-octane action and explosive adventures. He enjoys nothing more than entertaining his readers with death-defying missions, larger-than-life characters, and suspenseful stories that always find a way to keep you on your toes.

As the author of nearly a dozen titles, including the Orlando Black series and the Leroy Silver series, Alex combines his obsession for thrillers with a sprinkling of fantasy and sci-fi, so that readers will always find something to capture their imagination. He currently resides in North Carolina. When not writing his next novel, you can find him reading and practicing martial arts.

alexcage.com
connect@alexcage.com

GUMSHOE

Steven Van Patten

GUMSHOE

"The usual?"

"Sure, Doug!"

After the day I had, you're damn right I wanted a bourbon. And a manly brand, not one that the college kids are 'trending' about. Or for that matter, nothing the cheap old Irish guys are drinking because they've come to terms with hitting the grave a tad on the early side of sixty. Not that I'm not a candidate for that, but my grumpy cunt of an old man made it to seventy, so no reason to think I can't pull that off too.

Doug pours me a double without me saying anything. Fuck it, I tip him well enough, so why shouldn't he extend a courtesy? He lays it down and I take the first sip. So goddamn smooth. He knows what I like. If only Doug was a broad, who knows?

Speaking of women, that is exactly how this night went left. She walks in cool and slow. Barely seemed to touch the door. She was pretty. Dressed in black. A little too skinny for my taste, but it doesn't matter. I'm an old man. It's not like twenty years ago. I'm here to drink and wallow, not get hemmed up with yet another vagina owner.

Years ago, I used to frequent places like this, and my agenda was very different. And on those nights, I'd only get a whiff of most of the women in these places as they brush past me on the way to guys who were much better looking, and well-heeled. And there'd always be at least one young, talkative lady drowning some desperate looking old man with her words and the occasional caress. In turn, the old man would buy them drinks. Now that I am the old man, I really must be in the mood before I'd entertain that sort of mess. I mean, sure I'll buy a Cutie Patootie a drink occasionally. I might even entertain mindless conversation which would usually be about some rapper or singer I had never heard of and certainly didn't care about. But eventually I'd also clarify that this old man is not looking to adopt. They'd eventually excuse themselves and I would wish them well in their future endeavors.

But this woman, as she walked up, was giving a more serious business vibe. And a guy in my line of work, prides himself on reading rooms and situations. Still, she caught me off guard when she finally got to talking.

"Hey! You're that guy that helps the police find missing persons, right?"

That caused me to look her in the face. Maybe that was a mistake. Yeah, she was pretty. Chocolate brown skin. A dessert on a healthy pair of stems.

"You saw me on the talk show, I guess," I answered with a shrug.

"Yes. Can I say you're admirable? If you don't mind?"

"Sure. I can take a compliment," I said.

"Good. Can I buy you a drink?" I glanced over, and I mean glanced because I was trying to avoid eye contact. I saw the smile on her. Really nice teeth. Like either strong genetics or fucking a dentist nice teeth. I avoided gazing into her eyes on purpose, even though with a free drink on the table I almost felt like I was being rude. "I just ordered. But I'm not one to nurse, so if you give it a minute, you'll get your chance."

"Fantastic." She sat down on the bar stool next to me, close enough for me to feel the shoulder pad that flattened out that side of her jacket. I almost shot her a look, but instead I looked at Doug, who had decided he was going to polish a wine glass and pretend he didn't notice me being approached by a beautiful woman. Then I looked at her glass. Red wine. That seemed to suit her.

"There was the thing about you on CBS, right? You're big on catching human traffickers. You've rescued a few girls. Very courageous."

Doug looked up from his wine glass polishing. As far as Doug knew I was just another gumshoe, taking pics of people cheating on their spouses. Truth is, he assumed that from my appearance. I just never corrected him is all.

"I'm surprised you recognized me," I admitted. "It was a while ago and my hair is much longer now."

"I never forget a face."

"I just told you my face is different," I added. "Somebody with a grudge send you in here? You setting me up?"

"No!"

"Good, because you're kind of cute. I would hate to have to put a bullet in your esophagus just to make a point."

"Please don't. I come in peace and have no intention of leaving in pieces."

Anxiety brought on from having my past human trafficking busts become a sudden topic of discussion struck me, so I scarfed down the bourbon. "I'll take that drink now."

The lady inhaled her gimlet, then she waved a hand at Doug, who judging from his quick snap upright, was clearly paying more attention to the conversation than his intense glass cleaning would have let on.

"Another round for me and the gentleman. On me, please."

"You got it!" Doug answered.

As Doug went to whipping up the drinks, she turned to me. "What do you know about the occult?"

I shrugged. "I know there is a Satanic Church up the block. There is also a Catholic priest who says he performed an exorcism back in the seventies. He was in here bragging about it a couple of nights ago. He's two doors down from the Satanists."

"I was referring to your own personal experience."

Only now did I look in her face. Her eyes. Twin liquid black pools.

Now I must admit that this was when I became a little worried. I didn't say that though. What I said was, "I'm just a regular guy, ma'am."

Our drinks landed. She thanked Doug and held up her gimlet. "Cheers!"

"Salute!" I said as our glasses clinked. "How long have you been a witch?" I figured I would let her know I knew. I don't normally play all my cards on the first hand, but in this case, it felt like the way to go.

She smiled. "The eyes gave it away, huh?"

"Yes. And as far as my personal experience with the occult goes, you're it."

She raised an eyebrow. "But you figured out I'm a witch."

"I read a lot."

"You're lying. You've known other witches. In fact, you've been intimate with one."

I'm not sure if I was mad because she called me a liar or because she was right. "Yeah, I probably shouldn't lie to someone like you. But if you already know the answers then why ask the questions? And as far as witches go, their money spends just like everyone else's."

"First of all, to answer the first question, I'm not a mind reader."

"Just a know it all. Well, it's a relief you can't read minds. At least not mine."

"I'm sure your mind is a wonderful rollercoaster, but I must stress that I am actually here because I need your help in a supernatural capacity."

I looked to see if Doug were still eavesdropping, but other customers had arrived for beers and small talk. Probably a good thing he wasn't listening.

"You're a witch. I'm just a regular Joe. And we don't know each other from a can of paint. What kind of help could I have to offer?"

She put her hands on her hips. "The kind that involves money after you borrow a book from your ex."

She really knew more than I would have preferred. "Earlise? That's what this is about?"

The witch glared at me with narrowed, annoyed eyes. "Maybe."

I turned to face her. "Why do I get the feeling your use of the word, 'borrow' brings with it a very loose definition?"

"No, I want you to return it," she said. "After I'm done with it."

"And the reason you can't just stop by her place and ask for the book yourself?"

"Well, we kind of had a falling out..."

"That's funny. I also had a falling out with Earlise. Guess it's a trend."

She rolled her eyes. "Anyway, the book used to belong to my mother." Here she paused as if she suddenly had to hold back tears. "Yes, she was also a witch. She was amazing. Healed sick people. You were with Earlise for a time, so you know Hollywood has it wrong. Most witches are very nice people."

"Well, since you know I was with Earlise, then you know I know at least one witch who isn't a nice person. But I'll tell you what sister, I'll give you the benefit of the doubt."

I could tell the sarcasm was getting to her and that she was dying to slap me senseless, call me a few unflattering names and storm off. Either that or turn me into a sloth. The problem is, she was also assuming this was my personality. She didn't realize that I was being this way to gauge how badly she wanted me to take this questionable assignment.

"Some time ago, my mother loaned Earlise, your ex and my cousin, a book of homeopathic spells and such. It stayed with Earlise for a long time because no one really needed it. Most of the spells in this book we knew by heart. Things were fine until about a year ago when my mother was diagnosed with degenerative neuropathy. We asked for the book back several times, but she kept saying she wasn't done with it. We tried to explain that my mother was in trouble, but she would not budge. When we tried going to the house, we came to realize that she'd put a protective spell over her residence. We can't even stand across the street from her house without experiencing serious abdominal pains, much less, be able to knock on the door."

She had to stop to let out a few sobs. All the sarcasm seeped out of me like a slow gas leak. I waited for her to collect herself.

"My mother died last week and now my sister is ill with the same affliction. Even with my mother's death, Earlise will not speak to us, nor will she come out of the house."

"Not come out of the house?" I had to question that. Yes, Earlise is a witch. But she, at least when I was there, lived life like a normal person. That meant a job, grocery shopping and the occasional restaurant outings with me. And she had a mean side, but never would I expect her to just let a relative die. This didn't sound like the person I knew two years ago.

"Look, I can see you're upset and I'm sorry for your loss," I finally said. "But I must admit I'm a little taken aback. You want me to believe Earlise has become a crazy shut in? Like she's on some Greta Garbo shit?"

"I'm not sure how to categorize it, but she has shut down her life."

"All right, I'll go over there and see what's what. But I must ask. You're just trying to save your sister, right? You're not tricking me into going after this book so you can bring on the End of Days or some other heinous thing, are you?"

"How dare you!" she shouted as she slapped me. I saw it coming so I turned my head with the blow, so it didn't hurt so bad.

I was still pissed, though. "I think this conversation is over." I turned away and stared at Doug and the new customers. They, in turn, stared back at me all wide-eyed. Doug seemed to be figuring out if he needed to get involved.

Everyone except me watched her storm off and get to the door, only to realize she had to turn back. As she returned to my side, she did not look happy. "Were you this mean to Earlise? Because if you were, I'm surprised she didn't put a curse on you."

"Who said she didn't?"

She rolled her eyes again. "I apologize for hitting you. I still need your help, and I'm willing to pay."

I noticed the other customers still watching us. "The slap is gonna cost you extra. Not to mention the public humiliation."

And that was when she pulled a white plastic bag out of her purse. The bag was sheer enough for me to see through it. That meant that Doug the bartender and the other customers as well as I could see that there were banded stacks of money inside.

"That's ten..."

"I know what ten-thousand dollars looks like, gorgeous."

She took a deep breath. "Are you going to do it?"

"For ten-thousand dollars, I'd steal a book from that Satanic Church I mentioned earlier." I dismissed. I was lying again. I really did not want to talk to Earlise, especially if she'd gone all hermit crab. But these bills don't pay themselves. "Okay, I'll go ask her about the book."

The anger was back. "No! She can't know you're after the book. She must think you're trying to romance her."

"What?! Are you out of your mind? I can't. You don't know how we left things."

"But you do want her back, yes?"

I had to think about that for a second. Maybe more than a second.

"I think you may have something to do with her shutting out the world. You know, I have it on good authority that you are the last person to leave her house."

I practically snort-laughed. "That is ridiculous! That was over two years ago."

Her hands found her hips as she leaned into my face. I had to take care not to lose myself in those black eyes of hers. "I said what I said."

After a moment, I reached into the bag and pulled out a crisp one-hundred-dollar bill. "Doug, my ship has come in. Here! Keep the change! Go buy yourself a fresh pair of sandals."

Doug didn't move, but he saw the money. "Thanks, Gus."

I handed the witch my cellphone. "Punch in your number. When I have something, I'll call you." She took the phone and did as I instructed.

"There is more if and when you bring back the book."

I smiled as I waved and walked towards the door. "Under control, Money Bags!" Of course, it didn't feel under control. In fact, it felt like I was lying again.

Before I exited, I looked in my phone. My client's name, at least the name she typed into my phone was Lisa Longtooth. Good name for a witch, I suppose.

"Ms. Longtooth, you never told me the book's title."

Her face went the darkest it had been since our encounter started. "You'll know it when you see it."

That should have been my cue to give her the damn money back and go home. Instead, I waved goodbye to Doug and headed off to see the Wicked Witch of Nicholas Avenue.

———

Earlise Fillings and I dated for almost two years. It was as serious as a relationship could be without there ever being a mention of the word 'marriage' from either of us. Like many crazy people, she was a great lover. She was also very smart, and quick to help a friend in need. During our first two dates, she came across as normal as a rabbit coming out of a magician's hat. It wasn't until about five weeks in when I caught the first glimpse of who she really was.

Now, I'll admit to my partial guilt in this. I probably should have asked where she wanted the dress that she'd just taken off to go. But she'd jumped in the shower before I could ask. So, being an adult who knows what a hamper looks like, thought I was being helpful by tossing it in. The tongue-lashing I received when she'd realized what I'd done almost prompted me to break up with her right there. And by no means am I the overly sensitive type or a stranger to harsh remarks at my expense. But once she'd calmed down and I finally articulated that my putting a dress in a hamper when it should have gone to the unseen dry-cleaning pile was not so egregious a crime that my mother's parenting skills needed to be brought up, she apologized, and life went on.

These outbursts of disrespectful language continued unfortunately, as did the knowledge that she was a full-blown witch and not just some spiritualist who fancied mediation crystals and incense. About a year after the first dust up she cast a spell on me in the middle of a heated debate. As I stood there unable to open my mouth until her three-minute tirade was done, I realized I'd be foolish to stay with someone who had actual telekinetic powers and anger management issues. I didn't even say anything. As she stormed off, I quietly collected the random things that one leaves in someone else's abode during a romantic relationship and skulked off. Days later, she would blow up my cellphone with apology after apology, but by then I had taken on the child trafficking case that eventually landed me on the news and propelled me into even more dangerous adventures. And somewhere in there was my excuse to ghost her entirely.

And now, here I was standing in front of her so familiar front door. My hands were sweating so badly that I chastised myself. "Dammit, man. You have faced down Mexican drug lords and a heavily-armed child porn ring. You can do this."

I raised my hand to knock only for the door to swing wide before my knuckles hit the wood.

"Gus! What a pleasant surprise!"

She looked good, but different. Some new wrinkles around the eyes and a few grey hairs. Still shapely even in the flowing purple and black robe. It was hard to not think about the past. "Hey Earlise. What's happening?"

"You tell me, uninvited surprise guest!"

"Well, I was in the neighborhood, and I thought I would return something."

Her eyes widened. "I didn't realize I was missing anything. I mean, outside of you."

I held out a black crystal. Tourmaline. Supposedly it wards off bad juju. "Because of this thing I became famous. Caught some high-profile sex offenders. Really bad people..."

She shook her head. "I saw 60 minutes, Gus! I don't think the tourmaline, which was a gift by the way, facilitated your brilliant detective work."

"Still, I feel like a fraud!" I know I was pouring it on mighty thick, but it's all I had. It was either this or figure out when she went to bed and break in the joint.

"You're not giving yourself enough credit," she said after she stared at me for a minute to figure out if I was bullshitting her. "I mean, maybe the tourmaline helped, but not to any world-bending degree." She looked at me quietly for a moment. "Anyway, you want to come in?"

Now we're getting somewhere. "Sure."

As I walked across the threshold, I was reminded how great a set up her place was. The first floor was a wide-open space with a living room on the right and a thirty-foot-long kitchen area on my right.

Other than a fresh paint job, nothing seemed to have changed from two years ago. Not the furniture, nor the fixtures, nor the paintings. She even smelled of the same body wash that she was into two years ago.

The door slammed closed behind me after I was a few steps in. I jumped a little and Earlise laughed. "That wasn't me silly. The door is one of those self-closing jammies."

"Good to know," I said. "Anyway, are you going to take the tourmaline back?"

"No," she said with a head shake. "I am going to apologize for hurting you."

I guess I unintentionally gave a suspicious glare. Okay, maybe not that unintentional.

"Hey, I can admit I was wrong," she said.

Now it was my turn to laugh. "I didn't say anything." She scowled as my light chuckle grew to a full-blown belly laugh. "Sorry. No seriously, I'm only laughing because..."

"I was not the most self-aware person when you knew me a couple of years ago."

I stopped laughing. "Well, neither was I."

"Maybe, we've grown up a little? I know you have. Big hero and all."

"Just doing what needed to be done." I said it with the same tone as some western movie cowboy. And yes, I felt silly hearing the words come out of my mouth.

"Well, it's admirable," she said as she turned and walked towards the kitchen which was now on my right. On my left, I noticed that there was one new thing: a much bigger flatscreen TV. "Would you like a tea? Nothing questionable. Just chamomile."

"Sure," I said as I followed her and found a familiar barstool by the kitchen island. She circled to the nearby counter and prepared my tea. I sat quietly. While her back was to me, I started looking around. No books in either the kitchen or the living room. That meant I would have to somehow get to the bookcase, which was upstairs in the bedroom. I was about to get upset, but I remembered the bathroom was also upstairs.

When she turned with two cups of tea in her hands, I smiled and thanked her. My name was on it.

"You were in such a hurry, I guess you missed it," she said as she slid the cup in front of me.

"I guess," I said as I took a sip.

"So why are you really here?" She finally asked. "The tourmaline thing is a weak excuse."

"I was in the neighborhood," I answered. "And I was serious about the tourmaline. You always said you imbued these things with magic. I thought maybe you'd want it back."

She took a sip of her tea. "So, you just stopped by unannounced even though I might have a man up in here."

"Do you?" I had to play my usual feisty self, otherwise she'd know something was up. "Because he's being mighty quiet."

"Maybe he's sleeping," she suggested. "Maybe I fucked him to sleep like I used to do you."

"Lucky guy," I sneered. "Do you think he'll wake up if I use the bathroom?"

Her eyes widened. "Wait. Is that why you're really here? I was the closest bathroom?"

While I certainly hadn't thought to use that angle per se, I had neither the time nor the inclination to look a gift horse in the mouth. I needed an excuse to be upstairs and alone so since the conversation went in this direction, I gave a disarming shrug. "Well, I'm still prediabetic."

She rolled her eyes. "You know where it is."

"Thanks!" I got up and started walking towards the end of the kitchen to the spiral staircase that led upstairs. "The tea's good, by the way. I'll be right back."

She shook her head and chuckled. "Uh huh!"

To keep up appearances, I went to the bathroom, determined to will myself to urinate. As I closed the door behind me and pulled up the seat, I thought about the ocean until I was able produce a nice stream. As I stood there, I wondered if she would be able to hear me stumbling to the bedroom which was twenty paces away. I hoped not.

Just be quick, I told myself as I almost flushed. Then I realized, if she heard the flush, she would expect me down sooner. *No this has got to look and feel normal. Just flush, run in the bedroom, grab the book, stuff it in your coat and get back downstairs.*

And that's what I would have done if Earlise hadn't been standing in the bedroom doorway when I opened the door and made the turn. There was another unexpected complication. She was naked.

Earlise didn't say anything as she waved me inside.

"Hey, um..."

"Just shut up!" She kissed me, then abruptly broke off and started pulling off my clothes. As my arousal grew, I glanced at the bookcase. Longtooth had been correct when she said it would be obvious which book it was. On the third shelf of five, surrounded by what looked like a mix of romance novels and cookbooks.

Then, as goosebumps raised all over my body and cool air found my exposed body, I closed my eyes and resolved myself to taking care of other matters before I took the book.

———

I waited until I heard her snoring before I slipped out of the bed and made my way to the bookcase. If she were to wake up suddenly, my excuse would have been mild curiosity. No harm, no foul, right? After grabbing the book, I tip-toed across the room, collected my clothes and shoes that she'd thrown all around with reckless abandon.

Without making a sound, I made it all the way back downstairs and to the living room. There, I put everything down on her grey and white couch and got dressed. That's when I noticed my belt was missing from the collected pile. *Well, with twenty grand I can certainly buy a new belt.*

I got dressed in about sixty-seconds. Just me and the book. Something told me to just make a run for it, but I wanted to peek and see what the big deal with this book is.

Not sure what I expected. Pictures of Merlin the Wizard? Letters from Gandalf? Maybe just recipes with ingredients like frankincense and eye of toad.

I wasn't expecting two-hundred blank pages.

"Looking for this?" Earlise's voice called from the kitchen. I looked up to see her standing at the kitchen island holding an identical book, only I'm sure the one in her hand had words inside.

"You knew this whole time, didn't you?"

"Yes."

I took a deep breath. "Then why let me in the house?"

She smirked. "A woman has needs."

With dread filling my stomach, I closed my eyes. Turned out to be mistake. If my eyes had been open, I might have seen a dark object hurtling towards me.

"By the way, here is your fucking belt."

By the time my eyes shot open the airborne belt had wrapped itself around my neck like a living thing, like one of those big snakes in the nature documentaries. The impact alone had been hard enough to put me on my butt. As the belt tightened and my vision began to blur, I could hear her laughing. "Don't worry, I'll make sure my cousin gets her money back."

What a stupid way to die, I thought as I tried to pull the belt away.

"Please, Earlise..." I spoke out through the immense pressure on my throat. As tears filled my eyes, I could see that she was crying too, albeit for very different reasons.

"I loved you!" she shouted. "And you were going to give the book to my cousin. Do you have any idea what she would do with the book! She's completely evil! She'd bring on the End of Days!"

If I could talk, I would have joked about how this looked like the end of days for me, in any event. My amusement was short-lived as panic set in, and things started to go black. Close to being unconscious, I barely heard the flash bomb as the front door was ripped asunder.

As I turned to my side, I could see black combat boots and whirling lights.

Earlise gave an unearthly scream. "Get out of my house!"

"Gun!" a man's voice shouted. A hail of automatic weapon fire followed. The belt, still firmly around my neck, tightened as if her goal was to take me with her even as the bullets chiseled away at her. I remember being overcome with a deep sadness as I blacked out.

———

As I lay in the ambulance, slowly regaining consciousness, I overheard parts of a conversation. More of an explanation, really.

"So, when you ran in you saw the man on the ground and the woman holding what looked like a gun?"

"That is correct, sir."

"However, when the dust settles, turns out the man had not been shot and the woman was in fact holding a book. And to make it worse, the man turns out to be Gus Reynolds, the famous rescuer of human trafficking victims."

"Yes, sir."

A longer pause followed. I tried to wait to hear the rest, but suddenly I had a paramedic hovering over my face. "You neck is pretty bruised, sir. Don't worry, though. I told the police you wouldn't be ready to talk anytime soon."

Helpless in a gurney I nodded as I forced a single croak out of my mouth. "Earlise?"

The paramedic turned the proper amount of somber. "I'm sorry, sir. Your lady friend didn't make it."

I tried to sit up. I don't even know why. But when I did, I could see the ambulance doors were still open. Standing a short distance away, smiling at me, was Lisa Longtooth. Cradled in her arms was the book. I can only assume it was the correct one.

I heard a voice in my head. *Thank you, Mr. Reynolds. And hey, enjoy the money and what little time you sniveling humans have left. The next few days are going to be very interesting and it's all thanks to you.*

"All right, let's get out of here," the paramedic shouted to his driving partner behind me. The ambulance doors closed and so began a bumpy ride to the hospital.

"Fucking witches," I whispered to myself, and even that bit of vocalizing hurt terribly. As the ambulance gained speed and the siren sounded, I started to cry. Not just because my arrogance may very well have brought on the end of the world, but for the harsh realization that as toxic as she may have been, I was still very much in love with Earlise.

STEVEN VAN PATTEN

About the Author

Brooklyn native Steven Van Patten is the author of the critically acclaimed Brookwater's Curse trilogy, about an 1860s Georgia plantation slave who becomes law enforcement within the vampire community. In contrast, the titular character in his Killer Genius series is a modern day hyper-intelligent black woman who uses high-end technology as a socially conscious serial killer.

SVP's short fiction includes contributions to horror anthologies like Even In The Grave, Blackened Roots and the Stoker Award nominated Under Twin Suns. A collection of short horror and dark fiction stories entitled Hell At The Way Station, published by his company Laughing Black Vampire Productions and co-authored by acclaimed storyteller, Marc Abbott hit shelves in 2018.

Along with a plethora of other honors and accolades, SVP won three African-African-American Literary Awards in 2019, two for Hell At The Way Station (Best Anthology and Best In Science Fiction) and one for Best Independent Publisher.

laughingblackvampire.com
svp@brookwaterscurse.com

STONE

A Casey Stone Origin Story

Jonathan Staley

CHAPTER ONE

Terri Miller's lifeless face lay in a pool of blood, a gunshot wound marking the end of her struggle. The crime scene unit meticulously combed the area, documenting every piece of evidence, while detectives and uniformed officers took statements from nearby witnesses.

Detectives Chandra Parker and Patrick Garrett stood over the body. Chandra knelt beside Terri's lifeless form. She had earned a reputation as a relentless pursuer of justice, her no-nonsense approach feared by many. Patrick, also in his mid-thirties and equally sharp in appearance, stood nearby, jotting notes in his notepad. He was the epitome of a by-the-book detective.

Patrick broke the heavy silence. "Remind me why I came back to this cold-ass city?"

Chandra didn't look up. "Because you couldn't live without it."

Patrick glanced at the uniformed officer carefully examining the contents of Terri's pockets. "No one knew she was a cop until they found her ID."

"Damn," Chandra muttered, shaking her head. "Her husband's on the job."

"Yeah, he's being notified now," Patrick replied.

Chandra stood and scanned the desolate surroundings. "In the middle of nowhere."

"So you knew her, huh?" Patrick asked.

"We were in the academy together. This doesn't feel right," Chandra said, her voice tinged with unease.

"Maybe she couldn't handle the stress of the job. Narcotics is a mutha—"

Chandra interrupted him, leaning closer to the body. "They found her like this, you say?"

"Yes. What's up?"

"With the gun in her right hand."

Patrick raised an eyebrow. "Where are you going with this?"

"She was left-handed."

"You sure?"

"Yep, I used to tease her about it when we were in vice together. This was a murder through and through."

"Was she under on anything?" Patrick asked, flipping through his notes.

"No, she had just gotten back from vacation," Chandra replied.

Patrick glanced behind him, noticing I.A.B. Inspector Cooper approaching. Cooper, a well-dressed, hard-faced man, was never in a good mood. He epitomized the straight-laced, no-nonsense cop.

"Great, here comes I.A.B," Patrick muttered under his breath.

"Fantastic," Chandra echoed, her tone dripping with sarcasm.

Cooper stopped in front of them. "Detectives."

"Inspector," Chandra acknowledged, standing her ground.

"IA will take it from here," Cooper stated firmly, his expression unreadable.

"No, you won't. This is our murder scene," Chandra shot back.

"And she is a cop. Talk to your C.O.," Cooper insisted, his tone brooking no argument.

"He hasn't said anything," Chandra countered, crossing her arms defiantly.

Patrick's phone dinged, breaking the standoff. He glanced at the screen and sighed. "Speaking of the devil."

"Great," Chandra said, her frustration palpable.

CHAPTER TWO

Casey Stone's home was a modern marvel, a pristine sanctuary of sleek lines and minimalist decor. The large windows flooded the space with natural light, casting a warm glow on the polished surfaces. Casey, fit and handsome in his jeans and a T-shirt, stood in the kitchen, nursing a cup of coffee as he watched the morning news. His eyes flicked over the headlines, but the constant barrage of negativity finally became too much. With a sigh, he clicked off the TV, relishing the sudden silence. He scratched his scruffy beard and for a second thought about shaving it. This is the longest its been since hed left the SEAL Teams a few years ago.

The phone rang, breaking the tranquility. Casey glanced at the number and answered.

"Yeah... Fuck... On my way," he said, his voice a low growl of irritation.

He grabbed his pistol from the counter and holstered it at his waist. With his field coat and keys in hand, he left the kitchen, his mind already shifting to the task ahead.

Casey walked through the underground parking garage, his steps echoing off the concrete walls. As he approached his parking space, he saw his neighbor Sam stepping out of her car. She was stunning, a real head-turner with her confident stride and radiant smile.

"Morning, Casey," she greeted, her voice warm and inviting.

"Sam," he replied, nodding.

She walked over to him, her eyes sparkling with mischief. "When you get some time, I need you to look into a case for me."

Casey smiled. "Anything for you."

"And maybe we can do dinner later?" she asked, her tone suggestive.

"Well, you know I'm always up for dinner," he said, matching her playful tone.

She smiled seductively and walked off, leaving Casey to shake his head in amusement. He continued to his parked Land Rover Defender, ready to face whatever awaited him.

————

Sean Hill, a preppy-dressed sixteen-year-old, sat at the table in the aging, dimly lit interview room. The door slammed open, and Casey entered. This was hie sixth time this year bailing this spoiled rich brat out of trouble, but hey the kids dad paid well. He slammed the door behind him and pounded his fist on the table, startling the kid.3

"Do you ever stay out of fucking trouble!" Barked Stone.

"Stone, you gotta—" Sean began.

"There I was, enjoying my morning coffee, and I get a call from your father," Casey interrupted, his voice hard. "He's trying to run for Attorney General, and he asks me to get you out of jail."

"Man, look, I'm—" Sean tried again.

"What happened?" Casey demanded.

"That dude had it coming to him," Sean said defiantly.

"You live in Birmingham, you go to private school. Who could you possibly have beef with? And where did you get a gun? Better question: What are you even doing in the city?"

"I was hanging out with my girl, and the motherfucker stepped to me, so I stepped back," Sean said, trying to sound tough.

Casey raised an eyebrow, both amused and exasperated. "You stepped back. That's funny. Where did you get the gun from?"

"Just some kid," Sean mumbled.

"Just some kid. Okay, Little Glock 19, either you tell me where you got the fucking gun from, and we walk out of here. The arresting officer, who owes me a favor or two, forgets this ever happened. Or you can go with option B, which is you get booked, spend your sorry ass the night in this shithole, get a record, and kiss Harvard goodbye. You call it, kid."

Sean hesitated, the weight of the decision clear on his face. Finally, he sighed. "Alright."

"I want his name and number. And the next time your dumb ass decides to play gangster, don't."

"Don't talk to me..." Sean muttered.

"I can talk to you any fucking way I want as long as your dumb ass disturbs my Sunday morning. And your father calls me to get your ass out of trouble. My time is much more fucking valuable. Now sit tight."

Casey walked out of the interview room, his face a mask of controlled anger. He found the arresting officer, Davis, and pulled him aside.

"He's gonna give the name of the prick who sold him the gun. Do me a favor."

"Fuck, Stone, you are just about all out of favors. But I got you. It won't blow back on the dumb-ass kid," Davis said, resigned.

"All the money in the world, and this asshole wants to play gangster," Casey muttered, shaking his head.

"I'll never understand. Makes you wish you would've stayed in the teams instead of cleaning up rich people's problems?" Davis asked, a hint of sympathy in his voice.

"Well, rich people pay way more than my E-9 ever did," Casey replied, a wry smile tugging at his lips.

CHAPTER THREE

Sean and Casey strode down the precinct's hallway, Casey's hand firmly guiding Sean forward. They passed by two officers, Chandra and Patrick. Chandra's gaze lingered on Casey, curiosity evident in her eyes.

"Nice," Chandra commented, her voice low and intrigued.

"Trouble," Patrick replied, his tone wary.

"Lawyer?" she asked, glancing back at Casey.

"Bad news," Patrick said, shaking his head.

"You know him?" Chandra pressed.

"Yeah, I'll tell you that story another time," Patrick answered, a hint of reluctance in his voice.

"So what does he do?" she continued.

"Ex-special something, now an investigator of sorts," Patrick explained.

"Former FED?" Chandra asked, raising an eyebrow.

Patrick laughed. "I don't think he would pass an FBI psych eval."

"Copy that," Chandra said, nodding thoughtfully.

They arrived at Captain Hunt's office. The door was old, the paint peeling slightly, matching the rest of the building's aged appearance.

Hunt's office was cluttered with pictures and plaques, a testament to years of service. He stood behind his desk, imposing and stern, as Chandra and Patrick took their seats.

"You two are reassigned to the double homicide at the Casino," Hunt announced.

"What! We are working a case," Chandra protested, her voice edged with frustration.

"It's I.A.B's case now," Hunt replied firmly.

"I don't think so," Chandra retorted, her tone defiant.

"A detective fresh off of suspension should not be talking to her boss that way," Hunt warned, his eyes narrowing.

Patrick stepped in, trying to diffuse the tension. "We'll do the double."

"Smart man," Hunt said, nodding approvingly. He turned to Chandra. "You can learn something from this kid."

Chandra's expression was stormy as they left the office.

They walked down the hallway, the background noise of the squad room filling the space.

"This stinks to all hell," Chandra muttered, her frustration evident.

"Leave it alone, we have been reassigned," Patrick said, his tone resigned.

"You are just gonna roll with it?" Chandra asked incredulously.

"Doesn't matter what I want, we are off of it," Patrick replied, shaking his head.

"That's not good enough. I want answers," Chandra insisted.

"Well, we are off the case. IAB has it, so let them handle that shit. Maybe he was working for them. Or, if you got enough money, you can hire that fucker we passed in the hallway," Patrick suggested, his tone bitter.

"Who is he?" Chandra asked, curiosity piqued.

"Casey Stone," Patrick answered.

"Casey Stone. Sounds like an action movie star," Chandra remarked, a faint smile tugging at her lips.

"He's no action hero. Ex-Navy SEAL, who made waves with the department last year when his older brother was killed. Come to find out two cops were in on the murder. One of them ended up in prison, the other one was found at the old Packard Plant hanging from a beam with his head a few feet away from him," Patrick explained, his voice grim.

"I remember that case," Chandra said, her expression thoughtful.

"Yeah, apparently their other brother is Jackson Stone," Patrick added.

"The high-powered attorney," Chandra said, nodding in recognition.

"Yeah, him. He supposedly has proof that the Mayor is part of the group that had the other brother killed, but he's sitting on it. Of course, these are rumors," Patrick said, shrugging.

"Hmm. And no one ever looked at this guy for the murders?" Chandra asked, raising an eyebrow.

Patrick laughed. "You think someone who has done shit that this guy has done for the government is gonna get caught? Besides, no one gives a shit about two corrupt cops. I hate to admit it, but the guy is helping us out."

"How so?" She quizzed.

"Remember how that group of Iranian drug dealers that were terrorizing the east side just up and left town? Well. Rumor is they are still in town, just not about ground."

"Chandra, damn I get suspended for eight months and miss all the action."

"He takes on cases that no one cares about." Said Patrick

"Yeah, well, I care about this dead cop we got," Chandra said, her tone resolute.

"Leave it alone," Patrick advised, his voice softer this time.

Chandra's determination didn't waver as she walked off, her mind clearly made up.

CHAPTER FOUR

Casey stood in the cobblestone driveway of Stephen Hill's opulent home, the kind of place that spoke of wealth and privilege. Stephen, in his forties and impeccably dressed, stood beside him, gratitude etched on his face.

"How much do I owe you?" Stephen asked.

Casey shook his head. "I may need a defense lawyer in the future, so no charge."

Stephen smiled wryly. "What am I gonna do with him?"

"There's always military school," Casey suggested, a hint of humor in his voice.

"Funny," Stephen said, though his expression remained serious.

Casey shrugged. "He's a teenager. Be ready for more bullshit. Let's just hope it's not the kind of call you need to get me for."

"Thank you again," Stephen said earnestly.

"Don't mention it," Casey replied.

With that, Casey walked to his car, climbed in, and drove off, leaving Stephen to ponder the future.

. . .

Casey made his way into the building that housed his office, his mind already shifting to his next task, when a voice called out, stopping him in his tracks.

"Mr. Stone."

He turned, a flicker of annoyance crossing his face. "Sorry, you got the wrong person."

Detective Chandra Parker flashed her badge. "I'm Detective Chandra Parker."

"Okay, but you still have the wrong person," Casey replied, trying to brush her off.

"I'm here about Officer Terri Miller," Chandra said, her tone insistent.

Casey sighed. "Since you won't give up, you're talking about the one who killed herself."

"I think it's more, and I was told that you are someone who can get answers," Chandra pressed.

Casey motioned her to the side, away from prying ears. "I'm sorry, I can't help you."

"I know what you do," Chandra said firmly.

"Then you know I can't help you. Plus, what people are saying about me is all fantasy," Casey responded, his tone steady.

"Yeah, just like the disappearance of the fucker who killed that young recruit last year. A recruit whose aunt happened to be a U.S. Senator who your SEAL team rescued from being beheaded in Afghanistan," Chandra said, her voice sharp.

"Hypothetical," Casey retorted.

"This isn't a courtroom," Chandra shot back.

Casey chuckled. "You're cute, you know that."

"And this is not a request for dinner," Chandra replied coolly.

"I'm very expensive," Casey said, raising an eyebrow.

"Look, she was a friend of mine, and I need answers," Chandra said, her voice softening for the first time.

Casey thought for a moment, weighing his options. "Meet me at my office at one. Bring whatever you have, and I may help you."

Without waiting for a response, he turned and walked away, leaving

Chandra standing in the lobby, a mix of hope and determination on her face.

CHAPTER FIVE

Detective Parker rummaged through her cluttered desk, frustration growing with each passing second. Papers flew as she searched, her movements hurried and tense. Patrick walked in, taking his seat at the desk opposite her.

"What are you looking for?" he asked, settling into his chair.

"Who's been on my desk?" Chandra snapped, not bothering to look up.

Patrick shrugged. "Don't know. What are you looking for?"

"I pulled a file on Miller," Chandra explained, her tone curt.

"Cooper was in the squad room earlier," Patrick offered.

"Cooper," Chandra repeated, a note of suspicion in her voice.

"Whoa, we were taken off the case," Patrick reminded her.

"Something doesn't sit right with me," Chandra insisted, still rifling through the mess on her desk.

"Let I.A.B handle it," Patrick urged.

Chandra stopped and looked at him, her eyes narrowing. "Do you understand what's going on here?"

Patrick stood up and nodded toward the door, signaling for her to follow. She hesitated for a moment before complying, curiosity piqued.

The locker room was empty, the echoes of their footsteps the only sound. Patrick double-checked to make sure they were alone, then locked the door behind them. He turned to Chandra, his voice dropping to a hushed tone.

"Leave it alone," he urged again.

"Why?" Chandra demanded.

Patrick took a deep breath. "She was an informant for them."

"What?" Chandra's eyes widened in shock.

"Think about it. Who is her husband?" Patrick asked pointedly.

"Head of the mayor's security detail," Chandra answered slowly, the pieces beginning to fall into place.

"And who are the Feds investigating?" Patrick continued.

"Shit," Chandra muttered, the realization hitting her.

"So let it go. Let them take it," Patrick advised, his tone weary.

"Do you think it was a homicide?" Chandra asked, her voice barely above a whisper.

"I think I'm gonna let them handle it. I got enough shit to worry about," Patrick replied.

Without another word, Patrick unlocked the door and left the locker room, leaving Chandra alone with her thoughts. She stood there for a moment, the weight of the revelation settling over her. This case was far from over, and the danger was more real than she had ever imagined.

CHAPTER SIX

Casey sat behind his sleek desk, his eyes fixed on something on his computer screen. Across from him, Detective Chandra Parker sat in the guest chair, a look of frustration and determination on her face.

"So why don't you do what your partner said and stay out of it," Stone suggested, not looking up from his screen.

Chandra leaned forward, her annoyance clear. "She was a friend, and her mother deserves answers."

Stone finally met her gaze, studying her. "I see."

"How much?" Chandra asked, her voice firm.

"You won't back down, will you?" Stone observed, a hint of a smile playing at the corners of his mouth.

"No. How much?" Chandra pressed. "Look, I.A. took her file because she was an informant for them in their case against the mayor's security."

Stone raised an eyebrow. "So you think that got her killed?"

"Yes," Chandra replied without hesitation.

Stone leaned back in his chair, thinking for a moment. "I'll tell you what, let me look into it and I'll call you back."

Chandra nodded, a mix of relief and frustration in her eyes. "Ok."

She got up and left the office, leaving Stone to his thoughts.

Chandra exited the building, the sun glaring down on her as she made her way to the sidewalk. Suddenly, a white SUV sped around the corner, tires screeching. Before she could react, someone opened fire from the back window. Bullets tore through the air, and Chandra crumpled to the ground, blood staining her clothes.

The street erupted into chaos. Some people scattered, seeking cover, while others rushed to her aid. Stone burst through the crowd, his heart pounding as he knelt beside her. Chandra struggled to speak, her breaths coming in ragged gasps.

"Don't say anything. Just hold on," Stone urged, his voice steady despite the fear in his eyes. He yelled to the bystanders, "Call an ambulance!"

Chandra's eyes fluttered as she tried to form words. "Please...Please," she whispered, her voice barely audible.

"Shh," Stone soothed, his hand gently pressing against her wound in a futile attempt to stem the bleeding. "Just hold on."

As the sound of approaching sirens filled the air, Stone stayed by her side, silently vowing to find those responsible for this attack. The fight for justice had just become personal.

CHAPTER SEVEN

The hospital was a cacophony of police activity, a sea of blue uniforms and stern faces. Casey, blood still smeared on his clothes, navigated through the throng. The officers' eyes followed him, their gazes hard and judgmental. Stone didn't care. He had a mission. Patrick stood near the nurses' station. Stone approached, his presence drawing even more attention from the surrounding cops.

"Stone," Patrick acknowledged him, his tone curt.

"How is she?" Stone asked, his voice steady despite the turmoil inside.

"In a coma. What do you want?" Patrick's eyes narrowed, suspicion clear.

"She was shot outside of my office," Stone replied, his words clipped.

"Let DPD handle this," Patrick said, a note of warning in his voice.

Stone leaned in slightly. "When she wakes up, tell her my answer is yes."

Without waiting for a response, Stone turned and walked away. The hallway seemed to stretch endlessly, the stares of the officers boring into his back.

———

Casey strode towards his truck, his mind racing. As he reached the vehicle, a patrol car pulled in behind it, blocking his exit. Officer Kris White stepped out, a look of concern on his face.

"Stone," White called out, approaching him.

"Officer," Case responded, keeping his tone neutral.

"You good?" White asked, studying Casey's expression.

"I'll live," Casey replied, his voice gruff.

"Good. Do us a favor," White said, pausing for emphasis.

"What's that?" Casey asked, raising an eyebrow.

"Do what you do," White said, a hint of a smile playing at the corners of his mouth.

Stone nodded. "Copy that."

With that, White returned to his patrol car, and Stone climbed into his truck. He had work to do.

———

The small, secluded loft was a mess, cluttered with discarded clothes, empty takeout containers, and electronic equipment. A huge computer desk dominated the center of the room, three monitors casting a blue glow.

Carlos Hill, a disheveled young man in his mid-twenties, answered the door. His eyes widened when he saw Stone standing there, bloodied but resolute.

"Stone. This must be important. You're bleeding," Carlos observed, stepping aside to let Stone in.

"It ain't mine," Casey, replied, brushing past him. He reached into his pocket and pulled out a thick stack of hundred-dollar bills, setting it on the table by the door. Carlos picked it up and quickly counted it, his eyes lighting up.

"Ok, this is off the books. What do you need?" Carlos asked, pocketing the money.

"The case file from the federal investigation against the DA and the Mayor," Stone said, his tone leaving no room for negotiation.

Carlos's eyes widened. "Whoa, that's major. That's hacking into a government mainframe."

"Like that has stopped you before," Stone said, his gaze steady. "Are you in or out?"

Carlos grinned, a mischievous glint in his eyes. "Hell yeah. Where you gonna be?"

"You know where to find me," Stone said, turning to leave.

As Stone walked out of the cramped loft, he felt a grim determination settle over him. The pieces were coming together, and he was ready for the next move.

CHAPTER EIGHT

Casey Stone entered his penthouse, the weight of the night still lingering on his shoulders. The soft strains of jazz music floated through the air, instantly putting him at ease. He smiled to himself, tossing his coat carelessly onto the sofa as he made his way toward the bedroom.

As he stepped into the bathroom, he was greeted by an unexpected sight. Candy, his friend with benefits, lay comfortably in his tub, surrounded by bubbles that shimmered in the dim light. She looked up at him with a sultry smile.

"I thought you had auditions in New York," he said, leaning against the doorframe.

"I got back early," she replied, her voice smooth and inviting. "Want to join me?"

"Like I'm gonna say no with you naked in my tub."

The water had cooled, but the air between them was warm and charged. Candy lounged against the side of the tub, her fingers lazily tracing patterns in the remaining bubbles. Casey leaned back, his mind drifting to the night's events.

"So what are you gonna do?" Candy asked, breaking the silence.

"What I always do," he responded, his voice steady.

She turned to face him, concern etched on her features. "Be careful. If they have the balls to try to kill a cop, what do you think they would do to you?"

Casey reached out, brushing a stray lock of hair from her face. "I'm gonna be careful."

Candy's expression softened, and she moved closer, their faces inches apart. "You miss me?"

"Of course."

"How much?" she teased, a playful glint in her eye.

Casey grinned, pulling her closer. "I'll show you."

Their lips met in a passionate kiss, the worries of the world outside fading away as they lost themselves in each other.

CHAPTER NINE

The FBI Field Office in Detroit buzzed with activity as agents moved with purpose, some buried in paperwork, others engrossed in conversations. Casey Stone walked in, a visitor badge clipped to his jacket. He spotted his old friend Thomas Davenport across the room, and they met with a firm handshake.

"It's been a while," Thomas remarked, a hint of nostalgia in his voice.

"I know," Stone replied, a smirk playing on his lips. "I heard the new SAC was a real dick."

Thomas chuckled. "Funny. Right this way."

They navigated through the busy office and entered a conference room. Inside, a large board displayed gruesome photos of murdered girls. Stone took a moment to study the images, a frown deepening on his face as Thomas settled into a chair.

"Damn. Who caught this one?" Stone asked, his tone grim.

"Some rookie out of Alabama. He's in way over his head. What can I do for you?" Thomas replied.

"Terri Miller. I know you're on the case," Stone said, cutting to the chase.

Thomas's expression hardened. "And you know I can't help you?"

"Remember who helped you get to where you are," Stone pressed.

"You will never let me forget, but I can't comment on it. Off the record, it wasn't a suicide."

"Any suspects?"

"Her husband, his friends, anyone who can get burned by this," Thomas said vaguely.

Stone's eyes narrowed. "What do you mean?"

Thomas hesitated but remained silent.

"You flipped her?" Stone guessed.

Thomas sighed. "The honeymoon was over. He was cheating, and her revenge was to come to us and tell us everything he told her."

"Spousal privilege?" Stone inquired.

"We'll let his lawyer figure that out. She was gathering more info for us when she was killed."

"But you don't have enough on him, do you?"

"Nope."

Stone nodded. "Thanks."

He turned to leave, but Thomas called after him, "What are you gonna do?"

"Find a killer."

"Don't fuck up my investigation," Thomas warned.

"Never that," Stone replied with a confident grin.

He left the conference room and made his way outside. The sun was bright, a stark contrast to the dark thoughts swirling in his mind. He lit a cigarette and took a long drag as he walked to his car, an Aston Martin. As he crossed the street, a Detroit Police Department cruiser pulled up behind him, its lights flashing.

Stone turned, watching as the officer approached. "Morning, officer."

"Hands against the car," the cop ordered.

Stone complied, feeling the familiar pat-down. "I'm a licensed PI," he said, irritation creeping into his voice.

"No shit," the cop whispered. "Garrett said Chauncey's in one hour."

"He couldn't call?" Stone asked, eyebrows raised.

"His phone is bugged."

The cop finished the frisk and stepped back. "Am I free to go?" Stone asked.

"Yeah."

Stone got into his Aston Martin, the engine roaring to life as he drove off. Another layer of intrigue added to his ever-growing list of problems. The hunt was on, and he was ready for whatever came next.

CHAPTER TEN

Detective Cooper sat across from Franky Miller, who was attempting to look distraught over his wife's death but failing miserably. Cooper's irritation was palpable, his eyes narrowing as he scrutinized every word from Franky's mouth.

"So tell me why a cop as tough as she is just takes her own life," Cooper demanded, his tone sharp.

"Look, she had been depressed lately," Franky replied, trying to sound convincing.

"Yeah, so did you help her? Did you kill her and pass it off as a suicide?" Cooper shot back, leaning forward.

"You know what, you are crazy. I came down here on my own to talk to you," Franky retorted, his frustration mounting.

"So why do you think she killed herself?" Cooper pressed.

"I don't know! I loved her," Franky exclaimed, his voice wavering slightly.

"Is that why you two were heading towards a divorce?" Cooper asked, his voice dripping with skepticism.

"Who told you that?" Franky's eyes widened in surprise.

"Doesn't matter," Cooper said dismissively.

"I loved her. And I came down here without my union lawyer just to prove that I didn't have shit to do with it," Franky insisted, his anger flaring.

"Doesn't mean shit," Cooper replied coldly.

"You know what, next time you want to talk, do it through my delegate. I got a funeral to plan," Franky snapped, standing up abruptly.

Franky stormed out of the room, leaving Cooper watching him with a mixture of contempt and suspicion.

———

Franky sat in his living room, the weight of the situation pressing down on him. His best friend, Nathan Drake, the mayor's Chief of Staff and a real jerk, sat across from him, exuding confidence.

"This shit is going to come back on me bad," Franky said, his voice filled with anxiety.

"No, it's not. Look, keep your mouth shut and you will be fine. Go to the funeral, act like the grieving husband, take a few weeks off, then come back to work. This will all blow over," Drake replied, his tone dismissive.

"What about what she told the feds?" Franky asked, worry etched on his face.

"They have nothing. We are untouchable," Drake replied confidently.

"We didn't have to kill her," Franky said, a hint of regret in his voice.

"Yes, we did. Get some rest," Drake said, his tone final.

"Get some rest? Do you know I am their chief suspect? And that bitch cop went to Stone," Franky said, his frustration boiling over.

"We are fine, and Stone doesn't scare me. Now get some rest," Drake said, standing up to leave.

Drake walked out, leaving Franky sitting there, his mind racing with the implications of their actions and the mounting pressure of the investigation.

CHAPTER ELEVEN

Chaunceys, a popular strip club, had a subdued energy as dancers aimlessly wandered, trying to beat the boredom. A few patrons enjoyed the show, their attention fixed on the stage. Casey walked in, nodding hello to familiar faces before heading up a set of stairs.

In the VIP section, Patrick sat brooding. The dancers saw Stone enter and discreetly excused themselves. Stone took a seat across from Patrick.

"You sent for me?" Stone asked, getting straight to the point.

Patrick handed him an envelope. "There's ten grand in there. I'll get the rest to you. I want these bastards, but since I was put on disability, I can't do shit."

Stone glanced at the envelope and then at Patrick. "You look fine to me."

"That's how they shut us down," Patrick replied bitterly.

"How is she?" Stone asked, his voice softening.

"Still in a coma. You wanna start with her husband," Patrick said, anger simmering in his eyes.

"Will do," Stone said.

Patrick left. Stone sat there for a moment, contemplating his next move, then stood and exited.

Stone entered a sleek office building when Nathan Drake, flanked by two bodyguards, intercepted him.

"Flaky Drake, still an errand boy, huh?" Stone remarked with a smirk.

"I was told you were snooping around. Do me a favor and stay out of this investigation," Drake said, his tone menacing.

"I don't work for the police department," Stone replied, his expression unwavering.

"Listen to me, and I'm only going to say it once. Leave it alone," Drake warned.

"Actually, that was twice, and I don't know what you are talking about. Now, excuse me, I got shit to do," Stone said, attempting to walk past.

One of the bodyguards placed a hand on Stone's shoulder. With swift precision, Stone kicked him in the groin and then snapped his wrist. The second bodyguard lunged, but Stone chopped him in the throat, sending him to the ground.

"Where the fuck you get these pussies from?" Stone taunted Drake before moving on.

He was met by Carlos, as they both entered the elevator.

Drake, pulled out his phone and dialing a number, hissed into the receiver, "This is Mr. Drake. I have a problem."

Carlos handed Stone a file folder as the elevator ascended.

"Damn, your landlord is gonna kick you out," Carlos teased.

"We own the building, dickhead," Stone retorted, taking the folder.

"The feds have been using her as a C.I. for the last year and a half. She uncovered a lot of dirt on his unit that would bring back criminal charges against you-know-who," Carlos explained.

"Why am I not surprised. Anything else?" Stone asked, flipping through the folder.

"I broke into her home computer and intercepted an email to her sister asking for a reference to a divorce attorney," Carlos said.

"People get divorced every day," Stone replied, scanning the documents.

"And she was also sending emails to someone marked 'shadow99,' talking about all of her husband's exploits on the job," Carlos continued.

"Someone on the inside," Stone mused.

"Got to be, because the way he was talking, he knew a lot," Carlos confirmed.

"Thanks," Stone said as he stepped off the elevator.

CHAPTER TWELVE

District Attorney Patrick Connelliey stood behind his mahogany desk, his face flushed with anger. He was a man in his mid-fifties, tall and broad-shouldered, with a square jaw and piercing blue eyes that had seen too much. His hair, once jet black, was now streaked with gray, adding to his air of authority. Nathan Drake, the mayor's chief of staff, sat across from him, looking more composed but equally tense.

"Are you nuts? We have enough trouble on our hands," Connelliey growled, his voice a low rumble of controlled fury.

"I know this guy. He won't stop until he finds something," Drake replied, leaning forward in his chair, his eyes locked on Connelliey's.

"I've never heard of him. Who is he?" Connelliey demanded, slamming a fist on the desk.

"Casey Stone. Harvard law grad. After law school, he joined the Navy and became a SEAL. Most of his service record is redacted because he was part of DEVGRU," Drake explained.

Connelliey's brows furrowed. "What the hell is DEVGRU?"

"SEAL Team Six, the guys who took out Bin Laden. Stone left the Navy last year after his brother Nelson was killed," Drake continued.

"Wait, this is Jackson Stone's brother, the one who should be in prison?" Connelliey asked, his eyes narrowing.

"Yeah, that one," Drake confirmed, nodding grimly.

"Shit!" Connelliey cursed, pacing behind his desk. He stopped abruptly and faced Drake. "Okay, we send someone to take care of him."

Drake chuckled darkly. "Did you hear anything I said? Navy SEAL, SEAL Team Six—the best of the best. He'll spot a hitman a mile away."

Connelliey paused, then a cold smile spread across his face. "I know someone."

"Yeah?" Drake asked, skeptical.

"At the end of the day, he's just one man," Connelliey said, his voice dripping with confidence.

Drake nodded slowly, realizing that Connelliey had already made up his mind. The stakes were high, and the players were dangerous, but this was a game they couldn't afford to lose. As Connelliey picked up his phone to make the call, Drake couldn't shake the feeling that they were about to unleash something far more deadly than they anticipated.

———

Casey Stone leaned against his Aston Martin, lighting a cigarette and taking a long drag. He watched the entrance to the DA's office, his mind racing with the information he had gathered. Patrick's envelope weighed heavily in his pocket, a reminder of the task ahead.

He had a lead on Terri Miller's husband, but the deeper he dug, the more dangerous the situation became. The pieces were falling into place, but the picture they formed was one of corruption, betrayal, and violence.

As Stone exhaled a plume of smoke, he saw Nathan Drake exiting the building, talking animatedly on his phone. Stone's eyes narrowed. He knew that whatever Drake was planning, it wasn't going to be good for him.

But Stone had faced worse. Much worse.

Stone entered a dimly lit bar, a local haunt for cops and criminals alike. He took a seat at the counter, nodding to the bartender who slid him a glass of bourbon without a word.

"Got a lot on your mind, Casey," a familiar voice said.

Stone turned to see Thomas Davenport, an old friend and FBI agent, taking a seat next to him.

"You could say that," Stone replied, taking a sip of his drink.

"Heard you're stirring the pot again," Davenport said, his tone half-joking, half-serious.

"Someone's gotta do it," Stone said with a shrug.

"Just be careful. You know how this town gets when you start digging too deep," Davenport warned.

"I'm always careful," Stone replied, though they both knew the dangers that lay ahead.

As the night wore on, Stone and Davenport talked about old times and new threats, their camaraderie a brief respite from the storm that was brewing. But deep down, Stone knew that the path he was on was leading him into the heart of darkness, where enemies lurked in every shadow, and the price of the truth could be his very life.

CHAPTER THIRTEEN

Casey Stone made his way to the building entrance, his footsteps echoing through the dimly lit parking garage. As he approached the door, a man in all black stepped into his path, hands concealed inside his coat.

"May I help you?" Stone asked, his voice steady.

"Are you Stone?" the man replied, his tone cold.

"Yeah, and you are?" Stone inquired.

The man pulled a gun, aiming it directly at Stone's chest. "Your gun," he demanded.

"My gun?" Stone echoed, feigning confusion.

"Hand me your gun," the man insisted, stepping closer and pressing the barrel against Stone's chest.

"Turn around," the man ordered.

"If you say so," Stone replied nonchalantly.

In one swift motion, Stone disarmed the man, sending a fist crashing into his face. The man staggered but quickly regained his footing, drawing a knife and swinging it wildly. Stone blocked the attack and countered with the butt of the gun to the man's nose. Dazed and disoriented, the man stumbled backward, struggling to retrieve another weapon from inside his coat. Stone aimed the gun at him, eyes cold and focused.

"OK, who sent you?" Stone demanded.

The man pulled out a backup gun, defiance in his eyes. "Go to hell," he spat.

Before he could pull the trigger, Stone fired twice, the shots echoing through the garage. The man collapsed, gasping for breath, his life slipping away.

"Been there," Stone muttered, kneeling next to the dying man.

"Help me," the man wheezed, desperation in his voice.

"Now you want help? Who sent you?" Stone pressed.

"Help me," the man repeated, his voice weakening.

"Who sent you?" Stone demanded again.

"Drrr... Drake," the man managed to whisper.

"Too bad," Stone said, his voice void of emotion. With a swift motion, he broke the man's neck, ending his suffering.

———

Nathan Drake paced his driveway, phone pressed to his ear as he spoke in hushed tones. He was on his way to retrieve the morning paper when his eyes fell on the grisly sight: his dead assassin sprawled across the hood of his car.

"Get over here. We have a problem," Drake barked into the phone, his voice tight with anger. He disconnected the call and glared at the body, rage simmering beneath his composed exterior.

Drake knew this was a message. And he intended to respond in kind.

CHAPTER FOURTEEN

Mayor Tony Young, impeccably dressed in a tailored suit, sat behind his opulent mahogany desk. His calm demeanor starkly contrasted with the seething Nathan Drake, who sat across from him. District Attorney Connelley stood nearby, arms crossed and brow furrowed.

"You two go and get yourselves into trouble, and now you come to me for help," Mayor Young said, his voice dripping with disdain. "Jumping into bed with you two has already got the Feds looking up my ass."

Drake leaned forward, desperation evident in his eyes. "Remember, if we go down, you go down."

Young's expression hardened. "What does he know? He can't know much."

"I don't care," Connelley interjected. "Just having him snooping around is trouble enough."

The mayor's tone turned sarcastic. "We tried killing him, and that didn't work. What should I do, have him arrested?"

"I don't know, dammit!" Drake exploded. "All I know is this bastard knows where I live, and I'm scared shitless."

Young chuckled, almost amused by Drake's panic. "You should be.

If a man sent someone to kill me, I'd be pissed myself. Look, you two are going to have to figure this one out on your own."

Drake and Connelley exchanged frustrated glances before storming out of the office, their exit marked by the door slamming shut.

As Drake and Connelley descended the grand steps of the mayor's mansion, their frustration bubbled over into anger.

"This is a mess," Connelley muttered, shaking his head. "We need a plan."

"We need someone who can take Stone out without getting caught," Drake said, his voice low and urgent. "And we need it fast."

————

Drake stood in the dim glow of his porch light, staring at his phone. He'd made the call to a contact he swore he'd never use again. Desperation had driven him to it.

A dark sedan pulled up, and a figure stepped out, moving with lethal grace. The man approached Drake, stopping just short of the steps.

"Problem needs fixing," Drake said tersely.

The man nodded once. "Consider it done."

As the sedan drove off, Drake couldn't shake the feeling that he had just made a deal with the devil. He shivered, not from the cold, but from the icy dread that settled in his gut.

CHAPTER FIFTEEN

The suburban tranquility of the Miller household was shattered as Franky Miller stepped out into the cool night air, dragging a bulging trash bag behind him. The sound of cicadas filled the silence, but Franky's mind was elsewhere, lost in the chaos that had engulfed his life. He approached the trash can, his thoughts interrupted by a sudden movement.

Stone emerged from the shadows, his presence a stark contrast to the serene night. Franky's hand instinctively went to his waistband, drawing his gun in one swift motion.

"Jesus!! I could have shot you," Franky exclaimed, his voice a mix of shock and anger.

Stone's eyes were cold, unyielding. "Like you killed your wife?"

Franky's face twisted with a mixture of guilt and rage. "What do you want?"

"You know what I want," Stone replied, his tone calm yet menacing.

Franky's grip on his gun tightened. "I ain't got shit to say to you."

Stone took a step closer, his gaze unwavering. "Funny thing, a man loses his wife to suicide, and he's already throwing her stuff away. Seems like guilt to me."

"You don't know what you're talking about," Franky spat, his voice shaking with a mix of fear and anger.

"Why did you kill her?" Stone's voice was a deadly whisper.

Franky's anger flared. "Get off of my property."

"You found out she was spying on you for the Feds. How much did she know? How much did you tell her?" Stone pressed, his eyes never leaving Franky's.

"You got five seconds to leave before I start shooting," Franky warned, raising his gun.

Stone took a step back, his expression unreadable. "Tell Drake I'm coming for him."

Before Franky could react, Stone melted back into the darkness from which he had emerged, leaving Franky standing there, gun in hand, heart pounding.

Franky stormed back into the house, slamming the door behind him. His mind raced as he replayed the encounter with Stone. He tossed the gun onto the coffee table and sank into the couch, his head in his hands.

"Dammit," he muttered to himself, the weight of his actions pressing down on him.

———

Nathan Drake sat in his office, the dim light casting long shadows across the room. His phone buzzed, and he picked it up, seeing Franky's name on the screen.

"What is it?" Drake answered, irritation clear in his voice.

"Stone was here," Franky said, his voice trembling. "He knows everything."

Drake's grip tightened on the phone. "Calm down. We'll handle it."

"Handle it? He said he's coming for you," Franky almost shouted.

Drake's eyes narrowed. "Let him come. We'll be ready."

He ended the call and leaned back in his chair, his mind already working on the next move. Stone was getting too close, and it was time to eliminate the threat once and for all.

CHAPTER SIXTEEN

The night air was thick with an uneasy stillness as Stone leaned against his car, watching the shadows dance under the dim streetlights. The sound of gravel crunching under tires broke the silence as an unmarked car rolled into view. The vehicle came to a stop, and the cop inside scanned the area before stepping out.

Stone straightened up, his gaze fixed on the officer. The man, Officer Baker, extended his hand, and Stone shook it firmly.

"Officer Baker," Stone greeted.

Baker's face was lined with weariness. "Yeah. You know, I can get killed talking to you."

"Lot of that going around," Stone replied, his tone dark and unyielding. "You contacted me."

Baker nodded, his eyes darting around as if wary of unseen watchers. "I heard you were looking into Miller's death. It wasn't a suicide. Just like Vanity Klein didn't run off the road."

Stone's eyebrows shot up. "Whoa, the stripper."

"Yep. She was run off the road. Drake had it set up."

"Why?"

Baker took a deep breath, the weight of his knowledge heavy on his shoulders. "She was going to the Feds about her knowledge of the riverfront deal."

Stone's interest was piqued. "Tell me about it."

Baker's voice dropped to a whisper. "How does someone with a background and history like Rance Tillman get three prime contracts from the city? Plus, ownership in the new entertainment complex?"

Stone's mind raced. "I can think of five million reasons how."

"More like ten," Baker said grimly. "I was the bag man for the delivery."

"And Klein fit into this how?" Stone pressed.

Baker's face hardened. "Tillman made the mistake of sending her along with the bribe money as a gift to his honor. She tried blackmail, and Drake did his dirty work."

Stone's eyes narrowed. "Wow. How does Miller fit into this?"

Baker's gaze grew distant. "He and Young go back years. He was with the man at places we didn't go. Which means he knew a lot. That's how the Feds knew to go after his wife. Everyone knew their marriage was on the rocks."

Stone absorbed the information. "So why are you interested in this?"

A beat passed as Baker's expression softened. "She was leaving him for me."

Stone's surprise was evident. "Wow. So who pulled the trigger on her?"

Baker's face twisted with regret. "My guess? Franky. She was well-trained and tough. No one could get the drop on her except him."

Stone's expression turned serious. "That's gonna be a bitch to prove."

Baker reached into his coat pocket and handed Stone a flash drive. "Not really. I taped all conversations."

Stone took the drive, examining it with a critical eye. "I assume you have copies?"

"Yep," Baker confirmed. "Do what you can."

"And if your name comes up?"

Baker shrugged. "Who cares? I'm putting in my transfer papers."

With that, Baker turned and jumped into his car. The engine

roared to life, and he sped off into the night, leaving Stone alone in the lot, the weight of the new evidence pressing heavily in his hand.

Stone pocketed the flash drive and looked up at the night sky, his mind already racing through the implications of what he had just learned. The tangled web of corruption, murder, and deceit was beginning to unravel, and he was determined to follow it to its bitter end.

____

CHAPTER SEVENTEEN

____

The basement was a forgotten relic, its dusty corners and cobweb-covered shelves bearing silent witness to years of neglect. Stone moved methodically through the stacks of old boxes, each one brimming with relics from a life long past. The air was heavy with the musty scent of disuse, but Stone's focus was sharp as he searched for anything that might provide a clue.

As he rifled through the clutter, the sound of footsteps on the stairs made him pause. Claudia Fredericks, a striking woman in her mid-thirties, appeared in the doorway. Her beauty was undeniable, though it was tempered by the weariness in her eyes—a reflection of the hardship she had endured.

"I haven't been down here since, well, you know," Claudia said, her voice soft but carrying an edge of resignation.

Stone glanced up, his face a mask of sympathy and determination. "How you been holding up?"

Claudia offered a faint smile. "I have good days and my bad days. So, do you think this new case is going to shed some light on clearing his name?"

"I'm hoping so," Stone replied, holding up a worn, leather-bound book he had just uncovered. "Can I keep this?"

Claudia's gaze followed the book as she nodded. "Sure. Be careful."

Stone's expression softened as he leaned in to kiss her cheek. "I always am."

As he turned to leave, Claudia's voice halted him. "Casey."

He stopped and turned back, his eyes meeting hers. "Yes?"

"Be careful. If they did this to him and he was a cop, what do you think they would do to you?"

Stone's gaze was steady, his resolve unshaken. "Always."

With that, Stone stepped out of the basement, leaving Claudia to watch him go. The weight of her words hung in the air, mingling with the dust motes that danced in the shafts of sunlight filtering through the grimy windows. The stakes were higher than ever, but Stone's determination to uncover the truth.

CHAPTER EIGHTEEN

The beeping of medical monitors and the soft hum of machinery filled the sterile room. Chandra lay unconscious, her once-vibrant spirit now subdued behind the veil of a coma. The rhythmic pulse of her heart was the only sign of life, a stark reminder of the danger she had been caught in.

Stone stood by her bed, his expression a mixture of determination and sorrow. The room felt heavy with unspoken words and promises yet to be fulfilled. He knew he had to see this through, not just for Chandra, but for everyone affected by the web of corruption he was unraveling.

The door creaked open, and Patrick walked in, looking like he had been through a storm. His clothes were disheveled, his face lined with fatigue and worry. He moved with a resigned heaviness, his eyes betraying a depth of despair.

"I came by to check on her," Stone said, his voice carrying a note of empathy.

Patrick's gaze remained fixed on Chandra. "She's still the same."

Stone took a step closer. "Look, Garrett, I know you may not believe it, but I'm getting close."

Patrick shook his head, a tired chuckle escaping his lips. "Just give it up, man. You will never catch them. They are too dangerous, too smart, and anyone who gets close... they kill them. They've paid off the AG, judges, commanders—the list goes on. Just leave it alone and let the city be exactly what it is. The city."

Stone's eyes narrowed. "So while your partner lays in a hospital bed in a coma because she got too close, you're just gonna give up?"

Patrick's expression hardened. "If I do, I get my shield back and my job. This job is all I know."

Stone nodded slowly. "I read your file. You applied for the Secret Service. I know some people who can get you in if a job is what you're worried about."

Patrick's gaze met Stone's, filled with a mixture of hope and skepticism. "Can those same people assure me that when I jump in my truck to go to work, it won't blow up?"

Stone's jaw tightened. "Look, I am going to make them pay."

Patrick looked at him, doubt clear in his eyes. "For some reason, I can't believe that."

Stone's response was firm, his voice carrying the weight of his commitment. "Then you don't know me."

He turned to leave but stopped at the door, pulling an envelope from his jacket. He tossed it onto the bed next to Patrick. "Think about the offer."

Patrick glanced at the envelope, confusion crossing his face. "What's this?"

"Your money. This one is on the house," Stone said, his tone leaving no room for argument.

Patrick's curiosity got the better of him. "Question."

"Shoot."

"Why do you do it?" Patrick asked, his voice tinged with genuine curiosity.

Stone paused, considering the question. He took a deep breath before responding. "Good question."

With that, Stone walked out of the room, leaving Patrick to contemplate the envelope and the offer it contained. As the door closed behind him, the sense of resolve and purpose that Stone carried with him remained a beacon of hope in a world overshadowed by corruption and danger.

CHAPTER NINETEEN

Stone sat behind his desk, the room dimly lit by the late afternoon sun filtering through the blinds. The stacks of files and notes scattered across his desk bore testament to the intensity of his current investigation. He leaned back in his chair, lost in thought, when the door creaked open. Thomas walked in with his usual confidence, his tailored suit a sharp contrast to Stone's more casual attire.

Thomas settled into the guest chair, his posture relaxed but his eyes sharp. "You know, you need a receptionist. It would give this place the feel of a real PI firm or whatever you call it."

Stone's lips curved into a sardonic smile. "Funny. What's up?"

Thomas leaned forward slightly, his gaze steady. "I talked to my superiors. They somehow figure you can break this case before we can."

Stone's smile widened, though it didn't reach his eyes. "Again, funny. What do you really want?"

Thomas's expression grew serious. "I want this bastard big time. And if you get the goods, we want to slap the braces on him."

Stone leaned back, fingers steepled. "Garrett was right."

"About what?" Thomas asked, his curiosity piqued.

"This guy went to Princeton and law school at Yale. He's too smart to have any of this shit tied to him. The payoff to Tillman —everything."

Thomas nodded. "Ah, the five million dollars that was hidden oh so well..."

"Yeah, that," Stone confirmed. "What does your UC have?"

Thomas's eyebrows shot up in surprise. "Who said I have a—"

Stone cut him off with a smirk. "Cover your notes up on your desk when you have visitors."

Thomas's face reddened. "I don't know what you're talking about."

Stone's eyes gleamed with amusement. "How long have we known each other? The note that read 'Black Bird, City Hall, three p.m.' Still using the same call signs."

Thomas's expression turned to one of grudging respect. "You slick son of a bitch."

Stone chuckled. "Hey, you're the one using a call sign from your days in the sandbox."

Thomas's grin widened. "Well, not many motherfuckers I knew over there made it back except for you. Damn lucky bastard."

Stone's smile faded slightly. "Yeah, look who trained me."

Thomas's demeanor shifted. "He doesn't know shit. He's on to the detail. They don't talk about a lot of stuff around the new guys. So what are you gonna do?"

Stone's gaze turned steely. "Well, a trusted source of mine turned over tapes with Drake giving orders to pay off Tillman."

Thomas's eyes narrowed. "How does that help our dead cop?"

Stone's voice was calm but firm. "So you don't think it was suicide either?"

Thomas shook his head vigorously. "Hell no. But how do we prove it?"

Stone stood up, handing Thomas a flash drive. "Leave that up to me."

Thomas accepted the drive, his eyebrows raised in interest. "And your case at hand?"

Stone's gaze was unwavering. "Question the man."

Thomas took a moment to process the information, then tucked the flash drive into his jacket pocket. "Copies, I assume?"

"Yep," Stone confirmed.

Thomas gave a nod of approval before turning to leave. "Well, I'll be in touch. And Stone?"

"Yeah?"

"Good luck."

Stone watched Thomas walk out of the office, the door closing softly behind him. As the room settled back into its usual quiet, Stone felt the weight of the case pressing heavily on his shoulders. With the tapes in hand and the truth inching closer, he knew the real battle was just beginning.

CHAPTER TWENTY

The office was a stark contrast to the chaos that brewed outside its walls. Mayor Tony Young, immaculately dressed in a sharp suit, sat behind his imposing mahogany desk. Across from him sat a well-dressed man known only as Tank, his demeanor as unruffled as his crisp, tailored suit.

Mayor Young leaned back in his chair, his fingers steepled in front of him. "How far do we go back?"

Tank's expression remained neutral, his eyes steady. "A while."

"And how long have I had your back?" Mayor Young's voice was measured, his gaze piercing.

Tank nodded slightly. "A long time."

Mayor Young's gaze hardened. "I need a favor that will involve you doing a little time."

Tank's eyebrows raised, but his tone remained calm. "Let me know what it is."

The Mayor's lips curled into a tight smile. "I need you to take the fall for a certain incident. It's a dirty job, but you're the only one I trust to handle it."

Tank's eyes narrowed. "And what's in it for me?"

Mayor Young's expression didn't waver. "A promise that when this is all over, you'll walk away clean. No more strings attached."

Tank considered the offer, his silence stretching as he weighed his options. Finally, he gave a curt nod. "Alright. I'll do it."

Mayor Young's smile broadened, a mix of satisfaction and relief evident in his eyes. "Good. I'll make sure you have everything you need."

As Tank stood to leave, the Mayor's gaze followed him, a sense of finality hanging in the air.

———

Stone and Candy lay entwined in the soft light of the early morning hours. The tranquility of their sleep was shattered by the sudden, jarring sound of Stone's phone ringing. Groggily, Stone reached over to grab the device, his eyes squinting in the dim light.

"Have you lost your mind?" Stone's voice was rough with sleep.

Carlos's voice crackled through the receiver, urgency clear in his tone. "Your case just went to shit. Turn on Channel 2."

Stone didn't wait for further explanation. He hung up and flipped on the TV, his heart racing as he watched the screen.

The camera panned across a scene of chaos: a body bag being rolled into an unmarked van. The Reporter's voice came through, disjointed but unmistakable.

"That's right. The Mayor's chief of staff was killed by this man..."

The screen flashed with a picture of Tank, his face stark and unmistakable. Stone's mind raced as he processed the news.

Stone turned off the TV with a decisive click, his face a mask of determination and frustration.

Candy stirred beside him, her voice muffled with concern. "What's wrong, baby?"

Stone glanced at her, his expression softening despite the turmoil. "Nothing much."

He pulled her closer, trying to find solace in her warmth. They lay back down, the reality of the situation sinking in. Stone knew that this was more than just a bump in the road; it was a significant turn in the investigation that could change everything.

As he held Candy, his thoughts raced ahead, plotting his next move in the increasingly tangled web of corruption and deceit. The fight was far from over, and Stone was ready to see it through to the end.

CHAPTER TWENTY-ONE

The office was a disheveled chaos of cardboard boxes and scattered files. Hunt's recent promotion to Deputy Chief had not been accompanied by any effort to tidy up his workspace. He was absorbed in packing when Stone entered, a manila file folder in hand. Hunt's irritation was palpable as he set aside a box and straightened in his chair.

"Stone, what the hell do you want?" Hunt's voice was curt, his eyes narrowing at the sight of Stone.

"I heard about your promotion to Deputy Chief," Stone said, setting the folder on Hunt's desk with a deliberate thud. "Thought I'd drop by to offer my congratulations."

Hunt's face twisted in disdain. "I don't have time for your conspiracy theories."

Stone leaned in, his gaze unwavering. "I know this. Miller was killed, and somehow, you covered it up. Detective Parker was nearly assassinated, and you covered that up too. And Detective Garrett? He's sweating his ass off in Georgia thanks to me, removed from the force on some bogus psych evaluation. This mess has your name written all over it, and I'm going to prove it."

Hunt's demeanor shifted from irritation to arrogance. He leaned back in his chair, arms crossed, and scoffed. "See, that's your problem.

You were always asking the wrong questions. You think your brother's pull with the Chief can get you anywhere? Look at you—couldn't even solve your own brother's death. Now you're trying to save a drunk cop who ended up blowing his own brains out."

Stone's eyes flashed with anger. "Fuck you! You knew that woman was killed because she knew too much, and you covered it up and made my friend take the fall for it. But everyone has secrets. And here are yours, you bastard."

With a sharp movement, Stone flung the folder onto the desk. Hunt's eyes fell on the contents. The photograph inside was a damning image of Hunt and Conneliey, caught in a passionate embrace. The sight drained the color from Hunt's face, his hands trembling as he stared at the photograph.

Stone turned and walked out of the office, leaving Hunt alone with his mounting dread.

Outside, the midday sun was uncomfortably bright. Stone walked purposefully toward his car, the weight of the confrontation still heavy on his shoulders. His thoughts were interrupted when Inspector Cooper, a scowl etched on his face, grabbed him from behind. Stone's reflexes were swift; he twisted, pinning Cooper against a parked car with a forceful shove.

"Are you calm now?" Stone's voice was cold and controlled.

"Let me go!" Cooper growled, struggling against Stone's grip.

Stone released him, stepping back with a disdainful look. "Did anyone ever tell you not to sneak up on people?"

Cooper glared at him. "Stay out of this, Stone."

"I've been hearing that a lot lately," Stone replied, his tone sharp.

"Well, you should listen," Cooper snapped. "The cop will recover, the girl is dead, and I need this investigation to move forward."

"So you want me to ignore the facts?" Stone's voice was laced with incredulity.

"You're not a cop!" Cooper's frustration was evident. "Look, I know what Fredericks did for you overseas, and I know he's the one who helped you piece together what happened to Nelson. But this? You have to let me and the FEDS handle it."

Stone's eyes narrowed. "What's your stake in this?"

"A whole lot more than you realize," Cooper said tersely.

Stone's curiosity was piqued. "Well, I'm listening."

Cooper's expression hardened. "You know how close we are to nailing that entire crew. Don't screw this up. I don't want just a few cops taken down; I want the whole damn network exposed."

"I'll do my best," Stone said, his tone measured.

"For what it's worth," Cooper added grudgingly, "Nelson was a good cop."

Stone's gaze was distant. "Nelson should have joined the family business and worked for my father and Jackson."

Cooper's eyes met Stone's. "You didn't."

"I'm the black sheep," Stone said simply.

With that, Stone turned and walked away, leaving Cooper fuming beside the car. The city's bustle seemed to intensify around them, each step Stone took drawing him closer to the tangled web of corruption and deceit he was determined to unravel. As he moved forward, he knew the path ahead would be fraught with danger and deceit, but he was resolved to see it through.

CHAPTER TWENTY-TWO

The night was alive with the distant hum of the city and the sharp cool breeze. Stone parked his Harley in front of the house, the rumbling engine fading into the background as he approached the door. It was ajar, swinging slightly with each gust of wind. The unsettling silence was pierced by the sudden crack of a gunshot. Instinct took over; Stone's hand moved to his Kimber 1911, his senses on high alert as he inched cautiously into the house.

"Frank!" Stone's voice rang out, echoing off the walls.

He heard the faint sounds of struggling and another shot. The urgency in the situation quickened his pace. Following the noise, he made his way to the home office.

The scene that greeted him was one of chaos and violence. Franky stood amidst the carnage, two dead men in masks lying crumpled on the floor. Franky was holding a gun, his face a mask of rage and despair. Stone burst into the room, his own weapon raised and aimed directly at Franky.

"These assholes," Franky spat, his voice trembling with anger. "I did so much dirt for them, and this is how they repay me."

"Well, let's work this out, Franky," Stone said, trying to keep his tone calm and steady. "Put the gun down, and we can go in together."

"They made me set up my wife," Franky said, his voice breaking. "And shoot a cop."

Stone's heart sank at the gravity of Franky's admission. "Look, we can put an end to all of this."

"They've got people all over," Franky said, shaking his head. "I'm dead either way."

"I can help you," Stone pleaded.

"It's too late," Franky said, his voice taking on a resigned tone. He raised the gun to his own head, his eyes filled with a mix of defiance and despair.

"Franky, no—" Stone's protest was cut off by the deafening sound of the gun firing. Franky's body slumped to the ground, lifeless.

Stone stood there for a moment, the weight of the scene pressing down on him. The fight was over, but the cost was immense. The room, once a space of betrayal and violence, was now silent but for the distant sirens wailing in the night.

———

The Miller home was now swarming with police officers, their flashing lights casting eerie shadows on the surrounding buildings. Stone walked to his car, his movements slow and deliberate as he gave his statement to the officers. The weight of the night's events hung heavily on his shoulders.

As he finished, Inspector Cooper stepped into his path, a look of frustration etched on his face. "What did he say?" Cooper demanded.

Stone's expression was unreadable. "You've got an entire city to clean up."

Without waiting for a response, Stone pushed past Cooper, his mind already shifting to the next step in his relentless pursuit. Cooper's voice followed him, full of urgency and resentment. "This isn't over, Stone."

Stone mounted his Triumph Bonneville Speedmaster, the roar of the engine filling the night air. He looked back once, a final glance at the chaos he was leaving behind. "Yeah," he said, the word carrying a sense of finality.

The bike roared to life, and Stone rode off into the night, the city lights flickering in the distance. The road stretched out before him, endless and unforgiving. As he sped away, he knew that the fight was far from over, but tonight, the scales had tipped just a little.

The night was his ally now, and the journey ahead promised more challenges and revelations. The end of one chapter meant the beginning of another, and Stone was ready to face whatever came next.

JONATHAN STALEY

About the Author

Jonathan Staley, born and raised in Detroit, brings a unique blend of grit and heart to his writing, deeply influenced by the vibrant, resilient spirit of his hometown. A dedicated father, Jonathan is proud of his 21-year-old daughter, a college senior poised to make her own mark on the world. His 11-year-old son, who is on the autism spectrum, inspires Jonathan daily with his boundless curiosity and unwavering determination.

Jonathan's novels are known for their compelling characters, intricate plots, and a keen sense of place, reflecting the diverse and dynamic backdrop of Detroit. When he's not writing, Jonathan enjoys spending time with his family, exploring the city's rich history, and advocating for autism awareness and support.

His latest works, featuring the relentless investigator Casey Stone, have captivated readers with their intense action and profound emotional depth. Jonathan's storytelling prowess continues to earn him a devoted readership and critical acclaim.

jstaleybooks.wixsite.com/books
jstaleywrites@yahoo.com

OH, BABY WHERE ARE YOU?

Ryan D. Patterson Sr.

CHAPTER ONE

Loud clapping in the arena drowned out the ending of the last song and drumbeat. The crowd exited the arena to cold, wet, and breezy weather conditions.

Bobbi walked quickly to the exit, trying to get to her car. Ariana frowned and yelled. "Bobbi!" She stopped and waited for the girls; the crowd had separated them as they rushed to the parking lot.

"So where are we going from here?" she asked, walking closer to Bobbi.

"I'm getting kinda tired." Bobbi exhaled. "I think…"

"No, this is our lady's night out," another friend yelled before Bobbi could finish her thought. "This is also the prelude to your baby shower."

Bobbi's best friend, Ariana, started rubbing Bobbi's protruding belly. "I have a special surprise for you, and then, if you want, I will drive you home."

Bobbi looked at the three ladies and smiled. "You know I drove here just for this reason. All of you know Mike is at home waiting for me. He's only called a dozen times."

"He can wait; he has you all the time, and since y'all been married, we get very little of your time," Ariana smirked.

"Yeah." Bobbi laughed... "It's called being married."

"Aah, girl, just one more place, and you can go home to Mikey." Ariana laughed.

"Well, okay, but I'm not going to a bar; I don't drink, and I'm not going to sit around and watch the three of you drink till you're drunk. Besides, I don't need any drunk men approaching me, or any man for that matter."

"Calm down, baby girl." Ariana smiled. "We will have an early breakfast, and then you can go home. Unlike you, we can stay out all night long." She laughed.

"I'm good." Bobbi looked at all three of them. "There isn't anything good going on this late at night but trouble. You ladies can have that. I'm good at home." she stood up.

"Wait, girl. I'm going to walk with you. The ladies and I are going to the club after you leave." Ariana smiled.

"The car is out front; I'm glad I valet parked; my feet are killing me." Bobbi frowned.

Ariana and Bobbi hugged. Soon after, Bobbi plopped down inside the car. "Finally, off my feet," she thought aloud. She started the car and slowly rolled away.

The first traffic light she approached turned red, which gave her time to call home. She reached for her phone. "Hello baby, I'm finally on my way home. I should be there in about twenty-five minutes."

"Ok. Be careful getting here. The roads are wet and slippery from the rain."

"I wish you were out here with me so you could be driving. I'll be home soon."

The car in front of her changed lanes when they approached the next light and pulled off when it turned green. Bobbi hesitated and pulled off a few seconds behind them.

The car changed lanes when they approached the next light, which turned yellow midway down the street. Bobbi slowed down, and the light turned red. She exhaled and closed her eyes. When she opened her eyes, the light was green, and the other car was gone.

"I must've dozed off." Then slowly drove away.

After a few minutes of driving, Bobbi approached another traffic light, and just as she approached, the light turned yellow. Bobbi pushed down on the gas pedal and drove through the light, which had turned red as she was in the middle of the intersection.

Suddenly, she heard tires shrieking, and she pushed harder on the pedal. She made it through the intersection but heard a loud bang. She looked out her rear-view mirror and saw a car had swerved in an attempt not to hit her and hit a tree. She slowed down but continued driving without returning, trying to convince herself that the other car was moving too fast, and she was right.

Finally arriving home, in the driveway, She walked around the car to make sure there were no dents or scratches. After noticing nothing wrong, she walked to the door and entered the house.

Mike greeted her at the door and gave her a hug and kiss.

"Made it." she exhaled with a smile.

"They talked for a few minutes. Mike looked at the clock. Since you are home, the kids are asleep, so I'm going to bed."

"I thought you had the day off. Had I known you had to work, I would have stayed home and let you get some rest."

"It is my day off, but I picked up some overtime.

I need to make some money for the holidays." he walked up the stairs to the bedroom.

Bobbi sat at the table instead and looked at the coffee pot. *"Oh, he made some fresh coffee. I'll have a cup before I go up to sleep."*

Five Years Later...

CHAPTER TWO

Mike and Bobbi lived with their two beautiful daughters in Seattle, Washington's lively but cold city. Where the rain and the cold always made plans difficult. This year was frigid, with lots of snow on the ground and a steady brisk wind blowing mildly, just enough to keep it cold and soggy. This winter was one of the worst. But it made the city beautifully green. Mike worked at the largest parcel chain warehouse in the town. Bobbi, since having their second child, was a stay-at-home wife. But anxious to get back to work after being off for the last five years

It was getting close to the holiday season, so Mike decided to make this year different.

The following day was cold, and like most mornings, Mike woke up, kissed his wife, and ran to the shower. After brushing his teeth and washing his face, his next stop was to check on his little girls. He'd walk into their room, make sure the covers were over them, and kiss them. He stood over them as they slept, "I have two of the most beautiful daughters, *Kathy and Karen, I could have been blessed with.*"

He made it a ritual, and nothing changed for the last five years; that's how old Karen was. The ritual had not changed since she was born.

Kathy is a beautiful eight-year-old full of life who is just starting to be inquisitive. Karen is a five-year-old, and Bobbi says she isn't sure how her personality would go.

He continued staring and finally walked around the room to ensure the bedroom windows were locked before walking out. He left their bedroom; Bobbi was standing at the door.

"So, how are they?" She smiled.

"They are sleeping as always when I get dressed for work. By the way, don't forget I'll be getting home a little late this evening. The job is giving out some holiday overtime, and I thought I'd work some of it."

"Okay. But don't work too long. Your girls be driving me nuts when they don't get to see their dad."

"I'll be home for dinner." He walked into the bedroom to finish getting ready for work.

"I made you a cup of coffee and some toast; it's on the table." She yelled.

Mike headed for the door before he could open it. "Bye, Daddy." He turned around, and Kathy stood there smiling and waving her hand. "Hey baby, what are you doing awake? Come here and kiss Daddy."

She ran up and gave him a big hug and kiss.

"Tell Karen Daddy will see her when he gets home from work. You be good and do a good job in school today." He looked at Bobbi, who was smiling at their exchange, returned a smile, and left for work.

CHAPTER THREE

Mike walked into the warehouse. Pat was waiting for him in the breakroom. "Hey, what's good, Mike?"

"I'm fine, and you?"

"I'm good. I have some good news." Pat smiled.

"What's your good news?"

"Dee and I have been trying to have a child for the past few years." He smiled. "Dee is pregnant."

"What! You and Dee are expecting?"

"Yes, we are. Finally, it's not like we haven't been trying."

"Man, life begins for you now. There is nothing better than having kids. I wouldn't give up being a dad for the world."

"Well, you should know. I see you and how you interact with your girls and wish I could be you sometimes."

"Well, you no longer have to worry about being me."

"Well, for at least nine more months, I do." Pat smiled.

"Don't hurry it, man. Trust me; you have much ahead of you in the next nine months. Take it day by day and enjoy it. You are about to go on the longest rollercoaster ride you have ever been on."

The bell sounded to go to work, and they both found their equipment to get started.

"I'll see you at lunchtime, Pat." Mike walked away.

"All right, see you later."

They met in the breakroom at lunchtime. Mike looked at Pat. "Are you going to be working any of this overtime?"

"No, man! I'm going home. Dee needs me."

"That's right, she's pregnant?" Mike smiled.

"Yes, she is, and I want to spend all the time I can while she goes through her pregnancy."

"Yes, man, that's what you do, and if you need anything, just ask me. I'll be working overtime for the next few weeks to have money for the holidays. I want to make this holiday a good one for the family."

"Yeah, I understand. I'll be glad when I can start buying Christmas gifts for my daughter or son."

"Don't rush it; it will get here soon enough." They both Laughed.

"Yeah, but I bet you were just like me when your firstborn was due." Pat smiled.

"Yes, I was, Pat. Yes, I was."

After a long day at work, Mike slowly walked into the house, put his lunch box on the kitchen counter, and sat down.

The girls saw him and ran up to meet him, Karen first and Kathy second, grabbing anything they could on him.

"Hi, my babies. So, how was your day?"

"Mines was fine. I got an "A" on my spelling test." Kathy smiled. "Wonderful! What about you, Karen? Did you drive your mother crazy today?"

"No, Daddy, I didn't." she dropped her head, looking sad.

"No, baby. I was playing with you." He hugged her and left for the kitchen. "Hi baby, what's for dinner?"

"I fixed your favorite. Get washed up and come down. Today, we're eating dinner together."

"All right, but what's the special occasion?"

"Nothing, just go get washed up." Bobbi grinned.

After dinner, the family settled under the oversized linen comforter.

"It's your turn to pick a movie, Karen. Go pick out a movie while I go and get the popcorn." Bobbi left for the kitchen.

Karen walked to the cabinet and grabbed her favorite. "Beauty and the Beast," Kathy looked, "I bet it's Beauty and the Beast. She always gets the same movie."

"It's okay. Next movie night, it's your turn, and you can pick out whatever movie you like."

"I already know what movie I want to see." she smiled and walked towards the cabinet. "Come on back, It's Karen's turn tonight."

After the movie, Bobbi looked at Kathy and Karen. "It's time for bed. Kiss your dad and go on up to your room. I will be there in a minute." She put the girls to bed, walked into the room, and headed for the bathroom.

"Guess what?" Mike said.

Bobbi stopped and turned around.

"Pat and Dee are expecting a baby. Pat was the happiest person in the warehouse today."

"Oh yeah!" Bobbi returned from the bathroom. "We'll just see how he is in about seven months. He'll be the most tired person in town. Remember, that's how you started, twice. But by the time your daughters were born, you were dead tired."

"Yes, I was. And you had a lot to do with that, swearing at me in the hospital both times." They both laughed.

Bobbi left to go finish tending to the girls. Mike lay on the bed to wind down from a long day at work, but he thought quietly, tomorrow is another day.

CHAPTER FOUR

Saturdays mean house cleaning for the Pardee family. Mike jumped out of bed when he heard the trash collector, ran down the stairs, and took the trash to the curb just in time for the collector to pick it up. He began looking around the backyard, knowing he needed to cut the grass and the front lawn. Today would be full of work, But for now, it was too early to start. I'd only wake up the neighborhood if I started that loud old lawn mower; besides, I'm a little hungry.

He walked back into the house and washed his hands, then went to look in on his girls, both of whom were still sound asleep.

He kissed them both and went downstairs for Bobbi's coffee.

"Well, good morning, old man."

Mike looked at Bobbi. "Who are you calling an old man, old woman? I saw how you rolled out of the bed this morning." he laughed.

"Well, If you let me have my share of the bed, I would sleep much better."

"You have just as much of the bed as I have."

"Yes, I do until you sleep, then all the wheels fall off. You take all the pillows and all the covers and keep me on the edge of the bed."

"Whatever!" Mike grabbed his coffee and read the old newspaper on the table for the last two days. He stepped out the door into the brisk morning sun, went to the garage, and began making noises.

"Hey, Mike!" someone yelled from across the fence. Mike walked out of the garage, and Taylor smiled at him. Taylor was the next-door neighbor and a friend. Bobbi always thought he was a bit nosey.

"Hey, Taylor, good morning to you."

"Yes, Sir, it is a good morning; I see you have much work to do today."

"Yes, and I might as well get started. So, what are you doing today yourself?"

"Nothing, just hanging around and watching you do your work."

"Well, what else is new? You have your gardener; you don't have much to do."

"Yeah, and if you weren't so cheap, Mike, you could have the same gardener."

"Yeah, but this is my house, and I want to keep it pretty. Besides, I would get lazy like you if I let someone do what I can do myself."

"Funny, Mike. I'll come and check with you later."

"All right." Mike turned and walked back into the garage.

Just as Mike started the lawnmower and began working in the backyard, he heard a young, soft voice: "Good morning, Daddy." It was Kathy. She looked at Mike. "Karen is in the house getting her hair done; she will be coming out soon."

"Okay. Hey, try to stay off the grass until I clean the yard; then, you two can play, okay?"

"Okay, Daddy."

Karen ran out the door and yelled, "Daddy!"

"My baby, I need you to stay off the grass for Daddy for a little while until I finish, okay?"

"Okay, daddy her sweet voice answered. "Daddy, I love you."

"I love you too, baby." Mike smiled.

He hugged Karen and went back to doing his yard work. Finally, he finished, returned the mower to the garage, and went into the house.

"Hey, honey, I fixed some sandwiches and juice for you. Where are the girls?"

"They are in the backyard, why?"

"Because I don't trust anybody with my girls."

"They are my girls, too," Mike said.

"Well, I don't trust anyone with your girls either."

"Okay, I will get them, hey girls?" Mike yelled out the door.

But received no answer.

"Kathy! Karen!" he yelled again. Still, no answer. He walked to the front yard and called the girls again: "Karen, Kathy." In the distance, he heard, "Yes, daddy." He ran back to the backyard.

"Where were you two?"

"We were behind the garage playing with the ball, Daddy." Kathy laughed.

Mike exhaled. "Don't scare daddy like that." and walked them into the house.

Bobbi looked at Mike with an "I told you so face."

"Are you all right?" she asked.

"Yes, I'm fine. I'll be okay." he strolled up the stairs.

"We are about to go to the store; do you need anything?" Bobbi yelled from the bottom of the stairs.

"No, I am fine."

"All right, we will be right back."

She walked out the door with the girls, and there was Taylor again. "Hey ladies, good morning." They all looked at the fence and returned the morning greeting.

"I see Mike is about finished with his yard duties."

"I guess," Bobbi said without looking at him. "He is up there if you want to go in."

"Oh no, not now. I'm about to go to the gym. See you later." Taylor disappeared behind the fence.

The next day, the alarm went off. Mike jumped up and headed for the shower when he realized the day was Sunday. "Hey baby, why did you set the alarm today? I don't have to work."

"No, you don't, but I decided for us all to attend church today; we need Jesus. I'll get the girls ready, and you get yourself ready."

"I don't know what to wear or when I last attended church." Mike frowned.

"The more reason you need to go, besides "the family that prays together stays together." Bobbi reminded him.

"Yes, I've heard."

After church, Mike took the family out to eat at the neighborhood buffet. "We need to do this more often. I like it when we do family functions. This is becoming a good day, just me and my girls." He looked at the three of them.

Mike pulled into the driveway and looked at the fence. "Hey, baby, didn't I close this gate when we left?"

"I don't know, and I don't remember," Bobbi answered.

"I could have sworn I closed this gate." He slowly unlocked his seatbelt, exited the car, and walked through the gate, looking around the yard for anything else out of place. *"I know I closed this gate,"* he thought silently.

Bobbi walked through the gate. "Before you start checking anything else, can you let your girls in the house?"

"Sure, I'll let you in your house. Just wait a minute until I check out everything." He unlocked the door. "Wait, I'll enter the house first."

"Stop being so paranoid. Nothing, and nobody has messed with this house." Bobbi said and slowly entered the house.

Mike looked around and agreed with himself: Maybe he didn't close the gate, or maybe the wind opened the gate. He looked at the clock; wow, the game was on.

"Today, your favorite team is playing Bobbi," Mike yelled, heading for the TV. The Lakers are playing the Supersonics this afternoon."

"I don't have time to look at any of that. I have a lot of things to do, like cooking, laundry, and taking care of the girls while you watch the game. But I want you to relax. You have done enough this weekend."

The following day, Mike woke up, and the ritual began again. He kissed his wife, went to the bathroom, washed his face, and checked on his girls. They were sound asleep; he tucked them in, kissed them, and returned to the bathroom for his shower. When he left the bathroom, Bobbi was preparing his lunch and making coffee in the kitchen. "Good morning," he said.

"Good morning to you." Bobbi smiled. "Today, my vacation ends, and I must go to work."

"Did you call the babysitter for the girls?" Mike asked.

"Yes, I did everything I was supposed to do. Don't worry about the girls."

"I'll always worry about them girls and you. But anyway, I'll be late getting home again today. I will work overtime again, maybe three or four hours this evening."

"Okay, baby, but remember your little ladies will want to see you when you get home."

"Oh yeah! What about my wife?"

"I'll always want to see my husband when he gets home."

"Good." he smiled and walked out the door.

Mike returned home from work later that evening and walked into the house tired; he had worked more than fourteen hours.

"Hey baby, are you hungry?" Bobbi asked.

"I'm much more tired than hungry. So, how was your first day back to work?"

"Not bad at all. The ladies were trying to tell me how much they missed me, and the office runs a lot better when I am there."

"So, does that mean you will not take any more time off?" Mike looked at her, concerned.

"No, that's not what I have in mind. I needed the time off. And with everything I do between this house and that job, the time off is well deserved."

"I do understand, baby. I'll go take a shower and hit the bed."

"What about dinner?" Bobbi asked.

"I'm not hungry, only tired," Mike said, walking up the stairs. His voice started fading away.

"Check on the girls before you go to bed," Bobbi yelled.

Mike finished taking his shower and went to check on the girls. They were sound asleep. He tucked them under the covers and kissed them goodnight. He gave one last look before he turned the lights down. He walked to his bedroom, turned the lights off, and fell asleep in minutes.

CHAPTER FIVE

The following morning, at 4:30 a.m., the alarm sounded loudly. Mike woke up quickly; the alarm frightened him. He looked around the room and then at his wife. He went to sleep so fast that he never felt Bobbi get in bed.

"Are you all right?" Bobbi asked, adjusting the covers around her.

"Yes, I'm fine. I don't remember you getting into bed last night."

"You were sound asleep when I made my way up here. Lying in the middle of the bed with all the covers wrapped around you."

"Sorry baby, I need to get up and start getting ready for work." he kissed Bobbi on the forehead and left for the bathroom. Before he entered the bathroom, he felt a breeze coming from somewhere; the frigid air was circulating the hallway. He looked in all the rooms upstairs to see where the air was coming from, until finally getting around to the girl's room. He walked in and noticed the covers on Karen's bed were not there. "Hey baby, is Karen in the bed with you?"

"No!" she answered back.

"Then, where is she?"

Bobbi jumped out of bed and ran into the girl's room; she looked around the room and then ran downstairs. Mike was looking around the girl's room when the curtain swung, and frigid air began swirling around the room. He went to the window, which was open; one of the sheets to Karen's bed was on the back lawn. Mike ran downstairs as fast as he could, running out the door, hoping Karen did not fall out the window, but also hoping that Karen was there.

Bobbi ran out the door, calling Mike, and after seeing the sheet, she started yelling and crying. "Someone took my baby."

Mike ran into the house and called the police. He tried to keep Bobbi calm while being scared himself.

Kathy walked into the family room, asking where Karen was.

Mike looked at Bobbi, and she began crying again. "Where is my baby?"

CHAPTER SIX

When the doorbell rang, Mike walked quickly over and opened the door. He stared at the police with tears in his eyes and calmly invited them in. They walked around the house and returned to where Mike and Bobbi sat.

"Tell us, when did you notice your daughter missing?"

Mike exhaled lightly, "I got out of bed to get ready for work; I felt a cold breeze circulating the house, and when I finally got around to checking on the girls, I noticed she was missing."

The police approached the girl's bedroom, looked around, and slowly approached the window. Looked around and noticed some forced entry spots and called the precinct to report a kidnapping.

Detective Moore entered the Pardee's house with another detective and introduced him as Detective Crunby. Crunby stopped to talk to the first responding officers. Moore walked up to Mike and Bobbi and introduced himself as the lead investigating officer, and all information would go through him.

"First of all, Mr. Pardee, when did you last see your daughter?"

"About ten o'clock last night, I tucked them both in bed, then went to my bedroom. That's the last time I saw Karen." Mike said. "And please, detective, call her Karen, not the victim or my daughter. I want to talk about her in the present."

"Yes, I know what you mean, Mr. Pardee."

"Please, detective, call me Mike."

"All right, I can do that as well, sir."

"Now, Mike, I want you to realize there is an outside chance you may never see your daughter again, but we will work as hard as possible to ensure that does not happen. If you can get your daughter, Karen, back to you. We will do everything in our and your power to make sure it happens. Also, the F.B.I. will be notified of this situation. We intend to use every option available to us to get Karen back home to you."

"Thank you." Detective Moore. Mike said.

"Now I need to see the girl's bedroom again. "Detective Crunby walked up; I need you to take pictures of the crime scene and have them available for me this evening. I need a forensic expert and a C.S.I. here. Also, can you please call the precinct and tell Capt. O'Hara, what I have just requested?"

"Yes." said the detective.

"Okay, now let's go to the room." Detective Moore started walking away.

"I don't know if I can go back in there; it's upstairs and to the right."

"Mike, I need to know who knows your daughters and who would know which room your daughters sleep in. I also need to know the names of all the neighbors."

"I don't think any neighbors would do anything like this," Mike said.

"You'd be surprised. I need the names please. Let's not leave any stone unturned. I have called a female officer to take care of your wife and ask her questions."

"Okay," Mike said. "I need to call my job and tell them what is happening. Could you please excuse me, sir?"

"I'll just look around the room and the house. Take your time. I will find you when I need to know something or ask questions."

Detective Crunby walked up to the room, where Detective Moore looked out the window. "The Forensics and the C.S.I. agent are on their way, and you need to tape off the room and not let anyone other than yourself enter the room."

"No problem, Crunby, get the tape out of the car."

"No problem, sir."

Detective Moore was looking out the window when Mike returned to the room. "That's the window that was open when I was looking for Karen."

"Here is the tape, sir," Crunby said.

"Mike, I need you to step out of the room now. From here on out, until the investigation is finished, there will be no traffic in this room. I'm going to tape it off to make sure. I'll need to ask you more questions later. Can you please be available?" He waited for Mike's acknowledgment. But for now, you should go down and comfort your wife."

"Detective Crunby, can you take a picture of this?"

Detective Moore pointed at something in the window seal.

"I need Forensics to tell me exactly what type of material that is. He pointed to the window's seal and got this stain; it looked like blood. I need to know what blood type it is. Get the Forensics team on this right away."

Detective Moore walked out of the room and headed downstairs. On the way out the back door, he called Mike.

"Do you own a ladder?"

"Yes, I do, sir. It's in the garage. Why?"

"Because I need to get on the roof next to Karen's bedroom window to better look at the entry point."

Mike entered the garage and brought the ladder to Detective Moore, who climbed onto the roof. He called Detective Crunby from the roof, through the window.

"I need your camera; I have a set of shoe prints and more fabric. It looks like whoever was here was working fast, but the question is, how did he get up here? How did he get the little girl down? Unless two people were working together." he thought. "But there is only one footprint here."

Detective Moore stared at the window. "*Whoever did this was very methodical and careful not to leave any good evidence.*"

CHAPTER SEVEN

When Mike made it back inside the house, there were a lot more police walking around; they set up phone lines with earphone attachments. The press was there now, and his home was now a police precinct. He walked over to Bobbi. "Hey, how are you holding up?"

"Somebody has our baby, and no one knows where she is; there is no trace of her; it's like she just disappeared." She buried her face into Mike's chest and started crying again.

Detective Moore came back into the house and stood over Mike and Bobbi. "What I'm about to tell you might hurt a little, maybe even a lot, but whoever took Karen was a professional. They left little traces or leads of any kind. It will be tough to find them with what we have. But we're still trying to find anything that could tell us about what happened last night. Are you sure that you did not hear anything last night?"

"No, Sir!" Mike answered sternly. "We didn't hear anything."

Bobbi sat up. "I was the last one to bed last night, and I checked on the girls before I went to bed; they were asleep. I checked all the windows around the house and ensured all the doors were locked."

"Well, folks, whoever took little Karen went through the window. They had to have either climbed on the roof someway or used a ladder.

At any rate, there had to be some noise. Now, what I need to do is check your closets for shoes and check to see your shoe prints. We found some prints, and we need to ensure they do not match yours."

Mike stood up quickly. "Now I know you don't think we had anything to do with the disappearance of our daughter."

"Mike." Detective Moore stopped him. "I said I would not leave any stone unturned, which means you and your wife's stones as well. You will be asked questions you may think are absurd, but we will ask them, and you will need to answer them. Now I need to know where your closets are, and I don't need any of you to follow me to the closet."

"The closets are in our bedroom; all our shoes are in that closet."

"Thanks, Mrs. Pardee." He finished talking to the Pardees, walked upstairs to the master bedroom, opened the door to the closet, and took out all the shoes he could find. He took all the shoes out of boxes, and there were plenty. Then he and Detective Crunby matched them up according to the print they found on the roof.

A few minutes later, Moore came down from the room and looked at Mike. "Do you have any other shoes besides the closet?"

"No sir, I don't."

"Not even in your garage? Maybe old shoes you do the lawn with?"

"Yes, sir, I have a pair of shoes in the garage; they are old and dirty."

"And exactly where can I find them?"

"They are right next to the washing machine in the garage. When you open the side door, they are to your right."

Moore directed Crunby to get the shoes. He turned to the Pardee's. "I'm sorry for all this, but we are eliminating both of you from wrongdoings. Sorry, we must be so thorough, but we must be sure a crime did happen here."

Crunby walked back into the house with an old pair of shoes. He walked over to Forensics and handed them the shoes.

Then, Detective Moore was called over to the side; they whispered for about five minutes, and Moore went to talk to the forensics experts. They whispered for another ten minutes, and then Moore approached the Pardees.

The shoe material matches the material found in the window seal, and the shoe print matches the prints on the roof next to your daughter's window. "How do you explain this?" He asked, looking at them both.

"We have no idea, Detective," Mike said.

Detective Moore looked at Mike. "Where is your daughter? And what did you do with her?"

Bobbi looked at Mike, frightened.

"I didn't do anything to my daughter. She was sound asleep when I went to sleep."

"Well, are these your shoes?" He held up a clear bag containing the shoes he had gotten from the garage.

"Yes, those are my shoes," Mike answered.

"When did you rip them? Do you remember ripping them?"

"I never ripped them," Mike answered angrily. "I don't have any idea why you are accusing me of doing anything to my daughter."

"The shoe prints match the prints on the roof; these are the shoes used to abduct your daughter; you are the owner of the shoes. You have access to the garage; the ladder is in the garage; what should we think?"

"Where is our daughter, Mike?" Bobbi asked. "What did you do with her?"

Mike looked at Bobbi. "Are you serious? Do you think I would harm Karen? And for what? What do I stand to gain for doing anything like this? I love them girls too much to ever do anything to harm them."

"You need to come to the station with us, Mike." Detective Moore said.

"Am I being arrested?" Mike looked at Moore, confused.

Detective Moore looked at Detective Crunby. "Read Mr. Pardee his rights."

Detective Crunby started, "You have the right to remain silent. Anything you say can and will be used against you in a court of law. You have the right to an attorney. One will be provided for you if you cannot afford an attorney. Do you understand the rights I have just read to you? Do you wish to speak with me with these rights in mind?"

Mike looked at Bobbi, shook his head, and waited for Detective Moore and Detective Crunby to start walking him out. Wait, Detective Crunby, Detective Moore said. "Handcuff him."

"Mike, if you know where our daughter is, please tell me," Bobbi yelled.

Mike looked at Bobbi and just turned his head. "I can't believe this is happening."

CHAPTER EIGHT

Just as they made it to the door, the telephone rang.

Detective Moore picked up the phone. "Pardee's residence, may I help you?"

"Yes, you can. I need to talk to the person in charge."

"Who is this?" Moore Asked.

"Never mind that, are you in charge?"

"Yes, then Moore started motioning for other officers to pick up headphones.

"I see you are at the Pardee residence. I need to talk to the person in charge."

Detective Moore waited for everyone to get to the phone. "I'm the person in charge. How can I help you?"

"Alright then. I have the Pardees' child. I know you are tracing this call, so I will call back." He suddenly hung up the telephone.

Detective Moore looked over at Mike and slowly hung up the phone.

"Who was that?" Bobbi asked.

Detective Moore slowly began walking towards Mike, then glanced at Bobbi. "We are sorry, Mike. Take the handcuffs off this man."

"Who was that?" Bobbi asked again.

Detective Moore looked at Mike. "That was a man who said he has your daughter."

Bobbi fainted and fell to the floor.

Mike ran over to Detective Moore. "So, what did he say? What does he want? Where is she?"

"That's all he said before he hung up the phone. We must wait for him to call back."

"I told you I had nothing to do with what happened to my daughter."

"I'm sorry, Mike." Detective Moore said but got cut off.

"Did you really think I would harm my kid?"

"Well, Mike, it's not like it has never happened."

"It has never happened to me." Mike quickly answered.

"This stuff happens daily, and with all our evidence, everything was pointing at you." Moore quickly responded.

"Well, you need to point at yourselves because you almost blotched this up." Bobbi woke up and sat up.

"Well, we have already said sorry." Detective Crunby said.

"Well, you need to get the hell out of my house."

"No, Mike. Detective Crunby stays, as does everybody else here." Moore confirmed. "I know you are upset, but we must follow our evidence."

Mike walked away, talking under his breath. He passed Bobbi, looked at her, and kept walking. He went into the kitchen and out to the backyard. A few minutes later, Bobbi walked out. She hesitated, then called Mike.

"What do you want Bobbi?" He turned around abruptly. "You thought I would do something like that to Karen? What type of man do you think I am? That's my daughter we are talking about."

"Well, remember, she's my daughter too," Bobbi screamed.

"Oh yes, I remember. Of all the times you should have stood by me, that was one of them. You turned your back on me quickly. Just threw me under the bus."

"Mike, I don't want to argue. We need to start over and support each other to help find Karen."

"Be supportive. Are you kidding? What happened to be supportive a minute ago when I was in handcuffs when they were walking me out the door? If not for that phone call, I would be on my way downtown, but I guess you were being supportive, right? Give me a break, being supportive."

Bobbi ran back into the house, crying and shouting. "I just want my daughter back!"

"Hell, me too!" Mike said, shouting back.

Just as Bobbi walked into the house, the phone rang again. Mike ran into the house, and the detectives raced over to pick up the receiver simultaneously with the other officers.

"Hello." Detective Moore answered.

"Hello, is Mike there?"

"Who is this?" Moore asked.

"This is Pat. Who is this?"

"Never mind." Detective Moore said and handed the phone to Mike.

"Hey, Pat. I'm not sure this is a good time to talk."

"Man, I heard what happened," Mike interrupted him. "Wait, Pat, you need to call me on my cell phone. This line needs to stay open."

"Okay, I will call you on your cell phone."

Mike hung up the phone and looked at Detective Moore. Moore was looking at him. "I would appreciate it if you would have all your friends refrain from calling you on this house phone."

"I know. I have already told Pat to call me on the cell if he needs to talk."

"And one other thing, Mike, you don't need to tell too many people about what's happening here."

"I know! I'm sure he found out after I called the job." Mike walked away to answer his cell phone.

"Mike, are you alright? Is Bobbi alright? I know how much you love your girls and what you would do to get them back. If you need me to do anything, ask me." Pat asked, concerned.

"I'm doing all right, and Bobbi is fine too. Listen, I can't talk about what is happening here. Call me back, or I'll tell you what. Let me call you when I can."

"Okay, man, just remember I'm here for you."

Bobbi walked and kissed Mike on the cheek. "I apologize for what I said this morning. I know you wouldn't do anything to your girls, but I was just in so much pain that I wanted to believe in something. I want our daughter back, and I know you feel the same."

"I know you didn't mean that, Bobbi. It's just that when all was failing, it seemed you turned on me, which hurt me. I love you and my daughters so much. By the way, we need to take Kathy to your mother's house until this is resolved. Has she asked about her sister today?"

"Yes, she has."

"What did you tell her?"

"Nothing. Every time I think of Karen, I start to cry, and I don't know what to tell her right now. Because I know if I tell her the truth, she will be devastated."

"But Bobbi, we need to tell her something."

"I know Mike. Do you have anything in mind?"

"No, did she see me being taken away earlier?"

"Yes, she did. She was with me the whole morning. I'm already missing one of my daughters, and there is no way she was going to be let out of my sight."

"Where is she now?" Mike asked.

"She went up to our bedroom. I brought some of her things from her bedroom." Bobbi answered.

Mike hugged Bobbi to say we were good and walked away to find Kathy. He looked back while climbing the stairs. Please, God, *keep her safe and bring her back home to me.*

CHAPTER NINE

Mike opened the bedroom door and looked at Kathy. "There you are. Hey baby, how are you?"

"I'm okay, Daddy."

Listen, Kathy. "We are looking for your sister."

"What happened to Karen, Daddy?"

"Daddy doesn't know, but all those people are helping us to find her. Daddy loves you, Kathy."

"I love you to daddy."

"Daddy, do you love Karen?"

"Oh yes, baby, I love Karen and you. Why do you ask that?"

"Because I heard one of the policemen say you took her away."

"Daddy didn't do anything to Karen. They made a mistake when they said that. I would never do anything to hurt you or Karen." He reached out to hug Kathy. "Baby, we are going to take you to your grandma's house until we find Karen, okay?"

"Okay, Daddy, can I bring some toys with me?"

"You can bring anything you want with you, baby. I'll send Mommy up here to help you get ready to go." He kissed her on top of the head and walked away.

Mike walked back downstairs to where Bobbi was. "I talked to her and told her we were going to take her to your mom's house. She is waiting for you to go up there and help her get some things and toys together. So, when are you going to take her there?"

"I'm not leaving this house. There's no way I'm going anywhere."

"Well, then call your mother and tell her to come and pick her up, please."

"Okay, I'll do that, but I'm not going anywhere or leaving this house until my child is back." Bobbi frowned.

Mike gave Bobbi his cell phone. "Here, call your mother. I don't want Kathy to be around during this."

Mike walked out of the house, and Taylor was looking across the fence.

"Hey Mike, how are you doing? I was looking at the news and wanted to see if you needed anything, but there were too many Police Officers at your home. I didn't think they would let me see you anyway."

"No, they probably wouldn't have."

"So, are you all right? Can I do anything for you, man?"

"No, not right now, Taylor; I have to stay in the house. I will try to talk to you later."

"I understand, man; take it easy, and I hope you get your daughter back safely."

"Thanks, man." Mike walked away, looking at the ground.

Detective Moore stopped him at the door.

"Who is that?"

"That's our neighbor. He wanted to see if he could offer any help."

"The best thing he could do now is stay away from you. We are going to need you here and focused. Things will start happening fast, so be ready."

"I understand, and I'll always be available somewhere around here."

Suddenly, the phone rang again. Everyone got in their positions. Detective Moore answered the phone, but the person hung up. "This will happen all day," Moore said.

"What the hell does he want?" Mike asked loudly.

"We won't know until he tells us Mike." Detective Crunby said.

Mike walked around the house looking for Bobbi. Found her in the family room, looking at photo albums and crying. "Baby, you are torturing yourself. I understand what you are going through, but this is not helping you."

I have been looking at these pictures for a while. Do you know Karen is growing up?" Bobbi tried to smile. "She is almost as tall as Kathy and only five years old."

"I know everything about them, girls. She seems to be catching up with Kathy quickly and is very smart, which comes from hanging around you and Kathy. She sees Kathy doing something and wants to do it too, not even knowing the danger involved." Mike smiled.

"She just wants to be as old as her sister." Bobbi pushed the picture up against her chest and started to cry again. "Oh, Mike, I just want my baby back, please God, send me my child back." she started crying harder. Mike reached for her. "Baby, everything is going to be all right. Karen will be back with us soon. They have every police officer in the city looking for her. They will eventually find her."

Nightfall came in with no phone calls. Detective Moore walked around the house looking for the Pardees. "Oh, there you two are. We are leaving for the night. An officer will be outside your home; if anything happens, turn your front porch light on, and he will come to the door. I'll return early tomorrow. Please don't hesitate to call if you need to. Don't worry about the time; make the call." he walked over to the officer standing next to the door. They spoke for a few minutes, then he turned and walked away.

CHAPTER TEN

Bobbi sat up in the bed, "I don't know if I can sleep without knowing how and where my daughter is."

"Well, you must get some rest. I'll tell you what: I'll stay awake, and you get some sleep. Then, when you wake up, I'll try to get some sleep." Mike looked at her.

"Why don't you go first? That way, you'll be up later on in the night." Bobbi insisted.

"Alright, if you are sure about it because someone needs to get some rest." He grabbed the pillow and lay back, pulling the covers over himself. Bobbi grabbed the magazine off the nightstand and sat in the chair beside the bed. Mike sat up and looked at her. "Don't worry; I'm not going anywhere. I'll be right here when you wake up." She tried to smile.

The following day, Mike woke up, and Bobbi was asleep beside him. She popped up quickly, and Mike looked at her. "I guess that didn't work out the way we had planned. He tried to put on a smile. I guess we were tired."

"What time is it?" Bobbi asked.

"It's just two in the morning. Guess we both just took a power nap." Mike yawned.

They walked downstairs into the room with all the police equipment. Bobbi stopped abruptly. "Look at all this equipment they use to get our daughter back."

"Yeah, I see it, and I hope it works." Mike continued walking downstairs.

He hugged her. "I know this is hard, but it's just as hard for me. We have to be strong for each other." He grabbed some tissue and handed it to Bobbi. "I'm going upstairs to shower before all this starts again."

Bobbi walked into the kitchen and tried to clean up, but her focus always returned to Karen. "Oh, *my baby, where are you?*"

Mike had to pass the girl's room on his way to his room.

He looked inside; the yellow tape was evidence something was not right. He walked away, fighting back the tears in his eyes. He closed the door and looked up. "Please, God, take care of Karen wherever she is. Please bring her home safe."

He walked into the room and sat down on the bed. When the phone rang, he quickly jumped and ran down the stairs.

Bobbi was staring down at the phone. She looked at Mike. "What do we do?" She asked frantically.

Mike ran and turned on the porch light. Then returned to answer the phone before it stopped ringing. "Hello." Then again, hello, and the other end hung up. The officer quickly opened the door and ran in. "I called Detective Moore. What happened?"

"The phone rang," Mike said.

"And what did they say?" The officer asked.

"Nothing, just hung up after I said hello a couple of times."

Mike looked at the phone. "How many times did it ring?" he asked Bobbi.

"About three times before you made it downstairs and then a couple more times when you were here."

They walked into the family room with the officer. "What does that mean?" He asked.

"I'm not sure, but Moore and a few officers are on their way here. Maybe they can answer some of the questions you may have."

Mike looked around the room, and clothes were stretched over the couch. Bobbi walked into the room and sat down.

"What is this? What are you doing?" Mike asked.

"I can't stop thinking of Karen, and I need to do something to keep myself sane. And this is what I came up with."

"Baby, you are torturing yourself; you should go upstairs and try to relax. I will get you when Officer Moore and the rest of them arrive. I know you want to hear what they will say about that phone call."

"Okay, I'll try." Bobbi walked away.

On her way upstairs, Bobbi passed the girl's room and looked inside like Mike had. She stood in the doorway for about fifteen minutes, then left for her room. She sat down, grabbed her purse, and took out a picture of Karen. She rubbed the photo and tried to relax. As soon as she lay down, the phone rang again. She jumped up and walked quickly down the stairs.

Mike was standing over the phone. "Pick up the receiver." She said.

"I'll go and turn on the porch light again." Bobbi walked quickly to the front door and turned on the light. The officer was already standing on the porch.

"I heard the phone ring," he said and walked in.

He ran to the phone and motioned Mike to answer it.

"Hello, can I help you?"

"Yes, you may. I see you have an officer guarding your house; I just passed the house and noticed the officer." Then he hung up. Detective Moore came into the house just as the phone call ended. "What happened? Who was that?" he asked, looking at Mike and the Officer.

"I believe that was the kidnapper." the officer said.

"Was the voice muffed as before," Moore asked.

"The guy sounded the same. But he did say he just passed the house and noticed me guarding the house."

"Do you remember any cars passing in the street?"

"Yes, three cars went by when I stood out there."

"Can you remember what any of them look like?"

"No, not really; I wasn't

paying any attention; I was smoking a cigarette."

"You were smoking and didn't see any of the cars?" Mike screamed. "You were supposed to be watching everything. I can't believe you ignored what's going on outside. My daughter was in one of those cars, and you blew it. I want someone else outside Detective Moore." he looked at the officer. "I don't want this guy around; this guy is an idiot."

"Calm down, Mike. Getting mad isn't going to change the facts." Moore walked to a window and pulled the blind down just a little so that he could peek out.

"The fact is if the kidnapper just passed like he said he did, then he has your daughter not far from here. That is a good sign. Besides, we don't know if he passed the house."

"That's what he said." Bobbi walked over to the window.

"Yes, Ms. Pardee, but who knows when he passed by? Also, this may or may not be his first time doing this; he probably already knows how this works. Coming around late at night is dangerous and could be his first mistake."

"Well, taking a kid out of her bedroom of a window of a two-story house is dangerous too, but he did it." Mike frowned.

"We know we are working with a dangerous man who takes risks." Detective Moore said. "And that will be his downfall, trust me." Detective Moore found a good spot on the couch. "There is no point in going all the way back home. I'll rest right here if you two don't mind."

"No, we don't mind." They both said together.

"Hey, where is your other daughter?" Detective Moore asked.

"She's at my mother's house," Bobbi Answered. "She came and got her right after you all left."

"I don't want her around all this," Mike said.

"I understand." Moore laid his head down and was asleep in seconds.

CHAPTER ELEVEN

The next day, everything was quiet until the FBI arrived.

"I'm FBI Agent Aston. This is Agent Perry. Our offices have been staying in constant contact with the local authorities. Who is the leading detective? And what's going on this morning?"

"That would be me." Moore stepped up. "And what we have here is a kidnapped young girl of five years old. She was abducted from her own house in her bedroom."

"Can you show us the bedroom?" Perry asked.

"Sure, walk this way." an officer said and started walking away.

Perry looked at Aston and shook his head. "I'll finish down here."

"And who are the parents?" Aston looked around the room.

"They are the couple over there sitting on the couch."

Aston walked over and kneeled in front of Bobbi. "I'm Justin Aston from the Federal Bureau of Investigation. We have been given authority to help in locating your child." Bobbi looked at him and then to Moore.

"This is my husband." Mike stood up and shook hands. "Is there something wrong?" He asked curiously. "Other than your child not being here at home with you and her mom, we know exactly only what the officers who have been here the entire time know. We have been following up on this case since it started. After a day or so, something pops into your mind, something you may have overlooked, something that seemed out of place, but you just took it as nothing special. Have you thought of anything like that?"

Mike nodded no. Then he thought of when they returned from church, and the gate was open. "There was one thing he reminisced."

"And what was that?" Ashton asked while taking his notepad out of his pocket.

"One day, the gate was open after returning from church with the family. I thought I had closed it. But I found nothing out of order, so I just let it go."

"Was there anyone outside, walking around the neighborhood, that you noticed you were unfamiliar with?" Aston asked.

"No, there was no one on the street at all." Aston looked at Moore and then back to Mike.

"What!" Mike asked. "What's going on?" He walked up to Aston.

"Nothing, sir," Aston answered aggressively.

"Look, man. I have already been accused of kidnapping my daughter and would have been taken to jail had a phone call not come through here. You telling me nothing is happening makes it seem like you all are hiding something. I don't need any more surprises. What do you know?" Mike asked anxiously.

"There are things we understand, Mike, like patterns, things civilians like yourself wouldn't notice: habits and such. We write things down to feed into our database at the office to see if things match up with something already in the system. Open fences left open may seem like nothing to you, but it may be a misstep by the kidnapper. That's why we looked at each other. Trust me, the mistake made putting you in handcuffs will never happen again. You and your wife have been cleared of any wrongdoings. I apologize for you going through that, but the officers were following leads and evidence." Mike looked at Moore and walked away.

"Okay, let me see the bedroom." Aston turned to Moore.

Detective Moore led him to the girl's bedroom. "I taped it off, and no one has entered since yesterday morning." Moore opened the door and cut the tape off the entrance.

"You say the little girl was abducted from this room?"

"Yes, apparently, the kidnapper entered from this window and grabbed the little girl and took her out this window."

Aston began looking at the window seal and looking out the window. "Whoever took this little girl went through a lot to get her. He thought this out for some time. And he is very patient. This may take a long time to solve, depending on how patient he or she is. There could be more than one person because I'm trying to understand how one person could take a little girl of.... how old did you say she is?"

"She is five years old," Moore answered.

"So that puts her about thirty to fifty pounds. That's a lot of weight to carry, let alone climb with."

"So." Aston gestured with his hands. He takes her out this window and down this roof."

"We have an evidence board of what we have downstairs." Detective Moore said. "We found material and shoe prints here." he pointed to the window seal and on the roof. "The material found on the roof was also found on a pair of shoes we located in the garage; the shoe prints were on the roof and on the ground where we believe he came off the roof. More material was on the ground where we found the sheet from her bed." Moore explained.

"Where is the sheet from her bed?" Aston asked.

"We have it downstairs in an evidence bag."

"Has anyone done forensics on the sheet?" Aston asked.

"No, not yet."

"Well, there may be hair samples of the suspect on the sheet. I need Forensics done on the sheet immediately." Aston frowned.

"No problem." Detective Moore radioed Detective Crunby and had Forensics start on the sheet.

"Okay, Detective Moore, is there anything else you have?"

"Yes, there is just one more thing, and it's kind of strange."

"What is it?" Perry asked.

"The shoes where the material was found in the window and on the ground belong to Mr. Pardee."

"And where are these shoes?" Aston asked.

"They are also downstairs. Okay, let's see the evidence. There is no need for yellow tape anymore. The parents should be allowed to come into this room. They need to come into this room so they don't forget what this is all about."

Aston walked up to Mike and Bobbi. "All kidnapped cases are taken and sometimes turned over to the bureau. We will assist Detective Moore in getting your daughter back to you, but we will take over at some point, depending on the circumstances. We'll be asking questions that some of you may have already answered. I hope you don't get frustrated being asked the same questions again, but they are necessary to locate and understand what happened here.

I am sorry for this and would like it to go away as quickly as possible. The fact of the matter is kidnappers usually draw things out and usually have some crazy reason for taking little girls and boys. Some of the reasons you may already know, and then there are some that we do not even understand. So, let's try to work together if possible and get this over with. Detective Moore said you would rather be called Mike. Is it okay if I call you Mike also?"

"Of course."

"Alright then, Mike, I want to walk with you."

"Alright, let me get some shoes on."

Aston led Mike out the front door as he began to talk.

"Mike, I have talked to Detective Moore, and let me be the first to say I don't think you had anything to do with the abduction of your little girl. Let me get that out of the way. But I want to know how close you were with your daughter. Did you take time and play with her?"

"Yes, sir, we are close. I did everything with them."

"You have another daughter?" He asked.

"Yes, she is over at her grandparent's house."

"Does she know what happened here?"

"No, not really, but she was asking about her sister."

"I guess they were close, too, right?"

"Yes, sir, my whole family was close." Mike frowned, agitated.

"I understand, Mike, but I need to ask these questions in case the kidnapper wants to go through me to talk. I need to have an idea what the answer is."

"I understand, detective," Mike said.

"So, what kind of neighborhood is this? Is everybody cordial? Do you all talk to each other?"

"We talk to each other when we see each other. I have good neighbors." Mike smiled.

"Well, good, that's what's missing in these times. Everybody is so distant now, and nobody wants to be bothered. We will go house to house to see if anyone has heard or seen anything. Mike, I want you to know we will do everything we know. And we will use past experiences and tactics to get your daughter back. If there is something you don't understand, instead of voicing your displeasure aloud, I would prefer for you to approach me or Detective Moore; we will talk to you about what we are doing."

"Thanks, Detective," Mike said. "I'll do that."

CHAPTER TWELVE

As soon as Detective Aston and Mike returned, Mike hugged Bobbi. Aston went to look at the evidence. The phone rang, and all the

detectives looked at Mike and told him to grab the headsets. They put on headsets and told Mike to answer the phone.

"Hello, may I help you?"

"Yes, I have your little girl. I know you want her back. But there is more than one problem; I know this call is being traced, so I won't be on this line for long. I know you don't have much money, so money is not what I want."

"Well, what do you want?" Mike asked.

"Hey, I'm asking the questions and making the demands you just listen. I'll call back. He hung up abruptly."

"We have a trace!" the officer yelled loudly. Send all efforts to 1091 Macron Street." Detective Moore called the precinct and had squad cars sent to the address. He looked up the address and noticed it was in the next county.

"Wow, the guy is traveling with this little girl." He thought this guy was no ordinary kidnapper. When the officers arrived at the location, they noticed the phone call was made from a public phone located near a library. The phone was left off the hook. Detective Moore requested that the receiver be dusted for fingerprints. But they came back with negative results. The assailant used gloves. What looked like saliva residue was left on the receiver, and DNA tests were done on the substance.

Mike walked up to Detective Moore, confused.

"The kidnapper knows I don't have a lot of money and says that he doesn't want money. Then what do you think he wants?"

I don't know Mike. We have to keep talking to him and wait for him to play his hand."

Aston walked up to Mike. "It's all a process, and it takes time.
"

"I don't like talking to this fool." Mike frowned.

"I know Mike. But he's got your daughter; talking to him is the only way you will see her again. Eventually, he will tell you what he wants."

Detective Moore called Aston over to the side. "Last night, the officer we had guarding the house reported the kidnapper, saying he passed the house and seen him at the house. Today, the kidnapper is in another county. Do you think the kidnapper passed the house last night?"

"It's a possibility, but highly unlikely a kidnapper would travel with the kid in the car. However, he could have traveled and left the child behind." Aston answered.

"So, what do you think of the conversation on the phone?" Moore asked.

"I don't know what to say about this. I wondered what he could want if he didn't want money."

"We just have to wait for him to call again and see what he's asking for. Meanwhile, why don't you go to the station and see if the DNA matches up with anything you have in the database? If anything matches, give me a call." He walked away to talk to Perry.

CHAPTER THIRTEEN

The next day, Mike woke up to find Bobbi not lying next to him. He looked at the clock; it was six-thirty in the morning. He walked past the girl's room and saw someone in Karen's bed. He walked in, and Bobbi was asleep, holding Karen's pillow. He tapped her arm gently to wake her up. "Hey, are you alright?"

"No, Mike, I'm not all right. I have not seen my baby in three days. I miss my babies. I miss their laughter and smiles. I miss them being bad. I miss them arguing with each other."

"I know. I miss them too."

She rose to get out of bed and had a picture of Kathy and Karen under her. When she stood to walk away, Mike picked up the picture and stared at it. He looked at the sky, "Oh, baby, where are you?" He kissed the picture and put it on the dresser.

He walked back to his room and heard a vibration. He began looking for where the noise was coming from. Every so often, the vibration would come. Finally, he realized what the noise was: his cell phone. He picked up the phone, and the screen read fifteen missed calls.

"What is that, Mike?" Bobbi asked. "It's my cell phone. It must have been ringing for a while. With all that's going on, I put the phone on vibration and put it down. I haven't thought about it until now. Worrying about the kids, I forgot all about checking it. Fifteen missed calls, baby."

"Who is it?" Bobbi asked.

"Let me see." he checked his phone. "It's Pat; I better call him back. I know he is worried about what is going on."

"Hey, what's up Pat? I see you have been calling?"

"Are you and Bobbi all right? I can't imagine what you are going through."

"We are toughing it out. I won't say we are all right because we are not, but thanks for asking. So, how's everything at the job?"

"Everybody is worried about you. We know how you feel about your girls, including Bobbi. We know they are your heart and soul. If you need anything, and I mean anything, don't hesitate to call me."

"Thanks, Pat, I will remember that." "Oh yeah, what's going on with Dee? How's she dealing with the pregnancy?"

"She's doing well, man. Everything is okay."

"I gotta go, but I will call you again soon," Mike said.

"Okay. Don't forget what I said. If you need anything, give us a call. We gotcha, man."

"I appreciate it." Mike finished the call, then looked, and Taylor had called.

"Hey Taylor, what's up?"

"Oh, Mike, thanks for calling. I just wanted to know if I could do anything for you. I know it must be hard, but I wanted to say I'm here for you."

"Thanks, Taylor. I'm sorry for having all this going on next to your house."

"Look, Man! The most important thing is that they find your daughter. I know you can't stay on the phone, but I'm here if needed. We can stand by the fence and chop it up. You let me know."

"I appreciate it. It's hard over here." Mike stuttered. "Someone has my baby. It's tough."

"I can imagine," Taylor said. "But you hang in there."

"Thanks." Mike hung up the phone. You know what, baby? I have some decent friends; they want to help in any way."

Bobbi looked up with concern. "Mike, I don't have Kathy or Karen here. I'm not doing well. Please, someone, send my babies back. I wonder what I have done to deserve this," she asked, looking up to the sky.

"Baby don't go blaming yourself for what's going on. Some idiot came here and violated our home. It has nothing to do with you, and you must believe that."

CHAPTER FOURTEEN

Ten o'clock the following day, Mike was downstairs drinking coffee with the officers and sharing special moments with them about Kathy and Karen. He laughed. "Yeah, Karen has gotten into much trouble following behind her sister. But with those baby blues, she's always had me right in the palm of her hands."

"Yeah." one officer laughed. "I know the feeling. I have three baby girls at home right now, and we are trying to find a fourth child. I need a break from my daughters and get that boy. You ever thought of going after that boy Mike?" All the officers laughed.

"Shhhh. If she even thought we were down here talking about her having another child and going through that labor stuff, she'd kick all of us out of this house. Including me." They all laughed. Mike paused. "You know Karen likes to dance."

The phone began to ring. Mike ran over to the table. "Wait, Mike! Don't answer it yet!" Aston yelled. "Let it ring." The phone rang five times, and Bobbi looked at Detective Moore every time it rang.

"Why don't we answer the phone, Detective?" Bobbi asked.

"I'll answer the question." Agent Perry said.

"First, we need a plan of attack to go on the offensive now. We have been waiting for this guy to call, and every time he calls, we pick the phone up like we are desperate, and he knows that. So, for now, we will make it seem like we are not as desperate."

"But he has our daughter," Bobbi yelled. "What if he wants to return her." Bobbi cried.

"I think you know the answer to that." Ms. Pardee. Perry turned his attention back to Mike. "When the phone rings again, pick up the phone and ask him what exactly he wants since he doesn't want money. That tells him you heard him when he said he did not want money. When the phone rings this time, pick it up after the fourth ring."

"All right," Mike said.

"Mike, keep him on the phone for as long as possible. He knows he is being traced, so he will try to quickly say what he wants to say and get off the phone. Try to stall him for as long as he allows you to. We have patrol cars in all three adjacent cities, and we can get to any location in minutes."

"Okay, now that we are all on the same page, we will start our offensive."

Twenty minutes later, the phone rang. Agent Perry started counting rings with his fingers... " Three... Four, pick it up."

"Hello," Mike spoke into the receiver.

"Well, hello, Mike."

"How do you know my name?"

"Mike, the news is replaying everything you say and do. For instance, I know the FBI is there listening to this call, so for them, I will say this: This is not about money. This is about something that happened in the past; someone at that house knows what I'm talking about." He hung up abruptly.

Detective Moore hung up the phone and then started scanning the room. "Okay, what is going on here? This guy is playing a game with us. He is keeping us guessing." He looked at Mike. "Do you have any idea of what this guy is talking about? Think hard, Mike. Is there anything you can think of in the past that would make someone want revenge?"

"No sir, I don't." Mike quickly answered, slowly putting his headset down.

"What about you, Mrs. Pardee? Can you think of anything that would make anyone want to harm your family?"

"No sir, I have no idea what this is about," Bobbi said and sat beside Mike.

"Okay, we have a kidnapper who doesn't want money and has a personal vendetta against one of you. If he is telling the truth."

"The truth is he has Karen, and that is all we know of the truth," Perry said, looking around the room. There was a knock on the door, and the Forensics officer walked into the house and called the detectives to the evidence board. The blood type and the DNA evidence were back.

"What do you have?" Detective Moore asked.

"What we know is the blood type found was a rare blood type, "B," and we also know the blood type of Mr. Pardee is type "O positive," so there is no chance the blood found at the window was that of Mr. Pardee."

"Good," Moore said. "That eliminates him of all wrongdoings."

"Did you suspect he had something to do with this?" Aston asked.

"There were so many things pointing his way, with the shoes, the garage, the ladder, and the fact no one heard anything late that night. I mean, my thought was, why didn't Karen make any noise? She either knew who it was taking her, or they did something to her to make her not scream."

"Yeah, you do have a point there."

"Wait!" the forensics officer said. "There's more. The saliva DNA test came back, and the computer did a complete check with all computers around the country, and nothing came back. So, we are either dealing with a first offender, or this guy is being careful not to make any mistakes." Perry concluded.

"Thanks for all the evidence. Could you put all this next to the board for future matches?" Moore asked.

"Yes, sir, no problem."

"We need to start pressuring this guy to force some mistakes, make him do something that he is not ready to do," Aston said.

Moore interrupted. "We don't know where this guy is or why he took Karen. We don't want to push this guy too far into a corner and put him in a position where he must leave quickly. That could mean disaster for this family. Also, we don't know what this guy is capable of.

Will he kill? We don't know, so patience is the key here. Let him think he is in charge and let him get comfortable, and then he will get careless and make a mistake."

Day six came with nothing to report; the day was slow, cloudy, and cold. Aston walked up to Mike. "Can we talk to you again?"

"Yes, of course."

"Let's go in here." He pointed at the kitchen.

"Yes, what is it?" Mike asked.

"Detective Moore and I were looking over the evidence board and thinking, first let me let you know the blood tests came back, and the blood was not your type. I'm not saying we thought you were responsible, but we need to follow every lead, tip, or otherwise." Perry said.

"We want to keep you updated on what is going on here. You can tell your wife what we tell you. We're not trying to keep any secrets from her or you. Now think, Mr. Pardee. Is there anything you can think of that will make anyone want to harm your family?"

"No, sir. Like I said earlier, I live a very calm life. I go to work and then come home to my wife and kids; that is my life," Mike answered.

"Nothing you may have seen or heard would make anyone want you to keep quiet?"

Mike shook his head from side to side. "No sir, nothing."

"Okay, Mike," Aston said. "We try to keep ourselves ready for anything." Mike left to return to the family room, but the phone rang. Detective Moore held his hand and counted two...three...four... "pick it up."

"Hello," Mike answered.

"Hello Mike, again we talk. "Have you figured out what I want?"

"No!" Mike snarled. "I have no idea what you want."

"Okay, Mike, I will make it easier for you. Ask your wife what I want. I'm sure she can tell you." He suddenly hung up the phone. The call was so quick that there were no traces. When the officers put their headsets down, they all looked at Bobbi.

"What?" Bobbi asked. "Why are you all looking at me?"

"The kidnapper said you know what he wants and why he has Karen." Mike sighed.

"Well, I don't know. I have no idea what this is about."

"Are you sure?" Mike asked.

"Think Bobbi, think hard." Mike raised his voice.

"I don't know!" Bobbi said in a meaner tone.

"You don't have to get mad, Mrs. Pardee," Aston said. "We need to ask these questions."

The phone rang again...Moore ran to the phone again. Three... four...pick it up.

"Hello," Mike answered.

"Mike, I have someone on the phone that wants to talk to you." Detective Moore motioned for Bobbi to get on a pair of headsets.

"Who is this?" Mike yelled.

"Daddy...daddy, I want to come home. Come and get me, Daddy." She started crying, and then the receiver was taken abruptly. As you can see, I have your Karen with me, and she is all right, but if Bobbi doesn't tell you what this is about, I'm afraid I will have to do something to your Karen. This is between Bobbi and me." He hung up the phone again.

All faces turned to Bobbi again.

Suddenly, "We have another trace." yelled from across the room.

"Where?" Detective Moore asked.

2122 Croft Ave. Send all cars to that address." Aston yelled.

This time, the address was a house, so the officers responding to the call radioed back to determine the next action to take.

"Surround the location. I'm sending a helicopter to the location." Aston said.

Detective Moore yelled. "I have a car outside. Let's go."

Moore, Perry, and Aston ran out the door and sped away.

Detective Crunby let Mike and Bobbi know the call came from the next city.

"Why didn't they let me go," Mike asked.

"Right now, you would just be a distraction." A uniformed officer answered. "Things happen fast at the crime scene, and things and evidence get ruined if not correctly done. The best place for you right now is right here." Then he nodded his head to Mike to follow him. Mike looked at Bobbi. I'll be right back."

"Where are you going?" She asked.

"Nowhere just outside to get some fresh air."

When Mike found Detective Crunby, Crunby whispered, "Now is a good time to talk to your wife. You need to start asking questions because if the Detectives return empty, they will be on your wife hard, asking serious questions. I'm serious. Talk to your wife. Something is happening here, and she seems to be the person the kidnapper is targeting."

CHAPTER FIFTEEN

Moore, Aston, and Perry arrived at the scene. It was surrounded by patrol cars and helicopters flying high. The local press was there, and people started to surround the area. Aston and Perry walked to the first officer on the scene.

"Has anything changed since we talked?"

"No sir, nobody in or out of this location."

"Thanks, officer," Aston said.

"You want the lead, or do you want me to take it?" Moore asked.

"I'll take it," Aston said.

"Okay, officer, you can ensure nobody gets too close to this location. Perry, do you have your binoculars on you?"

"Sure here." He handed them over.

Aston looked at the house through the binoculars. "There's no movement in the house from what I can see. The curtains are not moving, and the door is closed. There's no car in the driveway, and the garage door is closed."

"Do we have a SWAT team here?"

"Yes, sir, we do," Moore yelled back.

"We are going to need them here.

"Okay." Detective Moore said. "I'll call the precinct and get them out here immediately."

"Alright, then, we'll stand down until they arrive."

Crunby arrived at the scene. Moore walked up to him. "For now, we have a quiet scene. We have the SWAT team in transit. Let's talk to the officers who arrived first at the scene."

"Finally!" Aston said. Watching the SWAT team arrive.

The team leader approached the detectives. "What's the situation here?"

"We may have a hostage situation, a kidnapped little girl inside this location."

"Alright, I will set up my men. I'll radio you when we are in position."

"Okay," Aston said.

A few minutes later, the call came back. "We are in position and ready. Waiting on your command!"

"Okay, wait for my signal," Aston said. He grabbed the loudspeaker and began talking. "You in the house. Your house is surrounded. Give us some signal to let us know you hear us." No response was generated. Aston looked into the area of SWAT and held up his hand, waving them to close in.

The team started from the south. They had a sharpshooter on the house directly across the street, aimed straight at the front door. Three men walked slowly towards the house, and two other men walked slowly around the driveway, working their way to the back of the house.

The call came back, "We are in position awaiting your signal to storm the house."

"Hold on," Aston called back on the radio. He looked around the perimeter and put his hand to his face. "Wait, something isn't right. Nothing is happening in this area; there is no movement in the house, and no one is making any demands. There's no one in this house." he said to Perry. He signaled the captain of the SWAT team to call him via landline.

When the call came through, Aston answered. "Move in cautiously, but I don't think anyone is in that house."

The team began to move forward slowly and came up to the porch of the house. Then, on the porch, then to the door. The captain yelled, "Engage!" The SWAT team slammed into the door, knocking the door off the hinges. They ran inside, throwing tear gas into the house, then walked around very rapidly from room to room. All clear came across the radios, and the Detectives and officers approached the house.

Aston was talking to Perry and Detective Moore. "There were no gunshots, and I heard the house was empty. Let's get in there and get all those officers out before they destroy evidence that may help us understand what we are dealing with. All right, everybody out of the house. I want Forensics and C.S.I. in here right away."

Detective Moore and Aston began going from room to room.

Across the house, someone yelled, "I got something here!" They walked quickly to where the sound came from and opened the door. There was a blanket that matched Karen's sheet set on her bed when she was taken, and there were little girl socks.

"I need a Forensics team in this room right away." Aston pulled some plastic gloves out of his pocket, put them on his hands, and picked up the sock. "This may not be a good sign. He pointed at the phone. I want fingerprints done on this. Has anyone found out who's the owner of this house?" He yelled. "And where they are at?"

"Yes, the owner of this property is a couple who lives in another state; they rent out the house until the summer. Someone reported. "We talked to the neighbors next door."

"Do the owners know who they rented the house to this time?"

"According to them, nobody is supposed to live in this house right now."

"Did you find out if they have children?"

"No, but I have a telephone number to contact them."

"Can I have that, please?" Perry asked. The officer handed him the phone number and name of the house's owner.

"Thank you." Perry quickly called the owners of the house.

"Hello, ma'am. I'm calling regarding the property you own on 2122 Croft Ave."

"Yes, sir, may I help you?"

"Yes, you probably can. As far as this house goes, do you have any children living at this address?"

"No sir, I am elderly, and my kids are grown."

"Do your kids ever stay at this address?"

"No sir, they never stay at that address."

"Well, the last people you rented out your house to, do you know if they had children?"

"No, sir. The house will never be rented out to families with children. They will ruin the place, and I always return in the summer. That's why I only rent the place for nine months a year. I like to be there for the summer; the summers are nicer there than here."

"I understand," Perry said.

"What's going on over there? Is there something wrong? Is my place on fire? Or damaged in any way?" She asked.

"No, Ma'am, there's nothing wrong with your property. There may have been some unlawful activity here over the last few months, and we are just following up on leads. But your property is fine. I have one last question. Do you keep records of who stays here?"

"Yes, sir, I do. I keep the records for about two years and then throw them away."

"Can you fax the records to me?"

"Of course, give me a fax number, and I will fax them promptly."

"The number is 809 777-1234. Perry answered.

"I'll fax them right now."

"Thank you, ma'am," Perry called the office and told the secretary he was expecting a fax and to let him know as soon as possible when it came through.

"No problem. Just as soon as it comes through."

He approached Aston. "This is what I have." He handed his notes over to Aston. After reading the notes, Aston told the Forensics to wrap the blanket and the sock in the plastic bag, and he would get confirmation from the Pardees if this were Karen's stuff.

Detective Moore walked into the room. "My, have you ever seen such a mess?"

"No, not really, but someone was here. I believe the person we want was here. I need officers to walk to the houses around here and see if we can get a description of who we are looking for. From the looks of this, he had been here for a while."

"I'll do this myself." Moore walked away and out the front door.

CHAPTER SIXTEEN

Moore grabbed a couple of officers and began walking down the block. At the first house he approached, an older man opened the door. "Good afternoon, sir. We are investigating the house next door. Could you describe the occupants that lived there?"

"I've only seen him once," the man said, walking out to the porch. I tried to speak, but he never spoke back, so I never talked to him again after that and never wanted to."

"And why is that?" Moore asked.

"Because I thought he was rude, he'd leave all his trash on my side of the property. The wind blows it over here, and I would have to go out and pick it up because the guy would never come out of the house."

"So, you never seen him at least leaving the house?"

"Just that once, but his back was turned to me."

"Not even getting into his car?"

"Officer, his car has tinted windows, and he gets in and out of his car in the garage, never in the driveway."

"That did not seem strange to you, sir?"

"Nope, none of my business. Sorry, I can't help you."

"Well, thanks for your help anyway."

Detective Moore went to the neighbor on the other side of the house. "Hello, sir. Can you help me out? I'm trying to get some identification on the man who has been occupying this house for the last few weeks."

"Oh, such a strange fellow, that man. He acted like he never wanted anyone to see him."

"Is that right?" Moore asked. "What made you think that? If I might ask."

"He did everything at night. But one day, I did get a glimpse of him."

"Oh, you did. To the best of your knowledge, can you describe what he looked like?" Moore asked. He looked at the officer with him. "Jot down the description."

"White man about five feet ten inches, medium build, dark hair, strong though, he used to carry a big sack of steer manure on his back when walking outside. And he didn't own any livestock. I thought that was kinda weird."

"The big sack or the little sack?" Moore asked.

"The large sack. I know this because one of the sacks fell and burst open; he waited until nighttime and spread the manure on the back grass. But the wind blew the bag out from the other side of his house to here."

"So, how long has he been occupying this address?"

"I would have to guess about four to five months. But I knew he would have to go soon because the owners always return to stay here in the summer."

"So, since he left, do you think it was someone who knows the owner?" Moore wrote down on his pad.

"I don't know for certain, but I know the owners always return for the summer. Be glad when they return too."

"Well, thank you for the information." Moore walked off the porch. And he looked between the two houses.

"No problem."

"Oh, one more thing? Do you know if the man had any children?"

"You know, it's strange you would ask because up until recently, I didn't think he did. Then, a couple of days ago, I heard a child crying in the house."

"Was she crying for a long time?"

"At first, she was, but now I hardly hear her crying at all."

"Did you ever see the child?"

"No sir, never seen the child. Sorry, that's all I know about the man."

"Well, you've been a tremendous help. Thanks again."

Detective Moore walked back over to the crime scene.

"What did you come up with?" Aston asked.

"One neighbor never seen the man and wishes he never will. The neighbor on the other side of the house said he had seen the man, and he was very strange, carrying a steer manure sack on his back."

Aston broke in to simulate a child. "What about the neighbors living behind the house? Did anyone go and ask them if they had seen anything?"

"I'm waiting for the other officers to return. I asked them to go over there."

Aston looked at Moore. "I think the manure bag was to make himself strong enough to carry a child around."

"Yes, maybe, but then check this out. The man was described as white, medium build."

"I'm done here. I'll let the CSI and forensic finish. We can pick up the faxed copies the owner sent me on the way back to the Pardee residence. They should contain information about everyone who has rented out this house for the last two years.

The other two officers returned from talking to the folks behind the house. They said they never heard anything and a tall brick fence separates the homes. They can't see over it. They took me to their backyards and showed me. They couldn't have seen anything from their backyards.

"Okay, thank you, officers," Aston said, returning to Moore.

"Maybe we might get lucky and get Mrs. Pardee to talk."

"What do you mean Mrs. Pardee to talk?"

"Well, Detective Moore. There is a connection there. The guy said so himself. Now, she has to come clean. She knows something, and the information she withholds keeps them from seeing their daughter. Let's go back to the house. When we get there, let's not go for the jugular. Let's take it slow and try first to pry information out of her." Aston said.

"Well, all the tough times we were giving her husband hell, and she knew it was not his fault."

"Well, maybe not; she looks also blind to what is happening here. But questions need to be asked and answered."

"Yes, sir, this is going on day seven, and things are starting to heat up." Moore exhaled.

CHAPTER SEVENTEEN

When the Detectives returned to the Pardee house, all was quiet. Detective Moore walked into the family room and told Mike and Bobbi that the attempt to capture the kidnapper had been unsuccessful. He had obviously left the house after the phone call.

"What did he mean saying that you know what is going on? He specifically said you know what he wants." Aston asked.

Bobbi stood up and looked at the Detective. "I have no idea what he is talking about. I don't even know how he got my name. Is this a game or something that he's playing with us?"

"I don't know, Ms. Pardee. It would be best if you started telling the truth. It would help if you started thinking of your daughter. This is no game; if it is, it's a game you cannot afford to lose."

"Well, what am I supposed to do? I work and come home and care for my family."

Perry nudged Aston and asked him to come into the evidence room. "Maybe you are being a little hard on her; maybe she doesn't know what is happening."

"Well, Perry, maybe she should worry about why he is trying to get us to talk to her." He walked out to the evidence board.

"Do you have the names that were faxed to you?" he looked at Moore.

"Yes, here they are."

"Let's go and see if she recognizes any of the names on the list."

"Ms. Pardee, I apologize for being so aggressive. The house owner we went to faxed us the names of the occupants who last lived or rented the house within the last two years.

I would like to know if you can recognize any of these names. Would you prefer that I hand you the list or that I read it to you?"

"You can hand me the list, and I will read the names." Bobbi frowned. "If I recognize a name, I'll tell you." He handed the paper to her and stepped back, looking for any reaction or any facial expression she might have. She looked at the list and then scrolled down the list again.

"I don't see any name I recognize, not a one."

"Okay, Mrs. Pardee, thanks for looking at the list for us."

The detectives walked away.

It was getting late in the day. "I'm hungry," Detective Moore said to the other detectives. I'll buy dinner; I know this excellent restaurant."

"Okay." Perry smiled.

"Sounds good to me, too. I could use a delicious meal." Aston said.

When they were seated, Aston looked at the four of them. "Okay, now that we are away from the house, we can speak freely. What do your guts say, Moore?" He asked.

"If you want to know what I think about this whole case." He paused.

"Yes, that's what I'm asking."

"The whole thing stinks and a child hangs in the balance. I don't know who is lying, the kidnapper or the wife. It seems strange the kidnapper would know her name. We did not mention her name over the phone until he said it first. So how does he know her? An affair? A one-night stand? A wife would never want to say these things in front of her husband. So, it's no wonder she is saying she doesn't know the man."

But Aston said. "Wouldn't you think she would rather tell what she knows than have her daughter taken away?"

"Maybe unless she knows the kidnapper would not harm her."

"I see what you mean." Moore grabbed his menu.

"So, what about you, Perry? What do you think?"

"I'm almost on the same page as Moore. But I hope that we're wrong. It takes an evil woman to put a child in the middle of something like this. We don't know, nor does she, what the kidnapper is capable of. We don't know how long this guy has been planning this. He obviously has planned this for a long time. Let's look at what we know: this guy knew a lot. He knew where the house was, how to get into the garage, where Mike's shoes were, about the ladder, what room the little girls were in, and how to get Karen, not Kathy. He did everything at his house at night. Remember the neighbor saying he did everything at night; he also carried a bag of fifty pounds on his back. That was to make his legs and body strong enough to handle bringing Karen down when he went up the ladder to the room. Kathy is much bigger and heavier. There is no way he would have taken Kathy. He knew in the dark which daughter to get. You would have to think he was trying to be quick about it. The last point I want to make is why Karen didn't make any noise. She didn't scream. There is no way she went along with this man voluntarily. So, what happened? How did he know all that? It's like he had been in the house before. Karen is the key."

"What do you mean by that?" Detective Moore asked.

"Why didn't Karen make any noise? It baffles me to no end."

"Great question; we figured that out and may break this case." Aston thought aloud.

"How long has it been now?" Crunby asked, carving his steak.

"Very close to two weeks now," Aston answered.

"Do you think he had to do something with Karen in his haste to leave that house? He did leave rather quickly." Crunby swallowed some water.

Aston put down his glass and began rubbing the back of his neck. "Damn, I hope he didn't harm that little girl."

"Are you all finished eating?" Moore asked and grabbed the bill. "I'll see you all outside. I want to make a phone call home."

"I have to make it back to the office," Aston said. "I have to check on the Dalton case. I'll see you all tomorrow." Perry walked out with him.

I'm going back to the Pardee's house. Look over the evidence we just received. See you all in the morning." Crunby said.

CHAPTER EIGHTEEN

Back at the house, Mike stood up and looked at Bobbi. "Would you like me to get you something to drink? I'm thirsty."

"Yes, Mike, can you please bring me some water?"

"Yes, no problem." He walked away to the kitchen.

"Here is your water, and let me say, baby, I don't think you have anything to do with our daughter being taken. I trust you, Bobbi."

"Thanks, Mike. I needed that."

"Bobbi, we need to be here for each other. Are you hungry? I'll get something for us to eat. It's been a long day."

"Yes, I can eat something," Bobbi said. "But I will not leave this house."

"No, baby, I said I would get something for us. I've seen how adamant you were when you told me the other day you wouldn't leave this house until your daughter was back, and I can respect that."

"Thanks for understanding," Bobbi said, showing no expression.

"Would you like to ride Detective Crunby?" Mike asked.

"Yes, I'll ride. But I've already had something to eat with the detectives. The officer on watch will stay with your wife while we are gone."

"Alright then, let's go." On the way to the store, Detective Crunby Mike exhaled. "I don't know what to think. I'm trying to get Bobbi's confidence. I think we have been ripping into each other the last few days, and if she did know something, right now, she doesn't feel secure in being able to tell me."

"That's a good idea, Mike. If there is a way to get her to open up and say something, provided she does know something, you are the only one who could get her to talk. When we get back, try to act normal and be yourself. She's already thinking you don't believe her, so anything you say will be scrutinized as you do not trust her."

"Yeah, but if she knows something, I want to know." Mike frowned.

"Of course you do, but you can't try to pull it out of her. She may never say anything. Anyway, if he is telling the truth, the kidnapper will give us the information we need."

"You are right. I will give her space and not scare her into a hole."

Mike and Crunby returned and walked into the house.

"Here is your food, Bobbi. Watch it. It's hot."

"Did anything happen while we were gone?" Crunby asked.

"No, still quiet around here. The officer started walking to the door. "I'll be in the squad car if you need me."

"Okay, then, I'm going home. I will instruct the officer to call Detective Moore if anything happens. Bobbi, are you okay?" Crunby asked. "You haven't been doing much talking lately."

"Yes, I am alright, considering what is happening here."

"Yes, I know Bobbi," Mike said. "Our daughter has been gone for what twelve days now, and we are no closer to seeing her than the first day she left."

Crunby walked out.

Mike, can I be honest with you? Bobbi asked.

"Of course, baby."

"I need to talk to you about something."

"What is it?" Mike asked.

"I've been beating my head inside and out trying to remember anything, but I don't have a clue what this idiot could be talking about."

"Maybe he's trying to pit us against each other," Mike said.

"If that's what he is doing, what does it say about getting Karen back? If that is the case, he never intends to return my child." Bobbi started crying.

"Baby, have you talked to Kathy since you sent her to your mothers?"

"Yes, but only once."

"We need to keep talking to her. We wouldn't want her to think Karen is more important than she is."

"I'll call her first thing in the morning. I'm going up and going to sleep. I'm mentally and physically exhausted." Bobbi said.

The following day, Bobbi woke up on the couch and looked for Mike, but he was not in the room. "Mike," she yelled.

"Yes, Bobbi. I'm in the laundry room."

"I just wanted to know where you were."

"You were sleeping so well; I wanted you to get as much sleep as possible."

"I don't want to sleep; I want my child."

"Well, what do you want me to do, Bobbi? I have no idea where she is and..."

"And what?" Bobbi turned quickly.

"Nothing," Mike said, walking back into the laundry room.

"Bobbi walked in a few seconds later. "And what, Mike?"

"Nothing."

"You still believe I have something to do with this, right? You don't believe a word I'm saying, do you? you don't have to believe me." She stomped back into the bedroom.

A knock on the door quieted things for the moment.

"Get the door, Mike!" Bobbi said. She left the bedroom and stood at the top of the stairs to see who was at the door. Mike walked to the door, looked at Bobbi, and she looked back at him.

"Please get the door, Mike, and leave me alone."

"Who is it?" Mike said before he even arrived at the door.

"It's Agent Aston and Agent Perry. Can you please unlock the door?"

"Yes, no problem."

They walked in and went straight to the evidence board.

"Let's see, the first phone call came from this location," Aston said. "The second call came from this address."

"What's the problem, detectives?" Mike asked.

"Wait a minute, Mike. Let us get our thoughts together. We will fill you in in a moment," Perry said without taking his eyes off the board.

"Okay, Aston, the officer on guard outside said the guy drove by that night, and then within minutes, he called. Something is not right here."

"What do you mean?" Mike asked.

"Wait a minute, Mike, please."

Bobbi walked down the stairs.

"There must be more than one person involved in this; the calls and times of the calls are too close. Someone is helping this guy, being his eyes and keeping tabs on what's happening here. Look here, Mike. The kidnapper said he drove by the house. Now look at this: the place we went yesterday is across here. He had no time to return to call within minutes, and I'm sure he wouldn't have stopped and called from a pay phone. Not if he had Karen in the car with him. So, there has to be someone else involved in this kidnapping. He has to have someone else."

The phone rang, and everybody looked at each other and stood still for a second.

"Okay, remember Mike, answer it on the fourth...no, no, now answer it on the second ring."

Aston looked at Mike after the second ring. "Okay, pick it up."

"Hello...hello, may I help you?"

"Mike, so we finally talk again. Are you ready to see your daughter?"

"Yes, when can I come and get her?"

"Not so fast. Have you talked to your wife about what she knows?"

"Yes, and she says she has no idea what you are talking about."

The phone hung up. Then rang again.

"Hello Mike, I know the police are trying to trace the phone call, so I will hang up abruptly when I know they are getting close to tracing me. So, have you talked to your wife?"

"Yes, she says she knows nothing about you."

"She's lying. Can Bobbi hear me?" He asked. "Tell her to get on the phone, or something will happen to your kid." The phone hung up.

Mike looked around the room. "He wants Bobbi on the phone."

The phone rang again.

"Hello, Mike. Put Bobbi on the phone. I'll wait."

Aston motioned for Bobbi to pick up the extra headsets and phone on the table. "He's asking for you. He whispered."

"Hello, Bobbi said with a whisper."

"I don't understand a woman like you who would put your child in harm's way to keep a secret. You are despicable, an insult to any mother caring for her kids. You are also a liar. You do remember, and you'd better tell it. Tell them, Bobbi, or the next phone call, I will tell them." The phone hung up.

The phone rang again.

"Hello," Mike answered.

"One more thing, Mike. Tell the two officers there they need to make her talk since you can't seem to get your wife to talk." The phone hung up again.

Mike waited for the phone to ring again; he stared at the receiver when Aston startled him. "I guess that was it, Mike." Aston looked at Bobbi. "Do you have anything to say?"

"Wait a minute," Perry whispered. "Think about what's just happened. How did he know there were only two officers here in the house? He either has to be close, or someone is feeding him information. And since none of us has been out of sight it can't be anyone here."

"What about the officer outside?" Mike quickly offered.

"Could be him, but I doubt that," Perry said.

"Well then, who?" Mike said.

"I don't know, but information is being sent to him."

Aston turned back to Bobbi. "What do you have to say about all the accusations this kidnapper is putting out on you? He's said you have a secret and are not telling us."

"I have no idea what he is talking about, Detective," Bobbi said with tears in her eyes.

"Young lady, your daughter is with a man she doesn't know, and only

God knows what he has already done to her or will do to her. I think you would say or do anything to regain your daughter. But you look uninterested and amazingly comfortable for someone who has a daughter kidnapped. I know you have been crying, but hell, anyone can cry. Do I need to get a polygraph test done on you to see if you are telling the truth?"

"You can do anything that you please, Aston!" Bobbi screamed. She looked at Perry and then at Mike. "I haven't done anything wrong!" she yelled, running into the kitchen.

"Mike," Aston said. "Are you hearing all this? Are you seeing what we all see in your wife?"

"Sir, I will not let you harass my wife any longer. You will not come in here and treat my wife like this. Based on what some psychotic felon have said. My wife is in pain, and you are scaring her. Your tone of voice is unacceptable. I would appreciate it if you would stop and return to trying to find our daughter."

"Well, Mike. I could find her if your wife would tell us what she knows." Perry grabbed Aston and took him outside.

"You have to calm down, man. You have nothing concrete to prove she is not telling the truth except the word of a criminal. Remember, he is the one who did the crime, not her."

Detective Crunby stepped out the door. "Are you folks all right? Do you need something?"

"Yes," Aston said. "We need to find that little girl before something terrible happens to her."

Detective Crunby looked over Aston's shoulder. "Keep talking. I just noticed the shade move in the window of the house next door. Someone is listening to our conversation in that house."

The Detectives went back inside the house and called Mike to them. They peeked out the curtain to the house next door. "Who lives next door?" Crunby asked.

"My next-door neighbor is Taylor. Why?"

"We believe he is listening, watching our every move, and sending info to the kidnapper."

"No, Taylor is my friend; I don't think he would do something like that."

"How long have you known Taylor?"

"He's been living there for about a year and a half."

"Did he make first contact, or did you?"

"Let me see. I think he did."

"Does he seem very friendly sometimes?"

"No, not really. Not overly friendly."

"Is there anything strange you can think he does or doesn't do?"

"The only thing Taylor doesn't do, I know everybody else does in this neighborhood, is clean up his yard. Everyone else cleans their property themselves. He's just lazy like that."

"Who cleans it?" Aston quickly asked.

"He has a gardener that comes and does it."

"Does he spend any time outside?"

"He peeks his head over the fence and greets us every once in a while. But no, not really, only mostly at night."

"Okay, Mike, thanks." The detectives walked away.

"One more thing, Mike, what does his gardener look like?"

"White man medium build, he stands about five feet ten to six feet. With dark hair."

"Has he ever spoken to you?"

"No, never."

"Okay, thanks again." Perry and Aston walked away, discussing what Mike had just told them. Aston called Detective Moore and asked him, "Do you still have the description of the man the neighbor gave you at the kidnapper's house?"

"Yes, I have it in my pocket in my book."

"How did the neighbor describe the man?"

"Let me see a white man of medium build with dark hair." Aston and Perry looked at each other... "same man."

"We'll need a search warrant to search the next-door neighbor's house. I'll go down to the precinct and get one." Detective Moore said. "Don't let that man leave the house."

"How long will it take for you to return, Detective?" Aston asked.

"The precinct is just five minutes away. I'll call ahead to request the search warrant; give me about twenty minutes for the round trip." Aston called the officer standing outside and asked him to come in.

"We are going to need another officer to make sure nobody leaves the house next door, the house to the south of us."

"Okay, detective, I'll post a car next to the house and make sure no one comes or leaves the address." Aston turned to Mike; this is what's happening. "We have reason to believe your neighbor. What did you say his name is?"

"His name is Taylor, sir."

"Do you know his full name?" Aston asked.

"No, he introduced himself as Taylor, so we have called him that."

"Okay, we have reason to believe Taylor is somehow involved with your daughter's disappearance. The description you gave us of the gardener is the same description the neighbor gave us of the man at the other house. We are going to search Taylor's house and see what we find. Detective Moore left to secure a search warrant for the property. When he returns, we are going into that house."

"Are you kidding, detective?" Bobbi asked.

"No, ma'am, we are not kidding. We are serious. We enter that house when Detective Moore returns with the search warrant. I must call Detective Moore to ensure we have more officers when we go in."

Detective Moore returned holding a search warrant. "Here, Aston, the search warrant is legal; we have authorization to enter that house."

"Okay, first, let's devise a plan. We will need officers around the side of the house and in the backyard." Aston looked around. "I'll walk up to the door and request he let us search his house. All right, let's go."

CHAPTER NINETEEN

"Is everyone in position?" Moore whispered into the radio.

"Yes, we are in position. We have officers in the front and the rear of the house," Crunby replied.

"Okay, everybody, here we go. Aston and Perry started walking towards the house, then to the door. The shade moved as they approached the door.

"Taylor, this is the FBI. We have a search warrant to search your property. We need you to open the door."

When no one answered, Perry knocked on the door. "Taylor, we know you are in there. We have a search warrant and need you to open the door immediately."

Still no answer.

The call went out to all radios. In three minutes, we were going to storm the house.

Aston and Perry walked away from the door to the side of the house; two uniformed officers walked to the door and waited for the signal. Aston nodded, and the officers kicked the door down. With guns drawn, they rushed into the house. Taylor was trying to escape out the side window when officers apprehended him. They walked him back into the house.

"Here is the search warrant." Aston slammed it into his chest.

"But since you tried to flee, we don't need it."

The Detectives searched the house to find it was barely furnished, with no furniture in any room except the bedroom. "What have you been doing for the last couple of years?" Detective Moore asked. Taylor just stared at the floor.

"Check all rooms and closets," Aston said. "If you find something, let me know." Perry walked up to Aston. "This house looks like a deserted home. It looks like only transients live here."

"Yes, looks like this house was used for one purpose," Aston said. "Got something someone yelled."

"Which room?"

"Room number four." He yelled back.

The detectives walked into the room filled with pictures of the Pardee family. There were pictures of Mike and Bobbi and plenty of photos of the girls. Paper pinned on the walls dictated when Bobbi was home, when she left for work, and when she returned home. There was also an illustration of the house showing where all the rooms were and who occupied them.

Aston walked up to Taylor. "Where is the little girl?"

Taylor continued to stare at the floor. "Alright, officers, read this man his rights and get him out of here."

Detective Moore walked back to the Pardee residence. "Mike, we found some evidence inside that house. We are very sure the suspect had something to do with the kidnapping of your daughter."

"Well, did he say where Karen is?" Bobbi asked.

"No, he didn't."

"We've taken him to the station for more questioning."

"Damn, Mike said, the next-door neighbor, who would have thought."

"He had been planning this for some time, and although I cannot tell you what we found yet, there is enough evidence to prove he was in on the abduction of Karen." Detective Moore continued. "We still don't know where Karen is, but hopefully, the evidence we have over there will guide us to her." We still must be ready for the phone calls, and now, with the kidnapper knowing we have his partner, he may be a little meaner because we are catching up to him."

"How does he know we have his partner?" Mike asked.

Detective Moore walked to the door. "Come outside, and I will show you."

Moore pointed up to the sky. "You see those helicopters up there?"

"Yes," Mike said. Looking up at the sky.

"Those helicopters are broadcasting everything, and you know the kidnapper is looking. He knows the news is broadcasting this investigation. That's how he tries to stay a few steps ahead of us."

"So why don't you tell them they can't be telecasting this?

Isn't this a private matter?" Mike asked. Still looking up but getting angry. "They are helping the kidnapper, not us."

"Freedom of the press, Mike. They have the right to freedom of the press. And there isn't a thing we can do about it. But in some cases, they help us. So, it's tit for tat. So, knowing that we must be a little more careful about how we talk to the kidnapper. He might want to flee now and take Karen with him."

"What?" Bobbi asked with tears in her eyes. "Is he going to kill my baby?" Bobbi asked.

"Never mind," Moore said, returning to the house next door.

"Have you found anything else?" Detective Moore asked Perry.

"Yes, look over here." A small undershirt thrown in the corner had blood on it. "Put that shirt in this plastic bag and take it outside to Forensics," Perry said.

"I need to know whose blood that is. I hope it's not Karen's."

"I hope they did not hurt that little girl." Detective Moore said.

Perry called Aston into the kitchen. "Look at this vantage point. The kitchen overlooked the Pardee's house." He pointed. Sitting right here, he could watch the house without anyone noticing he was even looking. Also, look at this... He pointed at the window. A cardboard box fitted the window with a hole big enough for a camera lens. This must have been the place where they took most of their pictures."

After closely examining the area, Perry pulled a piece of paper from under the table. He looked at it and called Aston and Moore. "I got something. Look, this is a receipt dated two weeks ago. There's a name on it. Robert Patton. Run this through the system and see what comes back. He handed the paper to a uniformed officer to take to the station.

"I can't wait for that to come back. We need that information right now." Moore said. "I'm going to call the name in, and hopefully, that will produce quicker results. Time is not of the essence now. Especially now since the kidnapper knows we're closing in on him."

Perry walked in and stood next to Aston. "Things are starting to move fast now." He walked away to continue searching the house for evidence. On the back service nook were more pictures, mainly of Bobbi. "Damn, I wonder what this guy got on her. He took more pictures of her than he did of the kids."

After turning over a few of the pictures, he found a note.

"If we can't get the girl out of the house, we'll just take the woman out in her backyard. But I'd rather get the little girl. She took mine, and now I want hers."

Aston tucked the note in his pocket. "I'll just let the wife read this if we have to ask her any more questions." Aston thought silently. After a full search of the house was complete and all evidence collected, the house was yellow-taped and nailed shut. The three detectives stayed before Taylor's home, discussing their findings.

"So, what do you think of all the pictures in the breakfast nook?" Aston asked. "It makes me believe these men wanted to get to Bobbi," Moore said.

Aston agreed. He took the letter out of his pocket. "Read this." He handed the letter to Moore.

"But for what? That is the question."

With all the pictures taken of Bobbi." Detective Moore said. "It makes me believe the kidnapper knows Bobbi in some way. But what is the connection?"

"Well, we may never find out if we have to depend on Mrs. Pardee."

They began to walk towards the Pardee residence, and the officer came to them with information on the receipt. The name Robert Patton comes with a full page of information.

Patton worked for Boeing just west of here. He abruptly quit after fifteen years of employment as head foreman of the flight department. The last known address was 9842 Beachwood Street, right here in town. We have sent Officers to that address and have had them talk to the neighbors. After speaking with one of the neighbors in the area where Robert Patton and his family lived, we were told the family had just disappeared about seven years ago. This is his picture, and his description is a tall white male, five feet nine inches tall, weighing in at one hundred eighty-five pounds. Eyes blue, hair brown."

Aston reached for the file. "Now that we have a picture and a good description of the kidnapper, all we need is the reason he did this. And the whereabouts of him and the little girl."

They began to walk into the house. Detective Moore called Mike to the evidence board and told him what other evidence they had found.

"So where is Bobbi?" Perry began looking around.

"She's upstairs in the bedroom; do you mind if I go up there and talk to her, Mike?"

"No problem, sir."

Perry headed upstairs and found Bobbi in the girl's room holding Karen's bedspread.

"You miss her, don't you, Mrs. Pardee?"

Bobbi turned around with tears in her eyes. "Yes, I do. Badly! My girls and husband mean the world to me, and someone is trying to take them from me."

"Well, we found a name. Do you mind if I invade this moment and see if you recognize the name?"

"No, I wouldn't mind. What is the name?"

"Robert Patton. Do you know of anybody by that name? Here is a picture. Does he look familiar in any way?"

"No detective, I honestly have never seen this man before."

"Okay, Mrs. Pardee, sorry to have had to come up here, but I needed to know."

"I understand, detective." Bobbi turned and started looking back out the window.

Before Perry could return downstairs, the phone rang.

"Everybody in your places," Aston yelled. "Mike, you come and answer the phone when you feel comfortable."

"Hello, may I help you?" Mike spoke cautiously.

"I have your daughter; you and your wife can kiss her goodbye."

"What are you going to do to her?" Mike asked curiously.

Bobbi came running downstairs. "Give me a pair of earphones. I want to hear for myself. Who are you, and what do you want from me? This is Bobbi."

"Bobbi, I have been waiting to talk to you."

"What do you want from me? And where is my daughter?"

"Not so fast, lady. You took much more from me than I'm going to take from you. And for all of you listening, this is personal for Bobbi and me. I see you have Taylor, so I don't care if I get caught as long as I get what was taken from me a little back. Now, as far as you go, Bobbi, you should know what this is all about."

Bobbi started crying and looking around the room. "I'm waiting for you to tell me."

"Think back about seven years ago, about ten o'clock at night, you were driving on Prairie Street on the east side of town. You ran the light. Do you remember almost striking a vehicle? The vehicle swerved out of your path, lost control, and struck a tree. Do you remember?"

Bobbi reached for a tissue and wiped her eyes. She remained quiet.

"Do you remember Bobbi!" the man asked again.

Quietly, Bobbi answered, "Yes." I was out late that evening with some friends. When I finally left them, I was tired. I remember running that red light. But that was an accident."

"Do you remember missing my car?"

"I remember a car, but I don't remember what happened to it. I slowed down and looked back after I passed through the intersection."

"Well, that car had me, my wife, and kids in it. I quickly decided to avoid a head-on collision with you and turned my vehicle right into a tree. The impact killed my wife and kids. You slowed and hesitated for me to get your license plate number. Then you sped off. I don't remember you coming back to see if my family and I were all right. You just left the scene."

Quietly, the officer tracing the call waved his hand and said he had a trace. The call was coming from 2015 Prairie Street.

All officers were dispatched to that address.

"Bobbi, do you remember?" he asked.

"All I remember is the red light," Bobbi confirmed.

"You are lying the man began to anger. You killed my wife and kids, and now you are saying you don't remember; then why did you slow down? Why did you not get out and check on my family?" The sound of the man's voice began to move. "The police have traced my call, so this is it. I don't have to worry about what will happen to me, but on the other hand, you have to worry about what will happen to your daughter. Mike, are you still on this line?"

Not believing what he had just heard, Mike whispered, "Yes."

"Were you listening to what we just talked about?"

"Yes, I heard."

"So, what would you do in my situation?"

"I would not have taken a little girl. But other than that, I don't know what I would do. But, mister, you are holding my little girl, and I badly miss my baby."

"How do you think I felt about my wife and kids? I will never see again because of your wife. She neglected to tell anyone what happened that night, and now she has to pay."

"But please." Mike pleaded. "Not with my daughter. She has nothing to do with this."

"She has everything to do with this. She has to be sacrificed because of your wife. I need to make this hurt the way I have been hurting since she took my family from me."

Mike broke down. "Are you going to hurt my daughter?"

Before the man could answer, Aston broke in on the conversation. "Robert Patton, we understand now what is happening, and you don't have to hurt little Karen. There's no statute of limitations on this kind of thing. I promise we will take up the case of what happened that night."

"You are too late; the day they buried my wife and kids is the day I planned to seek revenge on this woman."

"But this is unnecessary," Aston said. "We have Bobbi here with us, and she isn't going anywhere; you can attend the trial, and if convicted, you can tell the judge what you have been going through and what you would like to see happen."

"Let's be real. There's no happy ending to this situation." Patton said. "Just misery. We all know how this will end, so let me go on and get it over."

"Wait!" Bobbi said. "I'm sorry for what happened to your family, but please don't hurt my baby; they can do what they have to do with me. I remember that night."

"Oh, you do?"

"Yes. Yes. Bobbi lowered her head. "It was raining, and I left the club hanging out with a few friends. I may have dozed off for a few seconds, and when I looked up, it was too late to stop. Then I see a car coming straight for me. I closed my eyes and waited for impact, but it never came. I looked back to see a car hit a tree. I felt bad, but I didn't know what to do."

"You should have come to see what you could have done," Patton yelled. "The doctors said my wife died on impact, but my two kids would have made it if I had them to the hospital a few minutes earlier. If you had acted, the kids would still be here. So, the way I see it, you killed them, and your punishment is I take one of your kids. I would have taken both if it weren't for your husband. But I'm not mad at Mike, just you. I have to go; the police are calling me."

The call ended.

Aston looked at all the officers. "We don't need to put too much pressure on this guy; he may react badly. I'll radio the officer in charge of the scene and tell him to wait for us to arrive before they do anything. Let's go."

They all walked out of the house. Aston turned around, "Mike and Bobbi, maybe you should come with us this time." On the way to the scene, Perry told the Pardees what to expect when they arrived.

CHAPTER TWENTY

When the detectives arrived, the streets were blocked off; the house was surrounded, and the SWAT team was already in position. "I'll take it from here," Aston told the officer in charge. "We already know who we are dealing with, and this is the child's parents inside the house. Has the suspect asked for anything, made any demands or anything?"

"No, the site has been quiet. He looked out the window once, then closed the curtains."

"Do you have the phone number to this address?"

"Yes, but we have not attempted to call."

"Good. I'll try to make first contact. Mike, you and Bobbi stay close to me. Where I go, you follow me. I may need you to talk to the suspect, so stay close."

"Mike, Bobbi whispered."

But Mike didn't turn around.

"Mike, are you not talking to me?"

"Bobbi, I don't have any thoughts other than my daughter is in that house."

"But you haven't said anything to me since we left the house."

"Well, my concern is on my daughter."

"That's our daughter in that house," Bobbi yelled.

"We can talk when Karen comes out of that house safely." Mike walked faster to keep up with Aston.

Aston grabbed the phone and started calling the house. "I'm Aston; I was at the Pardee house when you told us about this. And although I sympathize with you about your family, this is not how to resolve it."

"Detective, right now, it does not matter what happens to me nor what you think. I'm seeking some comfort for not having my family around. I had a good life until Bobbi messed it all up for me. Now, I have no wife and no kids. My reason for living is gone. Bobbi took that all away from me.

The only reason I'm still here is to see her hurt like I've hurt for years."

I won't tell you I understand what you have been going through because I don't. But that little girl you are holding inside this house had nothing to do with this."

"I'll make you a deal," Patton yelled.

"And what is the deal?" Aston asked.

"You give me Bobbi, and I'll give you Karen. Ask Mike, or better yet, tell both. I'm looking at you from a spot in the house. I see Bobbi and Mike next to you, so you ask them if they want to make the exchange. That's the only way they can save their child."

Aston put the receiver down and looked at the Pardees.

"Hey, we need to talk."

Bobbi walked away with her face buried deep in tissue in the palms of her hands. Aston watched her walk away.

"Mike, the guy inside the house, has made some conditions to which he would let Karen out of that house."

"What are the conditions." Mike quickly asked. "We will do anything."

"He wants to know how you feel about this." he pulled Mike aside. "He wants to know if you'd be willing to exchange Bobbi for Karen."

"Why does he want to know how I feel about it?"

"I don't know why he wants it like this. It's a bad deal, but I will continue to talk to him to see what else he is willing to do."

Aston called back to the house. "I have told the Pardees what you said, and they are discussing it."

"Well, let me talk to Mike."

"I don't think that is a good idea."

"Right now, you have no choice; it's either you let me talk to Mike, or Karen dies right now. Remember, detective, I don't care about what happens to me. So, stalling is not too good for the Pardee family. And trust me, I have a gun. He let off one round to confirm what he was saying. I have a gun he shouted into the receiver."

After the gunshot, Aston shouted into the radio, "False alarm. He's letting us know he has in his possession a weapon."

"Mike ran up to Aston. What happened?"

"Nothing, Mike. He was confirming with me that he has a weapon. But it's good you are here. He wants to talk to you."

Mike grabbed the receiver and looked at Aston and Bobbi.

"Hello. This is Mike."

"Mike, one more time, we speak again."

"Hopefully, this will be the last time," Mike said.

"Mike, don't say anything too crazy or let your ego take control or get your kid killed. We both know you are angry. In this situation, I would be too. But listen to what I have to say. I'll give you Karen, and I want your wife in exchange. This seems like a fair exchange. What do you think?"

"If I go through with your plan, what will you do with Bobbi?"

"Mike, look around you. I don't plan to get out of this situation alive, and don't look for Bobbi to be alive if I'm not alive."

"I don't know what to say about your plans because either way, I lose." Mike was angered.

"Look at it this way: you gain a daughter and lose an unfaithful wife. She knew what happened and never told you. This could have been avoided, but she kept it a secret.

And now she must pay. It's either Karen or Bobbi. Mike, you cannot have both. You have about ten minutes to think about it before I start shooting."

"Wait, I need more time to think. Even you had a few years. And all you are going to give me is ten minutes? You don't plan to give me my daughter back because I can't decide that in only ten minutes."

"Okay, Mike, I'll give you exactly one hour, and that's all. And your hour begins right now." The phone went blank.

Aston reached for the phone. "What did he say, Mike?"

"He wants Bobbi, or he is going to kill Karen. He wants me to decide on who I want to keep. My wife or my daughter!"

Mike walked away, and his cell phone rang.

"Hey Mike, I saw you on television."

"Hey, Dad, how are you?"

"I'm okay. Are you alright, Mike?"

"Not really. I need about ten minutes of your time."

"Alright, what do you need?"

"The kidnapper holding Karen is willing to let her out."

"Okay, that's a good thing, right?"

"Yes, but there is one condition."

"What is that?"

"He'll let Karen out if I allow Bobbi to take her place."

"What! What kind of condition is that?"

"He gave me one hour to make my decision."

"That's crazy." His father insisted.

"I know, but if I don't send Bobbi, he will kill my daughter."

"Mike, I wouldn't want to have to decide that, especially because of the way I know you feel about Bobbi and your daughters. Have you talked to Bobbi about this yet?"

"No, not yet. I'm about to go and talk to her right now."

"Mike, I'll pray for you and your family, and hopefully, everything turns out alright."

"Thanks, Dad," Mike said and hung up the phone.

He walked back toward the scene and approached Bobbi. "Hi, baby. We need to talk."

"Oh, now you want to talk," Bobbi smirked.

"Bobbi, we don't have time to argue." He glanced at his watch. "We have to talk; I have fifty minutes."

"Fifty minutes for what?" Bobbi asked.

"Well, you heard me talking to the kidnapper."

"Yes, I heard you talking and saw you walk away when you were done. You should have come and talked to me, Mike."

"Look, Bobbi, you are not going to get an argument out of me right now, so please stop trying. I must talk to you about something important concerning our daughter, and I need you to listen."

"Okay, what is it?"

"The kidnapper is willing to let Karen out under one condition."

"No problem, let's do it."

"But you haven't heard the condition, Bobbi."

"Well, Mike, what is the condition?"

"The condition is he will let Karen out only if you take her place." Bobbi looked and paused.

"Okay, I will replace Karen if he lets my baby out. I'd rather be in there than have my baby in there."

"I know, but there is one more thing, Bobbi."

"And what is that, Mike?"

"The kidnapper is not willing to come out of there alive, and he has said if he dies, then you die. He wants me to choose who I want to let live. Do I allow you to go in and let Karen come out, or do you go in with me, knowing you will never come out alive?"

"So, what did you tell him?"

"I haven't said anything to him about this. He gave me one hour and said this was going to end."

Bobbi turned away and began to stare into the sky.

Mike looked at his watch, and thirty minutes had passed. "So, I guess knowing that changes things, doesn't it, Bobbi?"

Bobbi turned around. "So, he's making you make a choice, Mike?"

"Yes, baby. And he gave me one hour to do it."

"And so, what is your choice?"

"I don't know what to do." Mike grimaced. "All I know is my daughter is in that house, and I want her out. I can vividly see her face."

"But I'm your wife."

"Yes, I understand. But Bobbi, what would you do if the tables were turned? Bobbi, it will be Karen if I choose between you and her."

Bobbi looked at Mike. "I figured you would go that way."

"Given the same circumstances, I hope you will make the same choice."

Bobbi walked up to Mike and hugged him. "I love you."

"I love you too, Bobbi."

"Alright, I will replace Karen."

They approached Aston. He noticed the concern on Mike's face and the hurt on Bobbi's.

"We have decided, Detective,"

"We have decided to let Bobbi go in if the kidnapper will let Karen out."

Aston looked at Mike and Bobbi. "There's no way we could let that happen."

"Not even if it means saving my daughter's life," Mike asked.

"No, because he would probably not let either out."

Mike looked at Aston and glanced at his watch. "I only have fifteen minutes left; you must let Bobbi enter that house so my baby can come out. I have made my decision. The kidnapper gave me one-hour Aston, and now all's left is ten minutes. My daughter will die in ten minutes."

"Mike, you need to call back and request more time. Or you can call and try to talk to him. Here is the phone number."

Aston dialed the number and gave Mike the phone.

"Hello, Detective."

"Hello Robert, this is Mike."

"Mike, have you made a choice?"

"Robert, you are asking me to make a difficult decision."

"Yes, Mike, I know. So, what did you come up with?"

"Robert, I can't decide that."

"I felt you would not make a choice, so I have chosen for you, Mike. When I took your daughter, the choice was made then. So, you can say goodbye to Karen."

"No!" Mike pleaded. "Robert, please don't hurt my child."

A shot went off. Mike fell to the ground. Bobbi looked at Mike. "What just happened?"

He looked up at Bobbi, crying. "He just shot Karen!" Then he stood up and looked at Aston.

"I'm sorry, Mike, there was nothing else we could have done."

Then another shot went off.

"So, what was that?" Bobbi asked.

"We believe that was Robert killing himself," Aston said.

Mike looked at Bobbi. "All you had to do was go and see if the family was alright, and if you did, Karen would still be here."

"Are you blaming all this on me, Mike?" Bobbi asked.

"My daughter would still be alive had you just stopped Bobbi." Mike walked away.

Bobbi walked up to Mike. "I was scared. I didn't know what to do that night."

"And you never thought to call anyone Bobbi?" You just left and did nothing. What if it were your family? Would you be mad? What would you want someone to do, Bobbi? Just leave like you did?"

"I'm sorry, but I didn't know what to do. I wanted to tell you, but I didn't know how."

"You should have told someone!" Mike yelled. "Instead of leaving them to die."

Aston and Perry walked over to where Mike was. "I'm sorry, Mike and Bobbi, for your loss. Bobbi, a detective, will contact you about what happened that night." Mike looked at the detectives. "When can I see my daughter? I want to see Karen."

Perry looked at Mike. "When we get the scene secured, we will allow you to come make an identification of the body. But for now, no one has entered the house."

Bobbi looked at Mike. "You don't understand what I just went through these last few days."

"Oh, I don't Bobbi? I went through those days, too. And nothing hurts as much as the last hour. There is no way I was supposed to choose between you and my daughter. That was ridiculously hard to do."

Aston and Perry received a call over the radio: "We need you two in the house, and you bring the Pardees. "Okay, we will be there in a few minutes." They began to walk towards the house, and Bobbi broke down.

"I don't know if I want to see her, Mike. I want to remember her the way I saw her last."

"I understand, Bobbi, but I want you to accompany me. We may need each other."

When they approached the door to the house, Detective Moore came out of the house.

"Before you go in there, Aston, I must talk to you. Wait a minute, Mike and Bobbi."

The two men walked away and began talking, then returned.

"Alright, Mike, are you sure you are ready for this?"

"Yes, sir, I want to see my daughter." Tears began to fall from his face as they entered the house.

The house was fully furnished and clean. The shades and curtains were drawn closed. A hole in the wall leading to one bedroom around the hallway led to the kitchen, which was clean. A bunch of blankets were in the family room.

Mike looked at Perry. "Where's Karen?"

When they entered the living room, there was Robert. He appeared to be shot once in the head.

Bobbi looked at Mike and began to cry, "Where is my baby?"

"Hold on, baby, she is in here somewhere."

They walked down another hall to another bedroom. The door-knob had blood on it; there was blood leading into the room, and the walls leading up to the bedroom were bloody. When Mike saw the walls, he collapsed on the floor, looked up, and grabbed Bobbi.

Perry opened the door. The room light was on but very dim.

Blood on the floor and the bed. And over in the corner was Karen. Mike paused, then walked over towards her.

Karen moved, and Mike grabbed her. Her ankles were taped together, and her mouth was taped shut.

"She's alive!" Mike yelled. "She's alive."

Bobbi ran over and grabbed her.

Oh, baby, she looked at Karen; Mike ripped the tape from Karen's mouth.

Karen started crying mommy...daddy...they all started crying. And hugging each other.

A letter addressed to Mike was on the bed. Detective Moore called Mike over and showed him the letter.

"It's evidence, but it's written out to you. Please don't destroy this letter, Mike." He handed the letter to him.

Mike

"Hello Mike, you probably don't care what is in this letter, but I urge you to read it. You probably think badly of me, and I can clearly understand. For a long time, I held on to hate. I wanted to kill your wife and probably would have had you sent her in here. Your wife Bobbi hurt me in a way no man should be broken. And I wanted so badly for her to feel what I felt that night after I was told my wife and kids were dead. The pain was not as bad as the loneliness I endured. Raising a family and then having them snatched out from under you in the blink of an eye is very disheartening. I know this means nothing to you because you have your daughter back, but let me tell you something, Mike. The reason you have your daughter back is that after we talked this afternoon, I saw how much pain you were in when you were told to make a choice. It reminded me of the night at the hospital. After I saw you walk away and put your head in your hand, I knew you were feeling a little of what I felt. Mike, I want you

to know I didn't do anything to your daughter and never would have. I fed her and tried to keep her clean. Look her over. There will be no scratches or bruises on her. I'm not a sexual predator. I raised daughters, too. You have a beautiful pair of daughters. Take care of them and never let anyone take away their joy. Sorry, I had to put you through all this. I'm not evil; I miss my wife and kids terribly. I hope you never have to go through what I have endured. Bobbi, I don't know what to say to you except that if you ever get involved or cause an accident, please stop to ensure everything and everybody is okay. Karen, you probably don't know what happened the last few days because I ensured you were well cared for. You are a very precious little girl. You remind me of my own. I hope I didn't damage any feelings you have towards the world. I'll say goodbye and go see about my family."

Robert Patton.

After Mike had finished reading the letter, he went back to Karen and gave her a big hug and kiss. "Do you want to see Kathy?" she smiled at him.

Aston, Perry, and Moore approached Mike. "You are a strong man; take care of your family." Perry looked at Mike, smiled, shook his hand, and said, "Good luck."

Aston asked Mike to take a little walk with him. "Bobbi may be in a little trouble; I know what you have been through. But there will be an investigation into what happened that night. I will keep you informed of the progress of the case."

Mike looked at Aston. "Do you think she will go to jail?"

"I don't know. Running a red light is not like pulling a trigger. It's not like she tried to hurt anyone. The only thing not in her favor is that she left the scene. But I will do everything in my power to keep her from going to jail. Mike, I want you to know I'm proud of how you handled the situation. You are a lot more mature than most. Take care of your family. I'll be contacting you soon."

The two men shook hands and walked away in opposite directions. Mike was holding Karen's hand.

On the way home, they stopped by Bobbi's mother's house and picked up Kathy. Then they went home. When he opened the door to the house, it was clean. Pat and his wife Dee had come by and cleaned up behind the police after they had collected all their equipment.

"Hey, Pat. Thanks for this."

"No problem, this is the least we could have done."

Bobbi looked at Dee and said thanks, and they hugged.

"Well, we'll leave now." Pat grabbed Dee's hand. I'm so glad everything turned out all right."

"Me too," Mike said. After he closed the door, Bobbi walked up to him, and he had tears in his eyes. I love you and will never keep anything from you again." He kissed her on the lips. You know, baby, I don't know what I would have done either." They turned and looked at their daughters. Who wants McDonald's?"

Kathy and Karen stopped playing and ran up to Mike and Bobbi. "We do."

Bobbi turned and looked at Mike. "That's why they are spoiled."

"Yeah, and I intend to keep them that way." he opened the door, and the four walked out.

RYAN D. PATTERSON SR.

About the Author

Ryan D. Patterson Sr. is a fiction writer based in the vibrant city of Las Vegas, Nevada. His work tends to lean towards drama with a spiritual edge, as he explores the complexities of the human experience. Inspired by the art of writing and seeing stories come to life, he weaves compelling narratives that resonate with readers on a deep level.

When he's not busy crafting tales, Ryan enjoys spending quality time with his family and playing softball. His love for writing stretches back to his early years, and he finds joy in creating stories that captivate and inspire others. With a touch of spirituality, his writing delves into the inner workings of the human soul, offering thought-provoking insights and a sense of hope.

Ryan D. Patterson Sr. continues to pour his passion for storytelling into his work, With published books such as, "Whose Fault, Seven Days, Financial Stay of Execution, A Loving Encounter." His words serve as a beacon of light in a sometimes-dark world. Through his writing, he seeks to uplift and touch the hearts of his readers, leaving a lasting impact that resonates long after the final page is turned.

ryandpattersonsrpublishedauthor.com
rpatteo5@gmail.com

THANK YOU FOR READING THE COLLECTIVE

We hope you enjoyed The Collective and extend our most sincere thanks. If you have a moment, we would really appreciate it if you could leave a short review on the page where you purchased this book. The authors of this anthology is thankful for you sharing your feedback. It really helps new readers find this series.

James H Roby - *Ghost Guns*

jameshroby.com

jameshroby@gmail.com

Alex Cage - *A Deadly Chance*

alexcage.com

connect@alexcage.com

Steven Van Patten - *Gumshoe*

laughingblackvampire.com

svp@brookwaterscurse.com

Jonathan Staley - *Stone*

jstaleybooks.wixsite.com/books

jstaleywrites@yahoo.com

Ryan D. Patterson Sr. - *Oh, Baby Where Are You?*

ryandpattersonsrpublishedauthor.com

rpatteo5@gmail.com

www.ingramcontent.com/pod-product-compliance
Lightning Source LLC
Chambersburg PA
CBHW051213130726
47988CB00001B/80